GW00391572

COLONEL BLESSINGTON

Pamela Frankau's last novel was a new enterprise for her and one in which she delighted—a suspense thriller.

Colonel Blessington was an enigma. Half-English and half-American, he had magnetism and presence, but to Beryl Crawshaw he had spoken of having been 'haunted and hounded for years'. To Ivy Stone, his housekeeper, he was a source of fascination—and fear; to Anita Gilroy, twenty-year-old television star, he was the whole dazzling horizon of first love, the focus of her world.

But to Anita's father, the ex-commando, Matthew, the mention of his name revived a dark memory, an obsession that ran like a poisoned river underground.

Matthew becomes an outcast, on the run. Yet things are not quite as he believes; the horror which has engulfed him awaits one further revelation. The final truth about Colonel Blessington comes with as much shock to him as it will to the reader.

PAMELA FRANKAU

Colonel Blessington

Edited and
with an Introduction by
DIANA RAYMOND

THE BODLEY HEAD
LONDON SYDNEY
TORONTO

© Timothy d'Arch Smith
Ernest Vernor Miles and
Diana Raymond 1968
SBN 370 00638 0

Printed and bound in Great Britain for
The Bodley Head Ltd
9 Bow Street, London wc2
by C. Tinling & Co Ltd, Prescot
set in Monotype Baskerville
First published 1968

Introduction

THE ATTEMPT to follow a writer of such brilliance and originality as Pamela Frankau demands at least some explanation.

Pamela was my cousin; but our relationship was, I believe, much closer than that rather barren word usually indicates. Certainly, for my part, I have cherished a devotion to her from my earliest schooldays. For the wit and elegance of her writing I always had the utmost admiration; and when in adolescence I myself began to write, all my work was inspired, helped and influenced by her.

In the Spring of this year she became gravely ill. When she knew she had not long to live, she asked me if I would help her to finish *Colonel Blessington*, a suspense story whose central idea had haunted and excited her for many years. It was an idea, she said, which she was particularly anxious should not be wasted. I of course gladly agreed. She had often sat for hours discussing the book in full detail and with great enthusiasm; and revealing to me, under orders of secrecy, the solution of the 'Blessington mystery'. But then, to the grief of all of us, Pamela became suddenly much worse: before we could start work together, she died on the 8th June this year.

Her great friend Margaret Webster then gave me a pile of manuscript books (eleven in all)—the unfinished

5

Colonel Blessington—asking me if I thought I could complete it. Pamela had worked for many months on the book, and there was a great mass of material. Though the main body of the book was there, it was in some confusion, because she had decided to simplify a very complicated sub-plot: this had to be disentangled from the central story, and her new simpler sub-plot integrated with the whole. She had left a clear outline of this new sub-plot in her notes. Most helpful of all was a tape-recording which she made, not long before her death, explaining how the plot should work, and indicating the way in which she wanted the story to end.

From all these—the manuscript books, the notes and the tape-recording—I have completed a book which I hope fulfils the purpose of her design. I have tried consistently to shape the book as I believe Pamela would have wanted it, and to keep to her plan and method of thought. I have been much helped in this difficult and fascinating, but poignant, task by the goodwill and encouragement of all concerned.

I would like to offer my part in this book to those who loved her: particularly Margaret Webster, Ursula d'Arch Smith, and Margaret Kamm.

Diana Raymond
November, 1967

Prologue

ABSURD TO feel that he was followed. But the feeling persisted. Standing outside the St Francis Hotel, while the doorman called the yellow cab, Harvey Blessington looked over his shoulder: then looked right and left, taking in a wide-angle perspective from side to side of Union Square. This was the feeling that haunted his dreams. For years he had dreamed intermittently of being back, being followed.

Back here . . . in this cliché of a city. Everybody's favourite city. Well, he had loved it once.

He gave the driver the address on Montgomery Street. The driver began to talk. About San Francisco, naturally. Did San Franciscans ever talk of anything else? The changes. (Had the city changed? He, Harvey Blessington, saw the same bright confused pattern: tilting streets and wavy skyline, made of cable cars like self-conscious caterpillars crawling upwards, made of palm trees and sudden flat elegant façades, made of blue and dazzle and white, of Chinatown and Golden Gate Park and Nob Hill and Skid Row.)

The war, the driver said, the factory-workers moving in, the niggers . . . Harvey Blessington, though he had been here only thirty-six hours, was already irked by

7

this line. Particularly the nigger line. 'You from the deep South?' he asked the driver.

'How's that again?'

Blessington repeated the question. The driver, offended, said he was born in the Bay area.

'Then let's skip the racial talk, shall we?'

'Uh?' In Californian fashion, he made it sound more like Onk.

'I said skip it. The race-talk.'

'I don't hear you very well. You British?'

'When I want to be,' said Blessington artfully. He felt better. He had perplexed the driver, who shut up. He was alone. There was nobody after him; nobody following. All he had caught was an echo; a hint from his predecessor, the boy he used to be; the boy who had lived here a long time ago, more than a lifetime ago: the war—he decided—was a lifetime in itself and nearly eight years had gone by since it ended. He, today's Harvey Blessington, could not be afraid. He had learned the true meaning of fear in other places.

Paying off the sulky driver, he still looked to left and right.

Then he stared up at the burnt-orange façade of the sky-scraper building, on whose twenty-fourth floor he would find his fortune awaiting him.

As he went in, from the bright clanging street to the shadowed lobby, he looked back, just once.

The elevator rushed him up to the twenty-fourth floor. There he found a young man behind the desk in the old man's office. This, though he had been warned of it, gave him a small jerk of surprise. His mind had obstinately mirrored Joe Ashley, the old man, with his lanky limbs, his slow pundit's manner, his invariable dark blue suit and his silver hair.

Ashley Junior, he saw, was an eager beaver disguised

as the all-American boy. He was bronzed, his teeth were too obvious, his eyes were too small and he wore a terrible tie.

'Colonel Blessington—sir. It's a pleasure to meet you.'

'How do you do,' said Harvey, and settled to be bored. There was one advantage, he decided, in the death of the old man. The young man, like a new reader, beginning here, would know so much less about the past. He would hardly know anything at all.

'And—hold on to your hat—here's my estimate of the inheritance tax,' said Ashley Junior. His client studied the figures. His face was expressionless. No visible reactions from Blessington, neither to his wealth nor to the U.S. Government's share in it.

'He's too British to be true,' thought Ashley Junior. Blessington made him uncomfortable: the quiet war-hero, with the neat mask of a face and the grey flannel suit. Fair hair going grey at the sides, too . . . and only thirty-three. A manner that stopped somewhere short of friendliness: an edge of curt command in the voice. Peculiar eyes, green-gold eyes; straight-featured, to the asexual British pattern. The elegant mongrel—with only one side of his pedigree showing right now. ('And just why should that irritate me? Because he owes his luck to the other side? Maybe.') The luck, even allowing for the inheritance tax, was more than a million dollars' worth of luck.

Blessington handed him back the figures without comment.

'Anything else?' he asked.

'Let's see.' Ashley Junior looked through the file, disguising the fact that he was less and less at ease with this visitor to his room. 'Oh, yes. I'm still waiting for an assessment on the London property. No question of double-tax, under the reciprocal agreement, you don't need to worry. But it'll take time. Complex deal—always is.'

'The London property?' Blessington was frowning, the small impatient frown of one not accustomed to being puzzled. 'You mean the printing-press? That's in Bristol. I was down there three weeks ago. Anyway, it belongs to me. By Deed of Gift. Surely the estate doesn't—'

'I'm not talking about any printing-press. I'm talking about a house. A house in London—here. Minster House, Heath Hill, North Royal.'

'Minster House?' For the first time the war-hero gave a hint of emotion (though what emotion? The Colonel's emotions, Ashley decided, were obscure and disquieting.) 'I thought they sold it years ago.'

'No. It was rented on a long lease.' He glanced at the British lawyer's letter. 'Another twelve years to run.'

'It's a beautiful house. Last time I walked on the Heath I made a pilgrimage to it. I'd no idea. How extraordinary.' He brooded, tapping a cigarette on a case that bore a regimental crest. Ashley Junior's new secretary, a jittery blonde, coasted round the door, carrying two cups of coffee on a tray. As usual she bumped the tray against the door. As usual 'Take it easy' said Ashley Junior. Blessington continued to brood. Drinking the coffee he asked, 'Would I have the right to terminate that lease?'

'There I'd need the British lawyer's opinion. Want me to write to him?'

'Please.'

'You plan to live in London?'

'Not sure yet,' said Blessington. 'I was just remembering the house.'

'As I understand it, you have resigned from the Army?'

Blessington nodded. Now he looked shy, almost womanish. Yes, maybe. Maybe that was his problem. Homosexuality and heroism were not incompatible. Ashley Junior knew about Lawrence of Arabia. Blessington's next words had a suspicious ring: 'I'm a war-addict, I'm afraid. Give me a battle and I know where I am. Peacetime soldiering—office soldiering—doesn't really suit me. And now the future's taken care of—to use your idiom—I'll probably go into business.'

'In England?'

Blessington nodded again.

'I thought maybe you'd decide to settle over here now.'

'Not on your life.'

Ashley Junior's local patriotism flared. This fellow's legacies included a fine house on Pacific Avenue and the ranch on the Rogue River. Did his feelings show in his face? Blessington gave him a glance, half-amused, half - what? Contemptuous, perhaps. Ashley would, he decided, be glad when this visitor had gone. 'No need to take it as an insult,' Blessington said. 'I'm not a two-passport man any more: the American one died a natural death when I joined the British Army. Even before that I'd become absorbed into the scenery over there. You can imagine, can't you?'

Ashley Junior couldn't. Nor could he imagine why Blessington had never returned to visit his parents once the war ended. Peacetime soldiering could hardly be so restrictive. He found himself saying, 'I guess you wish you'd seen them again,' and hearing the note of reproach in his own voice.

'I do,' said Blessington calmly. 'Had I known they were going to die within a week of each other . . .' He broke off; the green-gold eyes looked into some distance that Ashley couldn't see. 'That *would* happen, of course. With those two. *She for a little tried to live without him, liked it not and died.*'

'Ah, you phrase it beautifully,' said Ashley Junior; he was easily moved; most of all by death.

'Not so much me as a poet,' Blessington corrected him. 'Happens to be a quotation.'

(So British he has to quote; they all quote.)

Ashley said, 'Well, that seems to be the lot. I take it you'll be here for a few days longer—'

'You take it wrong,' said Blessington; the voice cut sharply. 'I'm leaving at once for the ranch.'

Ashley stared at him. 'At once? But—'

'This morning.'

'You mean you're not staying in San Francisco—'

'No longer than I can help. I thought I made that clear. Too many people around, trying to get through on the telephone, trying to renew acquaintance. Not my idea. I want peace, and my own company. The ranch, I understand, is all prepared—'

'But the agent—'

'I know all about the agent,' said Blessington. 'He fell and broke his leg; he'll be laid up for quite a while. No problem. I'd rather be on my own.'

'Has he found someone to look after you?'

'Not yet. I can look after myself.'

You certainly can, Ashley Junior thought; that's the impression you give me.

'I'm going there to work,' Blessington said. 'I'm taking pen, paper, and a tidy pile of old note books.'

(Not only quotes, but writes.) 'Giving us your memoirs, sir?'

Blessington looked away beyond the room; his face was unreadable. 'Let's say my life story. Or part of it.

And if anyone wants to know where I am, fob them off. Tell them I'm travelling around and you can't get in touch with me . . . let's say, for a few weeks.'

Ashley Junior nodded. Unease was changing to curiosity; Colonel Blessington, it seemed to him, left a great deal unsaid. 'How'll you get there?' Ashley asked.

'Hired a car from one of those Hurt-Yourself companies . . . Well, whatever it is they're called. They're driving it to the hotel at noon. I should be there late this evening, given a bit of luck.'

With this, Blessington gave an unexpected smile, got to his feet, and shook Ashley Junior's hand. He moved to the door; then halted. More than halted—he froze. When he turned, a vizor was down. As if he had let a bright prisoner escape from inside and now turned the key on the prisoner. The eyes were cold again; meeting them Ashley felt a chill in his stomach.

'One question—'

'Sir?' said Ashley Junior.

'You've had no communication from—'

Ashley Junior guessed what name was coming. He didn't know the details; his father had always skipped them. Something tragically mysterious about that situation, the family problem, long hidden out of sight.

'Not a word,' Ashley Junior said. 'Not a word.'

Still the sensation of a dream, but a different dream. This was the knowledge of being rich and free: of having the whole round world to play with. He had known, he supposed, that these things would come to him one day. But he had never looked ahead to them; he wasn't in the habit of looking ahead. The war had taught him not to. He strolled two blocks, thinking of the ranch. In this

13

large and brilliant city, the image of the ranch beckoned, lone and far: he could see the bare place high up in the hills, the tall cliff sides and the wild river, flowing to the Pacific. He could see the cave in the cliff, boyhood's secret hiding place. The ranch held the best of his boyhood memories.

But boyhood memories were dangerous. They led his mind where it did not want to go. Presently he was looking over his shoulder, then saying 'Don't be a damned fool' and hailing a cab. Back at the hotel, safe in the anonymity of the transient, he finished his packing. He zipped up the hand case filled with note-books and diaries, and called a bell-boy to take his luggage down. He found himself aiming for the bar. He ordered a whisky and drank it while he studied his road-map.

Away now, away. Not yet. Another ten minutes till noon. He lit a cigarette. He strolled about the lobby. His bags were there. When the clock-hand moved past noon, he began to worry. A pedantically punctual person, he could not bear to wait; and besides there was no excuse. He had signed the papers and paid the deposit. 'When one says twelve o'clock one means twelve o'clock,' he raged inside, pacing to and fro. After five more minutes he went out to chivvy the doorman.

'I'm expecting a car. From Hackett's Drive-Yourself Company. The name's Blessington.'

'All ready for you,' the man said. 'Nearly an hour ago. I had them call your room. They couldn't get any reply.'

'Damn it, I said twelve o'clock—not eleven.'

'Guess they jumped the gun.'

'Idiotic. I told them—oh, never mind. Where is it?'

'The cop moved him on. He had to take it to the car-park. He's waiting there for you.'

'Which car-park?'

14

'This one; the underground park. Right in front of you.'

'New, since my day,' said Blessington. Unreasonably angry, he picked up his two bags, fending off the bell-hop. Still in a swirl of bad temper he dodged the traffic, walked down the concrete ramp and set the bags on the ground. Just ahead of him he saw a long black car waiting at the mouth of the tunnel. There was nobody at the wheel; nor was it the car he had driven this morning. A car of the same make, but this morning's car was grey. Harvey looked to left and right. As he moved towards the reception window, a figure detached itself from the wall and came to meet him, hands in pockets, with a slouch that managed to be graceful.

'Colonel Blessington? Looking for me?'

The figure wore a peaked cap, not a chauffeur's cap, more like a fisherman's cap, pulled down over the eyes. The peak made a mask's shadow there.

'You're from Hackett's?' Blessington asked.

'Sure. You kept me waiting quite a while.'

'Your own fault. The car was ordered for twelve.'

'Well, let's get going, shall we? I can use a ride.'

This put the last touch to Blessington's temper. 'That'll be enough damned impertinence. Put the bags in the back. Give me the keys. And take yourself off. If you're expecting a tip you're out of luck.'

Silence. His instructions were obeyed. The figure moved out of sight, then lingered still on the passenger's side of the car. Seated at the wheel, with the keys in his hand, Blessington put down the window. He said, 'You might tell your employers I don't think much of their service—or their employees.'

The only answer was a chuckling laugh. It came to him, horribly, that he knew this laugh.

'Why, Harvey . . . You've gone so British I could slice

15

you.' The speaker pulled open the door and slid into the passenger's seat. A hand went up, to pull off the cap. 'Want me to drive? Tricky in this town around noontime. For a visiting foreigner.'

It couldn't be happening. But it was.

'Come on now, start her up. Or move over and let me do the driving.'

'How the hell did you get charge of this car?'

'It's my car. I called Hackett's and cancelled yours. They're holding your deposit. I've confirmed it in writing. I can still do your handwriting. I've kept that up; it always came easy. Do we move?'

'No.'

'Okay, then we just sit here.'

'Is it the money you're after? I'll give you money.'

'Big of you. Crude, though. It's you I'm interested in.—Watch it. There's a fellow behind you, wants out. We're the centre of attention, aren't we? Or will be— any minute. You look kind of sick, Harvey. I'll take the wheel.'

'Damned if you will.'

'Move over.'

'Hey, mister! What's the matter with you? Won't she start?'

'We're okay. Just changing seats. Good boy, Harvey. I always did drive better than you, didn't I? I could do anything you did—and better. I've been following you around since yesterday morning and you never spotted me.'

'I don't imagine I was hard to track.'

'You can say that again. All I had to do was read the papers. War Hero Blessington flies in; nice going, boy.'

'I knew you'd be here,' he said, hearing the misery and rage in his voice. 'God damn it, I knew you would.'

16

'Well, isn't that fine? And—for the record—I'm still your friend: your best friend. There isn't a thing in this world I wouldn't do for you. I don't want your dough. I want to stick around while you're here, get acquainted again—tell you things. Boy, the things I have to tell you . . . got some of them written down, in case I forget any. *Forget*. What a notion. I'll be useful to you at the ranch, Harvey, you'll need a second string. Doesn't seem right for a Colonel in the British Army, doing his own chores, not to me it doesn't.'

A lilac coloured convertible cut in suddenly close to the black bonnet. There was a blonde at the wheel. Blessington's driver leaned out, calling, 'Take it easy, Araminta!' The chuckling laugh came again.

You ought to be dead. Not sitting here beside me, back in my life again; not someone making an old nightmare real. You should be dead . . . d'you hear me? Dead . . .

Six weeks on the ranch had, Ashley Junior thought, done much for Blessington. He was tanned to the colour of coffee. He had lost his formal manner. He wore a sports jacket and an open-necked shirt.

'So you had a good time,' Ashley Junior said.

'Wonderful. Hard to tear myself away.'

'Work went well, then?'

'Oh . . .' Blessington gave a small, lazy smile. 'Once there I forgot all about work.'

'No life story, then?'

'Not yet. Later, perhaps.'

From the ranch Blessington had been prompt with his letters and telephone-calls. Growing more amiable, too. And displaying a thirst for the details that had seemed unworthy of his earlier attention. 'Getting acclimated,' Ashley Junior thought. 'Not only to Cali-

17

fornia. To the size of his fortune. First time around, he didn't seem to know what had hit him.'

'You saw the agent?' he asked.

'The last couple of weeks.'

'Before that, you were on your own?'

'That was how I wanted it,' said Blessington.

'Well, we've wasted no time. There's another letter about Minster House. Came this morning. You may have difficulty in turning those tenants out. Housing's quite a problem over there.'

'No hurry,' said the Colonel, opening his crested cigarette case, but not taking a cigarette. 'No hurry at all.'

'Does that mean you've changed your mind?'

'Changed my mind?'

'About living in England?'

'Not exactly. I'm flying on Tuesday. Spending a few days there and then—taking off again. I've been thinking about it, up there at the ranch. Ultimately, I'll settle in England. But I've made a list of the places I want to see first. The Far East: thought I'd cover Japan; maybe call in on Hiroshima. India, Persia . . . perhaps Tibet. And Africa: bit of big game shooting . . .' The green-gold eyes were dreamy now, seeing the fabled places. 'After all, I've the time. And the money.'

You certainly have, Ashley Junior thought.

'It'll be good to get away. With all problems solved.' He repeated, 'All problems solved,' and gave a contented sigh.

'I had numbers of enquiries—'

'From friends and family? I'm sure you did. To use your idiom—keep stalling. Tell them I'm still away. No time, before I go, for one of those great here-we-are-again marathons.' He shut the cigarette case, without taking a cigarette. 'Trying to cut down on them. Now, what's left?' He scanned the papers with a far more lively interest than he had shown on his last visit. 'Minster House—yes, we'll have to wait and see. Offer for Pacific Avenue . . . Yes, good enough. We can close the deal. And the ranch. You still think we ought to hold out for more? Right, I'll leave it to you. And this, I take it, is the final list of holdings—H'm—h'm.' His nodding approval had a hint of complacency. He even laughed.

The blonde brought the coffee; she still managed to bump the tray against the door and Ashley Junior still said, 'Take it easy.'

'Take it easy, Araminta,' the Colonel supplemented, and laughed again.

1

BRIGHT BLUE letters on a background of delicate bluish grey: the leaflet had a certain distinction. It fluttered from eager hands; it was thrust into the less eager hands of housewives shopping their way down North Royal High Street. Throughout the Borough, True Tory helpers were busy forcing the message through likely, and unlikely, letter-boxes.

A sad mistake, thought Anthony Price, author of the 'Meet-Your-Candidate' scheme. He had meant each reception to be carefully planned, the company summoned by formal cards sent only to the right people. But the candidate, with the rest of the True Tories, had passed far beyond Anthony's control. Anthony was not, he realised, an effective character. A pity. His looks were effective. Writing last year's application for congenial employment, he had described himself as

21

Personable. He was thirty-two years old, brown-haired, blue-eyed, neatly built. His clothes were scrupulous and expensive. In reverie he saw himself truthfully as rather an old-fashioned young—no, youngish—man. He did not belong to Now; nor did Now belong to him, and this inclined him to take a jaundiced view.

At the moment he could hardly be blamed for taking a jaundiced view. He was aloft in a bitter east wind on a swaying platform. The loud-speaker through which he was announcing Rupert Ledyard had developed a kind of mechanical belch. Two West Indians at work in the Serve-U-Speedy garage were chanting 'Vote Labour' up at him. The ramshackle platform had been raised exactly opposite the garage yard. Anthony could not therefore avoid the four bright eyes, the two white grins, laughing out from the two dark faces mauve-tinted by the weather. 'Vote Labour!' The chant went on. Behind him, also aloft, endangering the small, perilous structure, was the fourteen-stone bulk of the candidate. (Ledyard had been told specifically not to come up until Anthony was down. At this rate they would both be down . . .)

'And that's all you need to hear from me. Breep, cluck, ack, ack, ack. Listen now to your True Tory candidate, Rupert ack, ack, whee-hee, Ledyard, the only possible choice for whing-whing-whing North Royal and for the country ram yam, prrrr, pee-ee-eek. Really think you'll do better without it, Rupert,' Anthony said as he detached the heavy equipment from his shoulder.

'All yours . . . Always did prefer the jolly old megaphone,' said the candidate. He stepped forward. There was a crunch and a crack. The boards trembled. Anthony leaped for the steps. *Herminius darted back*, he thought. (Who was the other fellow? Something Lartius.

22

Spurious Lartius ... Surely not *Spurious* ... *And as they passed, beneath their feet they heard the timbers crack.*) Scrambling down to the pavement, he awaited the worst. *But with a crash like thunder fell every something beam.* No. The platform held. Ledyard, like brave Horatius, stood alone.

A great pillar of a man: half-ruined, reddish good looks; curling grey hair; a clipped moustache. From below the moustache the familiar exhortations came roaring. A voice like Ledyard's could do without even the jolly old megaphone.

'Look to your left, up towards the Mac Fisheries! To the left, I said! Yes, indeed, ha-ha. The Left it is. You see that other platform with its red rosettes, its seditious pamphlets, its—'

'Vote Labour!' yelled the West Indians.

'Vote Labour and cut the country's throat, not to mention your own!' Ledyard yelled back. He pointed a scornful finger down wind, to the façade of Bloom the Chemist's. 'And there, ladies and gentlemen, look there! A small soap-box, a soft-soap box, ha-ha. Wreathed in some orange-coloured nonsense. The lone Liberal outpost. Scantily manned, as one would expect.'

'Vote Liberal!' called a cross-looking Jewish housewife.

'Vote Liberal and make yourself conspicuous. Not to say unique.'

'What's the matter with being unique?'

'What's the matter with anything?' asked a drunk of regular habits, emerging briefly from the door of the Rose and Thistle.

'Vote Labour!'

'Vote Tory!'

'Vote *True* Tory,' the helpers cried.

'And now I come to the most shocking sight of all—'

Ledyard pointed again. 'Opposite the windows of our famous North Royal Bakery—'

'Vote for the Bakery!' shouted a horrible young man with very long ringlets and leopard-skin jeans.

'Another platform. Another blue encampment. Under false colours. I repeat, false colours! The so-called Tories of this Borough. Tories, I ask you! The feeble compromising remnant of what was once England's proudest party. Those who have shaken hands with Socialism, with Liberalism, with traitors to the crown. Let us remind you of the Tory record, no less shameful than the Labour record.'

'Vote Labour!'

'Don't vote at all,' shouted the drunk. 'Sheer waste of time.'

Anthony Price, at a safe distance from the platform, though rather too near the West Indians, turned up his collar. A fantasy in his mind was creating the crash: the sudden, monumental collapse of Ledyard through broken boards to the pavement. A woman's cry. A shocked murmur all across the street. The ambulance dinging down through the traffic lights. Himself kneeling among the ruins, saying quietly to a policeman, 'Keep the crowd back, officer. He's dead.'

'We are alive! We are not the moribund Tories of the post-war decadence. Not the Tories of today. We are the Tories of tomorrow, the true Tories, who believe—'

The yard of the Serve-U-Speedy made a wide half-moon, with a sign at each end, announcing respectively IN and OUT. As usual, a car now drove smartly in past the OUT sign. This brought fierce yells from the West Indians; one threw a wet leather at the wind-screen. The car was a black Rolls Royce of apparently early vintage. Its shape made no concession to the new lines

24

answering popular demand. On a side-window could be seen a poster bearing the message VOTE *TRUE TORY*. Out of the car stepped the surprise supporter of the campaign, Colonel Harvey Blessington.

Anthony was delighted to see him; delight dimmed at once by that great beautiful Amazon of a girl leaping down from the left-hand door of the Rolls. There she was again. Miss Anita Gilroy—star of the television screen. She had intruded upon the meeting at Minster House last Monday. Obviously, then, Blessington's girl. Anthony's feeling was that Blessington (all of distinction and gentlemanly tastes) must be the hunted, not the hunter.

They looked entirely wrong together; the slender elegant Colonel and the huge girl. In her short, whitish fur coat, with the pale suede boots coming up to her knees, she was tall and bulky as a polar bear walking on its hind legs. Her large, lovely eyes glowed upon Anthony. 'Good morning, Mr Price,' said the polar bear. 'Good morning, everybody. I *do* think he's brave,' she added, gazing up at Ledyard. 'Agony, it must be, mustn't it?'

Blessington, murmuring 'Not for Rupert,' gave Anthony a wink. His profile then became expressionless, watching the candidate. He was a man of two faces: there was the sudden, positive radiance and there was this coldly thoughtful mask. Neat and elegant he might be; and graceful in movement; but that face, whether lively or solemn, was, in Anthony's view, the face of a leader. Blessington should be aloft on that platform.

'Our Empire clean destroyed—our glorious traditions brought low—yes, madam, I *will* tell you if you'll give me a chance.' The current heckler made a determined shape, thrusting herself into private battle with Ledyard. She was dressed to the fashion favoured by some North

Royal matrons, in a bright woollen hood, a shrouding tweed coat and narrow trousers. Ledyard leaned down to her. Nobody could hear a word of their dialogue and in any case time was up. The helpers, having disposed of about half the leaflets, were climbing back, as instructed, into their blue van. This, moving off, came across the path of the Borough dinosaur, the grey garbage-truck. Two policemen waved the van urgently downhill. The monster followed, clanking, groaning, evil-smelling; the men on the back of it shouting 'Vote Labour!' and making rude signs with their fingers.

Anthony, Blessington, Miss Gilroy and the heckler were now Ledyard's audience. It had been largely composed of the faithful. The runnel of hurrying women swept on, pushing lethally-beaked shopping-waggons toward their goals. The mixed, inaudible cries from the loud-speakers were quiet. Outside the Mac Fisheries, Bloom's and the Bakery, the rival parties were hauling down their colours, dismantling their stands. The True Tories should be doing the same. Saturday morning, as the police frequently pointed out, was a busy morning in the High Street.

'Yes, all right, officer,' said Anthony. Blessington moved towards the platform. Miss Gilroy, of course, ran after him.

'Have to get it down, sir.'

'It was supposed to go away in that van you brushed off,' Anthony grumbled. Here he saw that the big girl had her uses. No sooner was Ledyard off the platform than she picked up the whole top structure, toting it before her, crying gaily, 'Mind your backs, please!' until she set it down in the garage yard. 'Much lighter than it looks,' she declared, untroubled by the 'Can't stay there, miss' which greeted her alike from the West Indians and the police.

'It won't—or not for long,' said Miss Anita Gilroy.
'We can tie it on to the boot of the Rolls. Anybody got
some string?'

To Anthony's irritation, she was recognised; he left
her doling out her autograph. A small, quiet conference
had developed at the edge of the pavement. Joining it,
Anthony was mollified when Ledyard put up one foot
on the remaining plinth: being only an inverted orange-
box, it gave way with a crackle and enclosed the foot.

'Look out for nails!' cried the lady heckler, while
Blessington disengaged the hopping candidate. 'Do be
careful. I once pierced my hand on just that kind of—'
She broke off, staring hard at the Colonel. She was of
a type Anthony knew immediately. He classified it as
the Pink Aunt. He had several. They were all in their
fifties with overdone complexions like puckered sugar-
almonds, and touched-up hair; all smiling, and full of
vitality. A Pink Aunt, in the tradition, belonged to the
powerful majority of non-listeners, having so much that
was fascinating to say herself.

'Thanks, Harvey,' Ledyard rubbed his ankle. 'No
harm done. I am forced to disagree with you, madam,
forced to disagree. The United States is the nigger in the
woodpile.'

'Can't stay there, sir—' (the second policeman,
having torn himself from Miss Gilroy).

'What can't?'

'The woodpile,' said Blessington playfully as he kicked
the smashed orange-box into the gutter.

'So long as we go on truckling to America—'

But the Pink Aunt, unheeding, emerged from her
little trance of contemplation with a sudden glad cry.
'Of *course*! *That's* who you are. I knew we'd met. Your
name's Blessington, and you were at Bowood—1945.
You won't remember—'

Did he or did he not? Anthony saw the radiant smile turn on, but the forehead frowned; the green-gold eyes were watchful. He had forgotten, surely; this was well-mannered bewilderment; waiting to be told.

'Won't remember me, I mean. You'll remember Bowood—could hardly forget it, could you?' She gave a peal of organized laughter. 'Well, I was the Waff in charge—poor me.'

(Yes, the W.A.A.F. in charge; she would be. Anthony's own pink aunts frequently spoke of their wartime service with the W.A.A.F.s, the W.R.N.S. and the A.T.S.; he sometimes saw the Air Force, the Navy and the Army shuddering a little from the impact of their vociferous enthusiasm.)

'As I recall,' said Blessington, shaking her by the hand, 'you performed your duties to perfection.'

'Kind of you—but not true. I was in the most fearful flap—who wouldn't have been? How *nice* to find you again.' She surveyed him carefully. 'You don't look a day older—younger, if anything.'

'Those darling darkies are tying it on to the back,' Miss Gilroy interrupted and then piped down. The Colonel was telling the Pink Aunt, whose name proved to be Crawshaw, that she herself did not seem to have aged at all.

'*Nonsense*—just had my hair done, that's why. There's a lot to be said for a blue rinse.'

'Something I haven't tried yet—as you see.'

Blessington's hair was prematurely white: glossy, youthful hair. The effect above the lively brown face would, Anthony thought, account for the swoonings of other women besides Miss Gilroy. The Pink Aunt was obviously no swooner. She gave a brisk nod of approval, saying, 'It suits you.'

Nothing appeared to suit Ledyard, pawing the ground

impatiently, snorting and grumbling on about Americans until Blessington said, 'Couldn't we all do with a drink?' and Miss Gilroy said, 'Let's go to that blissful pub with the sausages.'

The Oak Apple, North Royal's most exclusive pub, so historic as to have place in a jig-saw puzzle called *Inns of Old England*, stood at a corner on Heath Hill, about two hundred yards below Blessington's house. Anthony heard the Colonel greeted with cries of comradeship from the early drinkers. The party was given a table by the fire. The sausages were brought. Blessington dominated the scene with easy grace; even though he didn't drink: ginger-ale for the Colonel. Anthony found this a depressant, being himself a devoted drinker at the right time.

Now was certainly the right time. He felt the gin make contact somewhere halfway between his frozen face and his frozen feet. Ledyard had forgotten the Americans and was having a gentlemanly kind of go at Anita. Snapped out of it by the Pink Aunt, he admitted to liking some individual Americans very much.

'Doesn't one's liking usually confine itself to the individual?' Blessington needled him: 'I mean, have you ever liked a whole nation—even the British?'

'There one cannot wholly bypass patriotism,' Ledyard replied and Blessington nodded, seeming to take him seriously.

Oh, but he *can't*, Anthony thought. Nobody can. How the Party had ever made the incredible mistake of nominating this mock-Churchillian dummy ... well, one knew how; one knew why. Ledyard had money and Ledyard had time. Besides, looking back, there was no one else to nominate. The emergency had occurred before Blessington sprouted so unexpectedly at stage-centre. The by-election thrust upon North Royal caught the True Tories unprepared. North Royal's perennially-returned member, Sir Falkland Hayes-Hartington, had done them a profound disservice by contracting some obscure disease which enforced permanent residence in the Bahamas. The promising Right Wing revolution was only just at the simmer. Another year, they all agreed, and they could have come to the boil.

'Excuse me, but have you ever *been* to America, Rupert?' The Colonel's voice was velvety. 'No? As I thought. You've got it all wrong, you know. The country's a vast, natural breeding-ground for the truest type of Tory.'

'I beg your pardon?'

'You 'eard,' said Blessington, with a grin. 'A *natural* breeding-ground. The only one there is. For an obvious reason.'

'H'm, can't say it's obvious to me.'

'My dear fellow, what other nation has ever begun with Socialism and grown out of it?'

'Begun with —sorry, I don't get this.'

'*We hold these truths to be self-evident* . . . what truths? Why, *that all men were created equal.* Look back through history and you won't find another community kicking off with that sublime mistake. Naturally they evolved in the right direction. What else could they do? Nowhere to go but up.' The orator in Blessington took over: 'You may say their class strata have been formed on a money basis, true enough. But all blue blood—always—everywhere—began to flow from property and power. We may laugh at their "old families". But the fact remains that the Western Hemisphere today is the world's Right Wing. And none the less powerful for loathing the doctrine that was originally their own.'

He had the gift of a stage-presence, Anthony thought; the voice though light, imposed itself; one expected a rattle of applause. None came. Mrs Crawshaw was looking pointedly, privately amused; Anita staring with such devotion that she seemed anaesthetized and Ledyard blinking, a sausage halfway to his mouth.

The Colonel soared on: 'The solution for America is a monarchy. I can't think why they haven't set one up long ago. With their automatic reflex of hero-worship, their love for parades, processions and ritual clothing, they only need a Royal Family and a full quota of peers to keep them happy. We'd like another round here, Frank, please. No, no more ginger-ale, thanks. Our misapprehension just now is to follow America instead of leading her. We should treat her as a promising heir, ready to inherit our traditions, or nearly ready.'

'That'll be the day,' Ledyard snorted. (What was Mrs Crawshaw's private joke? Pink aunts were seldom, Anthony knew, given to giggling.)

'Well, Rupert, perhaps it's time I unveiled my ancestry. My mother was a Californian, my father a naturalized citizen of U.S.A. and I was born in San Francisco.'

News to Anthony. It dropped into his mind like a clue, explaining—or partly explaining—things about the Colonel that puzzled him.

Ledyard sagged, saying, 'Good God! I beg your pardon.'

'Not at all.'

'I was wondering how soon you'd let *that* out,' said Mrs Crawshaw.

She had Blessington's full attention. 'Ye-es,' he murmured. 'Yes—of course . . .'

There was a moment of silence. Mrs Crawshaw gave him a knowing, intimate smile and he gave her the same sort of smile in return. Anthony was diverted. Had the

Colonel, perhaps, had a wartime dally with the Pink Aunt? The notion was, he saw, occurring to Miss Gilroy, who seemed all at once deflated, as though by means of some sharp puncture from the back. She went from outsize to no-size, asking in a miserably muted contralto, 'Where was this place—where you met?'

'Oh, my dear—' Mrs Crawshaw pealed—'it would take a genius to describe Bowood ... Here was this country mansion, this stately home, turned into our most important transit camp for all the V.I.P.s who flew from Lyneham. And it snowed, and it snowed, and it snowed. And nobody could get away. "Scrubbed" I had to tell them every morning. "Sorry, sir—flight scrubbed again." And there was the usual mix-up at top level. Security regulations were so tight that—'

'Forgive me, please.' The Colonel was looking at his watch, looking at Anita. 'I've asked my intimidating housekeeper to have our lunch ready ten minutes ago ... Your train—'

Anita nodded sadly. Anthony caught the look on Blessington's face, a look at once mocking and tender. And now the party was breaking up; Ledyard booming about a date at the Athenaeum and summoning a taxi, Mrs Crawshaw reluctantly putting on her hood; all of them out in the cold again.

'Ask him to tell you the Bowood story,' Mrs Crawshaw was saying to Anita. She then shook the Colonel's hand. 'Well, it's been great fun ... Thank you. See you at the party—Thursday, isn't it?' She flourished the grey and blue leaflet. 'I'll have a husband in tow,' she added winsomely. Oh, there must have been a dally, no doubt about it.

'Can't be certain. Only lending the house,' Blessington explained. 'If my dinner date ends in time ...'

'Oh. Well, we'll just have to hope, shan't we? Goodbye.' She looked him up and down. There was a medical note in her voice as she added, 'Splendid to see you looking so well. No "haunting and hounding" these days?'

Just what did it mean? Obviously it meant something to Blessington, replying without hesitation, 'That's all over long ago, thank God,' and treating the Pink Aunt to the full radiance of his smile.

The Rolls moved up hill, with its ludicrous burden lashed and wobbling in the open boot.

'Fascinating. *Quite* fascinating . . . Life's full of odd little adventures, don't you find?'

'Well no, not really. Ought I to?' said Anthony. She did not answer him, being—typically of pink aunts—in full cry. He suffered the cascade, making mean, italicized comments inside his head.

Never-a-day-passedwithout-some-intriguing-little-adventure. *Intriguing isn't an adjective.* She-was-going-to-the-Tube,-he-too?-The-short-cut-through-Heath-Square-and-up-the-steps-to-Mansell-Passage-she-hadn't-caught-his-name. *Butterfingers.* Mr Price? Meeting-her-husband-at-Leicester-Square-lunch-and-a-movie-Saturday-afternoon,-ha-ha. *What's funny?*

'Can't get *over* Colonel Blessington . . . The effect of inheriting a million? Or was it two million? An immense estate, anyway those Californian parents dying at the same time, the headline simply shot up into my eyes, I said to myself, Blessington that's the one from Bowood, lucky he didn't get killed after all, told me he only wanted to be killed in action, but Minster House, I'd no *idea* he was living there.'

She had temporarily run out of breath, and who shall blame her? North Royal specialized in flights of steps and narrow passages, all tilting at an uncomfortable gradient. At the crest of this particularly brutal steep,

Mansell Passage snaked its way on and upward. Jaunty little gardens and converted slum-cottages, proud with new paint, flourished on the right: on the left there rose the wall of the Public Baths. Mrs Crawshaw (Beryl she said her Christian name was, as if one wanted to know) halted at the top step and leaned for a panting moment on the iron rail. 'Minster House is enormous. He can't be living there all by himself.'

'Oh yes, he—'

'Can't have been there long, bought it from the Rushton-Courtneys, I suppose, must have paid a packet, they were there for years, such charming—'

'Inherited. Blessington family property.'

'Imagine nobody telling me that.'

Possibly you weren't listening.

'Poor Mr Ledyard put his foot in it about America, didn't he? Good-looking girl that but much too big . . . Divorced, I expect—the Colonel, I mean, must have married out there . . . oh yes, he went back to live off the fat of the land. Of course, you're too young to remember, but he was quite a name in the war. D.S.O. and bar; M.C.; all sorts of stories about him; nearly everyone at Bowood had a Blessington story, he wasn't a Colonel then, of course. And now . . . *goodness*, what a change. Used to sit there, grim and cold and quiet: we were all a little afraid of him. Kept right apart; never joined in anything. Don't think I ever heard him utter till that one night—he wasn't drinking ginger-ale *that* night, must have had a bottle of his own somewhere, we were running low. Not that it made him happier, just made him talk . . . Glooming on and on, that sad face and all those medal-ribbons. Haunted and hounded, he said, over and over again, been haunted and hounded for years. I said, why, whatever's haunting and hounding you, tell

34

your friend Beryl—cheek, I suppose, but I was used to their confiding in me, they always did, I don't know why.'

Me, I don't know how.

'And all he said was, "God forbid you should ever know the things I know." Then he turned on his heel and went off to bed.'

Does a person really turn on his heel? Just one heel? I'm sure I never have.

'They all flew at five oh-oh next day, so I never saw him again till now.'

Ah, no dally. Disappointing.

'Two to Leicester Square,' Anthony said at the ticket-office. Mrs Crawshaw paid him her exact debt. In the lift she said brightly, 'I suppose he's financing this campaign.'

Anthony gave a non-committal grunt.

'I wouldn't have thought him political, somehow— more the individualist.' Surprisingly she waited for Anthony's opinion.

He said, 'According to Blessington, politics are the natural explosions of the individual. "The fires down below" he calls them. In his view, there's nobody who isn't deeply, savagely partisan. The Philistine majority doesn't recognize this bias—any more than it realises its own impulses of sadism and aggression.' It was a direct quote: from his first talk with the Colonel, on a night when he was diffidently canvassing from door to door. The warmth of the Colonel's welcome was still an astonishment to him.

The Colonel's theory was, it seemed, an astonishment to the Pink Aunt. And a silencer. She spoke no word while they navigated the icy wind-tunnel from the lift to the hollow draughty cylinder, the catacomb, where it seemed that nothing would ever happen, least of all the arrival of a train. Looking at her, he saw that she was distressed.

'What a *horrible* thing to say. *You* aren't in politics for that reason, surely?'

'What reason?'

'Because you're a sadist.'

Anthony giggled. 'Certainly not. I'm a romantic, I want a world that's never existed in my time. The world I read about in books. Out-of-date books,' he added fiercely. 'I want God and good manners and guts. And privacy and quiet and space and a valet, and no television and a huge library of my own and enough money never to have to think about it. I want to take a world tour in vast luxury, all alone, without ever seeing a crowd.'

'You couldn't possibly—not on a world tour. There are always crowds in India—and Greece—and Johannesburg. Tell me, what does one *wear* at this party on Thursday night?

Since she was nearing her twentieth birthday, Anita Gilroy had, naturally, been in love more than once. But not like this. Looking back, the remembered symptoms were as those of the heavy cold compared with virus pneumonia.

The lightning had struck with her first glimpse of Harvey Blessington, twelve days ago. She had thought, He's too good to be true. He still was. The wave-length running between them gave her the illusion that she had known him all her life. (Not that one could have survived these sensations all one's life—one would have been dead of them long ago.)

How was it possible to be so unendurably happy and unendurably sad in the same second of time?

Because she was an innocent, Harvey said. She had never known what sort of person she was until she met him: other than one of those working girls whom Heaven would protect as long as she allowed Heaven the privilege. And that was her father's verdict, not her own. Vaguely she assumed that both verdicts, his and Harvey's related to her virginity. Anita was ashamed of her virginity. All her girl friends had disposed of theirs long ago. Nevertheless, she continued to counter the inevitable proposal in her own way. Sophisticated, intellectual reasoning, arguments founded in logical positivism, expoundings of the New Enlightenment, references to bourgeois beliefs, all were child's play to Anita. She simply listened, or appeared to listen, understood nothing and finally, simply, said No.

Unendurably happy; unendurably sad; seated in the Queen Anne dining-room of Minster House. Minster House itself added a dimension of grandeur to this paradoxical haze: its elegant façade fronted the Heath; in the old garden there grew a famous mulberry tree, allegedly planted by Sarah, Duchess of Marlborough. Moving, Anita thought, as she took another mouthful, and watched the clock-hand cut off the minutes, in a world of Duchesses and scampi. Something of fanaticism coloured Anita's feeling for scampi. They were adult and adventurous, they were gay. They were a sign of the times. They were also flavoured with a small taste of disquiet; with the question that needed to be asked. 'Say the difficult thing quickly,' someone had once advised her; for Anita advice was something that made sense until you had to act upon it. The question wouldn't come.

Instead, she was listening to Harvey: Her skin was made from a magnolia . . . There was no colour-scheme to compete with black hair and blue eyes—

There was. There was white hair and smooth brown skin and the green, gold-flecked eyes that made her think of a kind leopard. Eyes that were in no way diminished by the sparse, fair eyelashes. (But I can't say this, I don't know why not, can't be pride, I'm sure I haven't any.)

'And you desert me,' he said, 'for Yorkshire—of all places. I find it impossible to believe you come from Yorkshire.'

'Why not? Everybody comes from somewhere.'

'Stern and unyielding, Yorkshire. Stern and unyielding—like your father.'

'Like *Matthew?*' This made her laugh.

'He must be. Or you'd cancel your week-end, you'd stay here and play with me.'

'My conscience,' she pleaded, 'and his birthday. And I haven't seen him for nearly three months. And all those letters he writes give me guilt. Anything that strikes Matthew as funny gets written down and posted to me. And press-cuttings. And all the new rhymes.'

'Rhymes?'

'Sometimes his whole letter comes in rhyme. Obscure, quite often; anagram sort, so that I have to work at it to get the meaning. With my kind of brains, I have to work hard.'

Harvey was looking amused, curiously interested. 'Nothing wrong with your brains my darling,' he murmured.

'Oh, there is. His last card read:

Gospeller and Arnold
North East Two and Three.

And *that* was a reminder of his birthday. St Matthew; Matthew Arnold; NE—born—2nd March. Get it? It took me ages. He's slightly bonkers,' she added, 'But no trouble.'

'Bonkers,' Harvey murmured absently, still interested

and amused. 'What else does he do, besides writing letters in riddles?'

'He makes Christmas cards. And birthday cards.'

'Well—well, I've always wondered who did.'

'He said he was such a bad painter and such a bad poet that it came to be the only thing. But he composes a horrific highbrow crossword on the side. The "Syntax" crossword, in *New Outlook*.'

'Good God. Syntax . . . my sworn enemy. Always defeats me at one point, however hard I try to finish it. Tell him, will you?'

'I will. Puzzles are his thing, you see. In the war, before he joined the Commandos, he worked in M.I.5. They put him, he said, in a kind of incubator where he hatched out codes.'

'Fascinating,' said Harvey, looking as though he meant it. 'Codes and Commandos. Go on.'

'About Matthew?' said Anita, wondering now if she didn't want to talk about something else. 'I don't know that there's much more to say . . . Except that he did a marvellous thing once, years ago, when I was small. He joined up with an anthropologist—is that what I mean?—and travelled right across North America and down the west coast, digging about for bits of bone. Now *that*,' said Anita, 'I should like to do; I'm always hoping that he'll do it again, now that I'm big enough to hold the spade, but he never has. Just lives alone in Hawkeswell.'

'And your mother?'

'I don't remember her. Only two when she was killed . . . Matthew says he still doesn't believe she's dead. He's always expecting her to walk in and give him hell because the house is so untidy. That makes me cry; it doesn't make him cry at all.'

She thought she had lost his attention. He was

staring past her with the cold, vigilant look she had remarked before; as though the leopard were watching its prey. Rather frightening, this look.

'How dead *are* the dead? That's the question.' His voice was toneless, grim; he seemed to have gone a long way away.

She didn't like it; her forehead felt suddenly cold. 'What does that mean, Harvey?'

He came back, blowing her a kiss and quickly pretending that he was merely fondling his upper lip. This because the alarming housekeeper had come in with the cheese and the celery. Mrs Stone, christened Stonehenge by Anita, had presided over Minster House for eighteen months, apparently to Harvey's liking. Anita was less pleased: there was today a definite atmosphere of pity emanating from Stonehenge, a patronising, You-Poor-Thing look in her eyes. Just Another of His Ladies, said the eyes. Leading You On with a Cynical Disregard, the eyes said.

'Saw you again last night, Miss Gilroy,' the thin lips said, smiling a little.

Ah yes, the serial ... Anita suffered the serial as she suffered other regular irritations, crowded buses, insurance stamps, young men who lusted, young men who were queer, drip-dry dresses—which, for all their boast, needed ironing. And writing to her father.

The serial depicted a life of mixed sentiment and squalor in the Midlands. It concerned a perfectly beastly family beset by what were called contemporary problems. Anita played the beautiful saintly sister who sewed when she wasn't cooking, wheeling her crippled mother in a chair, heartening her neurotic brother or refusing the attentions of a comedy-moron who wore a fringe down to his eyebrows.

She had the good sense to smile at Stonehenge and seem pleased.

'The scampi were splendid. You cook them much better than I do.'

Stonehenge replied briskly that they were none of her doing; Miss Gilroy must thank the Ring-For-Your-Supper service (a North Royal institution by which exquisite food was delivered in blazing hot metal boxes on wheels). For herself she was allergic to all shellfish. They Brought Her Out. Stonehenge left the dining-room with the air of one who had scored a point.

Harvey said, 'She's intolerable today. The fact of next Thursday's party has finally penetrated. I've told her three times, but she wasn't listening. She never does. Has her "pardon?" at the ready before I'm halfway through my simplest sentence. Is it a sign of my advancing years that nobody listens any more?'

'Enough of your advancing years. My presence seems to bring them on.'

'So will your absence,' he said, looking at the clock.

'Oh don't . . .' (And could I ask the question now? No, I couldn't.) 'Why is Stonehenge against the party? Political views?'

'No. She imagines a mob of undisciplined vandals let loose, today week, all over the house . . . Foolish . . . Twenty at the outside, there'll be. Did you ever go to a party on the strength of a pamphlet?'

She giggled. 'No . . . I see what you mean. But— *why* are you a True Tory?'

'Because revolutions on behalf of the weak, the un-skilled, the loutish and the lazy have sent humanity halfway to hell. This little local eruption interests me as a symptom. For my bet, it's the earliest beginning of the Right Wing Revolution.'

'You don't think Rupert Ledyard will get in?'

'Forfeit his deposit, more likely.'

'I *was* a Socialist. I have to tell you. I'm not any more.'

'Growing up, my darling.' He handed her the silver cigarette box. A non-smoker, he was scrupulously attentive to the smoker's need. Her glance lingered, as it had done before, on the particular beauty of his hand; it was like the slim hand in a Vandyck portrait: one saw it fringed with lace, or decorated with a ring.

'Well, I want you to know everything about me—not that there's much to know.'

'God forbid you should know everything about me.'

That meant bed ... Women in bed. As though she cared. She was still kicking herself for the heart worn on the sleeve, the plunge of misery in the pub, guessing that he had once slept with that voluble lady. Ridiculous. He must have slept with dozens, voluble and taciturn.

'Time to drink your coffee and away.'

'I know.' (And if I don't ask it now ...) 'Harvey—just one more thing—'

'What's on your mind, my beautiful?'

She swallowed; the words still stuck. He smiled, and gently touched her hand. 'Take it easy, my darling. Take it easy, Araminta.'

(And 'Araminta' wasn't all that comforting: some other love, perhaps?)

She said, 'What was it the pink lady said to you—I was round the other side of the car—that made *you* say, "That's all over, thank God"?'

'Ah ...'

Her heart was knocking disproportionately. She could not read his look; the green-gold eyes were quite closed to her, as if some light in them had been switched off.

She started to speak again; heard suddenly the click of the outer gate. It was set between two pillars under

42

a slated gable, a Victorian anachronism, the slate and the bright red brick, making a defensive porch upon the hill.

She stared through the window.

'You have a visitor,' she told Harvey.

'He's out of luck.'

'Looks like a queer.'

'Darling, who doesn't? Probably a tradesman too idle to go to the back door.'

A sudden collision of argument from the hall brought him to his feet.

The boy stood just inside the front door, lowering at Stonehenge. Anita's eyes took a brief snapshot; curly fair hair, a pouting lip, a candy-striped shirt. She heard Harvey's officer-to-man voice.

'I don't recall inviting you.'

'You didn't. I've only just seen these bloody things.' He flung a whole scatter of True Tory leaflets across the floor. 'I jumped on the first train I could get.'

'Mrs Stone, would you please fetch Miss Gilroy's coat? Thank you. I have to take this lady to King's Cross, Quentin.'

'How could you? How *could* you?'

'Quiet, please. You just jump on the next train you can get—straight back to Bristol, there's a good boy. And don't do this again. *Remember what I told you.*'

The boy gave a petulant sniff. There were tears on his long lashes.

'Come along, Anita,' said Harvey; he was laughing now. He patted the boy's arm, then turned him briskly toward the steps.

'My poor Quentin. When I choose to give an order for leaflets, then my firm does the printing. The firm belongs to me—remember? Which means, among other things, that you're my paid employee. Your private pink politics have nothing to do with the transaction. Have they? . . . Goodbye.'

'But he's in love with you,' Anita said in the car.

'If that poor little Communist is in love with anybody but himself and Karl Marx . . . Don't look sad, my darling.'

'I'm not sad. I just have a very deep longing *not* to go to Yorkshire.'

2

THE SKETCH on Matthew's drawing-board presented the outline of a dear little boy seated in a big armchair. To these outlines must be added a stack of birthday-parcels heaped around the chair, Mummy's kind face peeping over the top of the chair and—up to the left—a table set with a birthday cake. Easy. But he was temporarily deflected by the look of the chair itself. He had somehow given it a personality. Not a pleasing person-ality. It seemed in its monstrous embrace to be swallow-ing the little boy. At once he began to improvise, pacing the floor, chanting aloud:

> 'I'm Moloch, the chair that eats children.
> They'd better keep out of my way.
> I gobble down lots
> Of succulent tots.
> A toddler's my natural prey.'

Pleased with it, he gave today another good mark. For Matthew Gilroy, all days had different flavours, auras, colours and characters. He could size up a day as soon as he awoke in the morning. He could like or dislike it long before it got a chance to prove itself; even before he knew if it was to be clear of pain, or if the old head-wound was going to muffle his apprehension with its dull, aching cloud.

Today was bearing out the truth of his six a.m. diagnosis. It had a most pleasing personality. Unlike the chair.

'I'm Moloch. I cuddle the kiddies.
My soft-padded seat seems to fit them.
Then they slip through the crack
And they never come back
For a hair of the horsehair that bit them.'

He ran it through in a muffled snorting voice with a tinge of Cockney accent. By the third run-through it was fixed in his head; he would remember it for the rest of his life. On the other hand he could remember nothing of practical importance—least of all when his head ached—and he had now forgotten who was driving his daughter into Borrowgate to catch the London train. Both the aunts had offered, Doctor Bates had expressed himself as more than willing. He, Matthew, was obviously the person to do it. What was the problem—if there was a problem? What had been decided? And what time was the train? And what was the time now? His watch had stopped.

He shouted for Anita, who was clashing in the kitchen and could not—most obviously—hear him. The kitchen opened off Matthew's long, chaotic living-room. He had made and hung the green baize door himself, about fifteen years ago. It needed attention. He nudged it carefully open. Anita was chasing the last fish-cake round the frying-pan with a spatula. The other fish-cakes, nicely browned, though a little shaggy at the edges, sat on their plates on the top of the stove.

'Sod you,' Anita was saying in her beautiful cello voice to the last fish-cake.

Matthew eyed her doubtfully. He found his daughter strange but magical company. Entertaining her was always like having a unicorn about the house. But this week-end she had provided him with a new perplexity.

46

The unicorn had come near. It had shed its mysterious magic. It presented the aspect of a large, solemn-eyed ...what? He would have said donkey, were donkeys known to be thoughtful. It was plain to see that Anita had taken up thinking.

Not only thinking ... thinking about him. Of all people. As though every facet of his life had suddenly acquired importance for her. The question that put an end to each solemn silence was a direct, personal question:

'Do you *really* like living alone?'

'Did you *never* fall in love again?'

'Have you *no* politics these days?'

'Where *exactly* were you in America? Tell about it. Will you go again?'

More surprising yet was an appetite for information about the war, his war, the 1939–45 adventure. Until now her mind had seemed to run it concurrently with the Wars of the Roses.

Curiouser and curiouser. Any normal father would, he supposed, be delighted. For himself delight was darkened by the sense of a waiting disclosure, of a change in things. He didn't want things to change for Anita; he wanted her to stay as she was, beloved and magical; the unicorn that went on its aloof way, walking through private, enchanted groves.

Reflecting thus, he found he had now forgotten what it was that he had forgotten and therefore needed to ask Anita. He could only remember, 'I'm Moloch, the chair that eats children.' He watched her spooning the grilled tomatoes into place beside the fish-cakes.

The aunts said she was beautiful. Aunt Dorothy, ecstatic as always, claimed that her looks were enhanced by the current fashion: 'purely mediaeval—straight hair—tabards—tights!' cried Dorothy. Aunt Mary had said, 'Lucky she's got Laura's figure and not ours', which Aunt Dorothy took ill. Both aunts were well-padded. Mary had no shame about it. In a peevish tone Dorothy had pointed out that *all* the Cattle family had the same eyes; her own eyes, Mary's eyes, dear dead Laura's eyes and Anita's eyes were more than blue—or less—but in any case a rare blue, a light silvery blue. (She was right.) 'She doesn't take after Matthew at all. Not one *bit,*' Dorothy had continued, as though this were cause for congratulation. She was right again. All Anita had inherited from Matthew was his height, his black hair—and a certain smile. He would recognise this smile because he smiled at himself in the glass, while combing his beard. The beard was the result of a calculation that in a normal lifetime he would gain six weeks by not shaving. It was a neat black valance: it was the only thing in his life that he enjoyed keeping tidy.

('Matthew looks like an avenging pirate,' said Aunt Dorothy; 'Particularly in that red shirt. Why does he always wear a red shirt?' 'In mourning for my past politics,' said Matthew.)

'Soup's on,' said Anita. 'Are you in a trance?'

'I've forgotten what I came to ask you. Why weren't you bored? That *wasn't* what I was going to ask you,' he added, helping her carry in the fish-cakes, 'but it will do for now.'

'Why wasn't I bored when?'

'Last night. With the aunts. All the personal remarks. Mostly made as though you weren't there. At your age I'd have been screaming.'

'Careful—there's a sock or something just where you're putting your tray.'

'Not a *sock,*' said Matthew indignantly. 'Only the two egg-warmers left from breakfast.' He steered them out of the way.

They were picnicking at one end of the gigantic table that carried the jig-saw at the other end, with a miscellaneous pyramid, mainly books and papers, in the middle. The jig-saw was Anita's birthday-present; a beguiling beast, *Il Cavaliere* by Picasso; unrelieved blue-and-white and wholly unintelligible: obliging him against all his rules to begin with the outside edge.

The puzzle would, he thought, be a consolation after she went . . . 'Ha, got it,' he said now. 'Got it.'

'Got why I wasn't bored?' said Anita.

'No, got what I'd forgotten. Who's taking you to your train and why, and what time? There was a thing about it and that's all I can remember.'

Anita said, 'Quite simple. The train leaves at four and the thing was about the car. If Ken couldn't get it right . . . But he did . . . While you were working.'

'Splendid. Then I'm driving you in?'

'Yes.'

'Well, that was all I wanted to know. These are very good fish-cakes.'

'I think so too . . . that wasn't all you wanted to know. There was why I wasn't bored.'

'Ah.'

'The aunts don't bore me. They're cosy, reassuring; part of the family pattern, Yorkshire pattern. Aunt Dorothy can take off into grand opera, but Aunt Mary's terribly intelligent.'

'Too intelligent . . . What *does* bore you? When were you last bored?'

He needed to make these explorations: she was growing up so fast and he saw her so sledom. She never objected, though she was always slow with her replies.

'When was I last bored? Let me think.' Finally she said, 'When I was taken to a Lesbian club called Scylla

49

and Charybdis. November, I think it was. Generally speaking, I don't bore easy.'

'Good God!' said Matthew.

'Now you really do look like Dorothy's avenging pirate.'

'Who on earth took you to—'

'Well, a Lesbian. She was quite nice. Didn't make a fuss or anything—just sorry I wasn't. Oh, and I know another thing. Boring thing ... Bisson. Bodkin. Fardels,' she added with her mouth full.

'Come again?' said Matthew.

'Hamlet.'

'Blinding glimpses of the obvious. And what's so boring about those words, d'you mind telling me?'

'Not *them*—taking them out ... *That's* boring. Shakespeare for the teen-ager. B.B.C. School prog.,' she explained. 'With the most disheartening producer— a sad breathy little man who's rewriting it all. Any words the teen-agers wouldn't know are out. I can't see the point.'

'Then you're a very silly girl,' said Matthew; 'haven't you grasped the fact that *nothing* must be difficult for today's tots—not even learning? They must be kept clean of religion, discipline, poetry, morals, magic, manners, inspiration and other old-fashioned misapprehensions. All of which cause trauma and psychosis, as I'd have thought you knew. Be a kind girl and give me some bread.'

The telephone rang, and Anita shot up from her chair. 'For me,' said Anita. She went running into the hall. As she ran one foot tripped over the other. 'Take it easy, Araminta,' she said.

'*Take it ...*'

No. She could not have said that.

She had said that.

'*Take it easy, Araminta.*'

Thought stopped. The sun went out, the day departed, there was no day, or not this day. There was a swirl of cloud and Matthew alone, his memory hawkish, soaring and swooping, ringing above a prey that was four words.

Faintly through the shut door he heard Anita talking on the telephone.

Black ripples down below, chasm opened on the old river running at the bottom of his mind; the forgotten river. A rush of blind shapes in the dark. The cliff and the light. A snake of fear sliding through his bowels. Hands and hurting and killing, the killing of something too young to die.

But this is insane.

He shut his eyes. He opened them. The room came back: today's room, the always room; with the log-fire, red-pointed grey plumes rolling under the brick arch of the chimney-piece; the bookshelves, the massy comfortable furniture, the tool-basket on the floor, the wide windows. The drawing desk, tall in its corner, the stool, the rack of paints and pencils. Through the windows, he could see the river, could hear the always-sound of the river. This river, the Garfe, with beyond it the slopes of brown moorland that rose behind the bare trees like a great steep wave.

This river. This room. This day. He was here, himself, in Garfedale where he was born. He was Matthew Gilroy, aged fifty-two; purveyor of literary pranks and pretty-pretty postcards.

I am I. This is now.

Now. Not then. Not that river. Not the black ripples washing. Not the run through the dark. Not the cliff. Not the cold voice saying 'Take it easy, Araminta.' The killer's voice.

Forgotten, it's forgotten, so long ago, it has to be forgotten, but what am I thinking? Why is Anita taking such a hell of a time? It's unbearable sitting here not knowing what I'm thinking.

Or not daring to know.

Snap out of it. She might have heard the phrase anywhere. Look how words travel, any words, from mouth to mouth, across cities, across continents, across oceans . . . the easiest currency, the lightest luggage . . . four words.

In all probability she won't have a notion where she heard them.

He rose from his chair and plucked the door open. He stood, looking into the hall, looking at Anita. She was obviously unaware of him. Stooped forward, bowed from the waist, with her elbows on the ledge where the telephone was, she presented rather an odd view; the lower, horizontal half of her being draped by a swathe of old coats and mackintoshes slung from the hatstand. The effect, he decided, was that of a palfrey in its trappings.

She talked on. 'Absolute bliss, to be met. Do you *really* want to bother with King's Cross? I could get a taxi . . . Proves I'm lacking in what? Acumen? An acumen-deficiency . . .? Don't let Stonehenge put herself out as they say, I'll be dining on the train, I'll . . . of course I do. In fact I could burst,' she added and then stared in a dazed way at the telephone before she said, 'Oh—you've gone,' and hung it up. Turning slowly, freeing her hips from their ill-matching draperies, she looked to be in a stupor.

'So it's Love—ha?' said Matthew.

She gazed at him a moment before she said, 'I don't know about Ha.'

First, as they moved back into the room, he saw that

she was blushing. The magnolia skin emphatically exposed the blush. Then he saw it fade and cool. Reaching her place at the table she stood still; frozen suddenly, becoming her public image, Miss Anita Gilroy, six feet high and in trained command of the whole structure. It was a dignified lighthouse that shone coldly upon him. He got the message. He said, 'All right, all right. None of my business. I'm sorry.'

She said nothing. She helped herself to coffee and lit a cigarette. She drifted away to the window. He grumbled, 'Don't be cross,' still seeing that she had reason to be cross. In the last two years, there had been other calls from London, plenty of them; there had been names spoken, despite her obvious efforts, with an overtone; sudden changes of plan respecting arrival times and departure times: all the signs, he said to himself, and I never intruded, never asked, before. That is my rule; and now I've broken it.

Easy to put this right; easy, could he say to her, 'I promise you I've no intention of prying. I won't ask you a thing about your chap. All I want is to know where you picked up that bloody little phrase.'

Here he sat, saying this in his head. But not aloud. No words would come.

'You look *most* peculiar,' said Anita's voice above his head. She had returned to the table for more coffee.

'Do I? Do I indeed? Well, I must ask you something . . .' He might, he thought, approach it by way of an ellipse: 'Do you remember what you said when you heard the telephone ring?'

She frowned. 'I said "that's for me" . . . didn't I?'

'And something else.'

'Are you playing a game?'

'No. What was it you said *after* "That's for me"? As you ran into the hall?'

'Goodness—don't remember saying anything, do I?' She laughed suddenly. 'Yes, I do. I said, "Take it easy, Araminta".' This time she spoke the words with a kind of caressing bravado. 'Any objection?' she asked.

It was absurd that he should find it so difficult to ask the simple question. He had to push out every syllable, as though this were a breathing-exercise. 'Where—did —you—get—it—from?'

'From Harvey.'

'Harvey being the telephone, if you see what I mean?' She nodded.

And now—remembering your questions—I realize I am quite well-informed about your Harvey. Harvey is my age; or thereabouts; he fought in the war. A widower too, likely; at least he lives alone. What else? Ah, yes. He has some tie-up with America. Myopic of me not to see what the change in you meant. I knew I didn't like the change.

But it's still a thousand to one against his being—this Harvey's being . . . The thought lost track, lost shape. He heard his own voice, 'I'd like to know—if you wouldn't mind—a little more about him.'

She was looking at him, as if she wanted to go on being the lighthouse but had a doubt about it some-where. 'I don't get this—'

'Just the name.'

'Blessington. Harvey Blessington. Colonel Harvey Blessington.' The bravado was still there, the caress too.

'And he lives?'

'I don't under*stand*—'

'Just tell me where he lives.'

'In North Royal. A place called Minster House. But I don't—'

54

'Never mind,' he said. 'Never mind.' He became silent then, sitting still.

Anita drank two more mouthfuls of coffee without tasting them. She looked steadily at her father, having the sensation of one who hears a familiar person talk in an unknown tongue.

I don't know him. I don't know anything about him. It came like a slap in the mind, a sudden window banging open. I know the outside, the person who writes to me, who makes up crosswords, my-father-who-lives-in-Yorkshire. I know the widower who's lived alone for seventeen years; who has the aunts for company, my mother's sisters; the man who belongs to this village and these moors. I know the soldier, the ex-Commando who survived the legendary horror of the Labrière raid, two years in a prison camp, and whose wound can still put a cloud over the day. Sometimes I've wondered a little, about his life: about the life of a man alone ... dimly perhaps I saw a woman somewhere, but she had no face: just an idea, taken from the books I read.

I thought that was a real person. But it wasn't. *This* is real. This sudden window opening; this stranger.

She watched him as he swung to his feet, and went about the room, savagely tidying it, as if someone else had made the mess. He punched the cushions, and, taking an armful of papers from the middle of the table, put them finally on the window sill. He said with his back to her, 'I've forgotten what time's your train.'

'Four. I don't know what's wrong.'

One hand went irritably through the plumy dark hair, turning it into confusion. 'Nothing wrong ... nothing wrong.' He had found a pair of bedroom slippers under the table and with an expression of mingled triumph and disgust, put them outside in the hall. 'Four, you said? Then we've got time—got about an hour—'

'Time for what?'

He gave her a smile then, a sudden savage smile. 'For a game. Scrabble ... game of words ... spelling out words ...' The odd smile was still on his face, making her uneasy.

She said mournfully, 'I always lose.'

'Never mind ... never mind.' He had found the box, was putting out the board and the little letters. He let these run through his hand, saying, 'So few letters, and so many words ... the easiest currency.'

'The easiest what?'

'Doesn't matter. Don't look so perplexed ... Come along. Set up your side ... Blessington,' he muttered with his head down. 'What else about him, eh? Anything more?'

'Golly Moses, he's a *friend*—'

'Of course, of course. Just like to know ... interested to know ... Age?'

'In his forties.'

'Which end of them?'

'I'd think, about the middle.'

'Job?'

'One wouldn't call it a job. Business,' she said, watching him, as he shifted the letters on the board. 'He's quite rich.'

'A tycoon! Well, well.' His brow was creasing; he looked puzzled now.

'No. Retired Colonel. Ex-Army. You ought to like that.'

Matthew gave a suprising angry laugh. 'Last sort I'd have put you in love with, a retired Colonel.'

'Oh, but not what you think.'

His near-black eyes were suddenly on her, wicked and

alight. 'And just what do I think? Suppose you tell me.'

'You think red face and white moustache and whisky —and the-country's-going-to-the-dogs, don't you now? Prehistoric. At least pre-war . . . Harvey was a Colonel at twenty-seven. And he's perfectly beautiful, so there.'

'Beautiful? So what we have is a beautiful rich retired colonel.'

'Yes,' she said, still watching him.

He began setting the letters up in their stand. 'And how did you meet this hybrid?'

'At a party.'

'Some noisy pile-up of wine, drugs and girls in a basement?'

'Not at all: elegant six-till-eight in Kensington; I saw him across the room and the whole place turned over.'

'Love at first sight. I see.' He rubbed his jaw with one finger. 'For a man determined not to pry, I don't seem to have done too well. But I'd still like to know more—'

'More what?'

'Oh—have no fear. Not my intention to ask what your relations are.'

'If by relations you mean what people usually mean, we aren't having them. I want to marry him.'

'The devil you do.'

Silence then. In the silence there seemed an opposition stronger than words; she felt forced to speak, to gabble at speed: 'He's been everywhere and done everything; he's a widower; his wife died years ago; tragically; he hardly ever talks about her; he doesn't drink and he doesn't smoke—he takes pills, sometimes, to make him sleep, (you'd disapprove of that, of course) but you have to do *some*thing, don't you? And he has a family business in Bristol; he goes there at week-ends. I'd like you to

57

meet him; you could come to London and meet him; he's most enormously kind.'

'Ah!' His head came up and he gave her the smile again. '*If I give my body to be burned, and have not charity* . . . Let's begin. We can play for an hour. And then you can get on your train, and go back to him.' His eyes were still on her, and indeed the smile was still there, but it was without light or warmth, as if he himself had gone away and left it there.

Yes, a stranger. Not just the man of wild changes of mood, the almost childish sweep from fury to laughter, of whom she had sometimes said, 'He's pathos', without knowing why. This was a man in torment.

And it has something to do with me, something to do with Harvey, something to do with 'Take it easy, Araminta.'

And I don't like it, one bit.

Mary Cattle drove with steady care up the village street. A large woman of sixty, she drove with an air of authority, of one who is going to stand no nonsense from the engine. The authority was placid, not belligerent; in her days as a schoolmistress, before her retirement, Mary had kept order without fuss; the broad snub-nosed face had commanded obedience, not fear.

Driving back from Borrowgate, with the shopping on the seat of the small car, she welcomed the village again. Sometimes, on such a day as this when you could feel the Spring, she saw the village with a new eye, as if she had not known it for a lifetime. How did it come here, this sudden pucker of the valley road drawn up to your left, encircling a patch of green? The river winding on beside the road: the strange river which at one point ran for some distance underground; the church, twelfth century, with its green and its gravestones toppling down to the Garfe; the beetle-browed village store and the bus-stop by the green . . . What was the point of this tiny place that never changed? From time to time Mary had been moved to write about the village: one of those vast Yorkshire-family-sagas, full of hard-swearing fathers and pregnant girls—'Nobody wants to read *those* any more, dear,' Dorothy assured her. Mary remained untroubled; the book was a fancy, something for her mind to play with; it would never be written. Only sometimes the words went through her head, *Strangeness in the valley*, and she would see in her mind's eye Matthew's house, as she could see it now, with the mountain of moorland rising behind it, and the river at its side. She could see too in a drift of pale sunlight the little grey bridge, like a humped lizard, that grew straight from the garden and spanned the waterfall.

As she came to her own house, she saw Dorothy standing on the step looking out for her. Dorothy was by nature a looker-outer, ever on the edge of anxiety, eager to give news. A head taller than her sister, moon-faced, big-eyed, the tragedy-queen lacking a tragedy (unless one counted her short theatrical career, under the stage-name of Desirée Castle, and the long sad aftermath of elocution-lessons, eurhythmics, amateur opera, school pageants and the rest of it.) She was dressed in a huge embroidered shift, with great swags of amber beads hurling themselves about between her active chin and the shelf of her bosom. She cried, before Mary had got out of the car, 'There you are! I've been waiting—'

'Not,' said Mary, retrieving her shopping from the car—'really necessary, since I told you when I'd be back and I am, if anything, early.'

'I know, I know; but *Matthew's* rung up. Just now. He wants to come to dinner.'

Mary felt a small twinge of recognition, having had him so recently in mind; but said only, 'Ah. Well, the cottage pie will spread over three.' She smiled to herself, rather liking the image this presented, but Dorothy went plunging on. 'He sounded just a little odd, you know how he can sometimes; I said we'd be delighted to have him, but he said delight wasn't exactly what he was after. I think he had something on his mind.'

'Ah,' said Mary again; 'well, everybody has, of some sort or another. Perhaps you'd carry the eggs.'

In the kitchen Dorothy billowed about, getting in the way. Mary put the vegetables in the rack, the bread in the bread bin. (And there's something reassuring about them, I don't know why; part of the established structure of life.) Dorothy, blocking the path to the refrigerator, said, 'I suppose he misses Anita; I expect that's what it is—'

'Well, of course he does; he sees her so seldom, he's devoted to her and he makes no claims.'

'Claims,' said Dorothy, who had a habit of picking up the last word of a speech while she gave her attention to something else. 'I thought—if you don't want me for anything—that I'd go into Borrowgate this afternoon.'

'But I've just come from Borrowgate—'

'I know, dear, I know. I thought I'd just go in and have my hair done.' The big-eyed moon face looked supplicating, apologetic. Dorothy retained a profound interest in make-up and hair-dressing; she could spend an afternoon swimming dreamily through the pages of coloured magazines, admiring exotic young women, lean enough for her to make three of them; absorbing articles on face cream and how to improve your bust. Mary did not so much despise these things as look on them with detachment; she scrubbed her face with soap

60

and drew her hair firmly into a bun. Nevertheless Dorothy, coming into the house with her hair bright blue and smelling like an over-heated conservatory, always looked guilty, as if she'd been caught stealing jam.

'Well, of course have your hair done,' Mary said, putting onions in a bowl. 'You'd better ring up now to see when they can do you.' She knew of no way to absolve Dorothy's guilt; it all seemed to her rather childish, but there was no need to fuss. Matthew was coming to dinner, and a man in the house was so rare a diversion that to Dorothy it called for the hairdresser. It was quite unnecessary; Matthew wouldn't notice if Dorothy was wearing a tarbush; to him they were 'the aunts'; his dead wife's sisters, known in the village as the Misses Cattle, and therefore, sometimes, as 'the two old cows of Squaretrees'.

When Dorothy had gone, Mary began to make the cottage pie. Knife, chopping board, mincer. As she used these she became aware of a liveliness in the day, an air that sparked. Due to Matthew? Perhaps. She had no wish like Dorothy to fly to dressing-table or hairdresser; nevertheless Matthew appealed to her strong, adventurous curiosity. 'Brother-in-law' did not sound a likely phrase: Laura, the youngest sister, had been dead so long, the time of marriage so short; the connection seemed lost. True, Dorothy would take off sometimes into a sentimental orbit, weeping a little and saying How Beautiful it was that Matthew had been True to Laura's Memory. Mary made no comment. She didn't think Matthew had been true to Laura's memory, or if he had, that it was much to the point. He did not, she thought, any longer grieve for her. He was a lone tiger, pacing over the moors, working with sudden feverish fury at the Christmas cards or the crossword puzzles:

she was aware in his presence of some explosive force kept insecurely down.

Something on his mind. Strangeness in the valley . . .

Held between contentment and disquiet, Mary went on mixing.

The dark was on fire. The noise that stunned his ears had in it the elements of pain; he did not have, in this storming confusion, wit to know whether he himself was hurt. Some thread of understanding conveyed to him that he was still moving through this desperate dark; that he was not in the launch, not in the black, blazing river, slipping and turning, a body alight with the petrol that flared like an evil carnival there. Quickly on. Away from the base of the cliff. The heart's thunder drowned in the louder guns; the dark through which he ran threatened by searchlights, moving with sinister silence amongst so much sound. Death close about him, at his shoulder, in his nostrils: no longer the quiet passing in hospital bed or home, the dignified melancholy of lament and funeral: something now without grace or mercy: a body there with both legs torn off; a man with the blood running from his bowels. Quickly on. And the awareness of the man beside him, a stranger, not of his company; face blackened by the fiery light reflected in his eyes, memorable eyes . . . And now the true horror was coming close; he had to meet it again: the figure that had no place here, the boy who came running with odd lunatic lilt, head swaying to one side; a half-wit, a harmless French fool, tow-headed, coming with innocence towards—

Matthew shouted '*No!*' and stared, for a moment uncomprehending at the firelit wall before him.

His room; his house; the logs flaring in the hearth,

making the light swarm upon the wall; the gargle of the river, this river with its always-sound, slipping placidly, with no danger there.

He sat up on the sofa and rubbed his face with his hands. Bad time of the day to sleep; nearly six o'clock: he had gone out over the moors, striding into the grey blowy afternoon, with the occasional patches of sunlight opening over the bare waves of ground. Once home he'd taken a drink and flung himself on to the sofa, with the nagging thought of yesterday still in his head; he must have suddenly slept.

He poured himself another drink; the dream stayed sourly in his mind. Some weeks since he'd had the dream; but Anita had brought it vividly back.

Brought back too it seemed the throb of the old wound; brought back the climate and memory of the raid, which sometimes seemed the seeding ground of all memory. He stood with the glass in his hand, head a little turned, as if over his shoulder he caught echoes of the guns, and heard across a wide plain of time and difference, the voices of men, friend and enemy, close in that fevered dark. (And it had been March then as it was March now; the dangerous time of year, when the moon and tides were right: the first of spring.)

In the lamplight he saw the small golden gleam on the spines of books: *The Great Raid; The Story of the —th Yorkshire Regiment; Prisoner of War*. In the silence he heard the old names: Philip Carlson, David Ballam, Jack Forge. The raid had lasted a few hours of a March night, yet it seemed to combine a whole history: training, climax, and aftermath. Young men together: young men of a special kind, fearless, quick-witted, stung with the gadfly of adventure, leaping death as if it were a wide ditch, a challenge put before them. They had seemed careless, even happy, and there were times when

63

he had matched them in gaiety. But, at the test, he had been aware of a darkness in himself: not fear, especially, but a lonely place of brooding and reasonless despair.

Quickly he finished his drink; slightly rubbed his forehead where the pain was with the palm of his hand. That was all past. It was only so vivid in this quiet room because Anita had brought it back.

He put down his glass. Dinner with the aunts; the prospect of Mary Cattle was strangely healing. He had made his decision. He would, for the first time, tell the whole story; and she would hear him with understanding and without surprise. And when he had told her, the plan would be clear in his mind; he would know whether it was the right thing to do.

'I expect you'd like some more coffee.' Dorothy rose from her chair with the suddenness of an unwatched soufflé; Mary waved her down again. Dorothy was always in danger of wrecking a mood by jumping up and offering drinks or coffee or little biscuits: an over-stressed anxiety to please.

Matthew didn't answer; Mary thought he hadn't heard. She watched him; he sat leaning forward with the firelight on the craggy piratical face, his pipe in his hands. She stayed with her hands folded in her lap, willing Dorothy to keep still. For he was telling them, as he had not done before, the whole story of the raid. (And in this placid room, with the knitting on the sofa's arm and the clock measuring the harmless hours, she caught a whiff of the unknown male world: the extremes of chaos and fear. It gave him a difference; it was like talking to someone come back from the grave.)

'By then,' Matthew said, 'we had done all we could. It was about two o'clock in the morning. The clouds had lifted and there was a misty moon. We had to get down the cliff, to the beach. It seemed our only hope of escape; there was a motor torpedo boat still alive; if we could get to it . . . The river was a kind of funeral pyre of wooden motor launches; their engines exploded as the guns fired on them, and there was a huge drift of black smoke that almost dimmed the searchlights.' He paused; Mary kept her eyes on him. He was still looking into the fire; at the small, innocent flames. 'There were four of us,' he said. 'Jack Forge and I of the demolition party; David Ballam of No. 3 Commando; and—a stranger.' He looked up suddenly, away from the fire, as if someone had lightly knocked on the door. 'An officer of the fighting troops; not of our company; I hadn't seen him before. I was sure of that; even with his blackened face, he was a stranger.'

He paused again. Mary sat still. She could hear the wind thrumming against the house: the bullying, Yorkshire wind.

'We reached the top of the cliff. We began to climb down. And then the searchlight swung, and a machine-gun opened fire. We could hear the bullets, striking the chalk of the cliff. Suddenly I heard Jack Forge cry out. He'd been hit in the chest. He was a little way above me. I still had an ampoule of morphia. As I moved up towards him I called to the stranger who was below me, "Come and help me get him down." I could see the blackened face turned up to me. He said, "Don't be a bloody fool. Leave him. He's had it, anyway".'

Mary saw him put his head in his hands as if the old anger was still beating there.

'I gave Jack the morphia; somehow I climbed down with him. But as we got to the beach, a heavy gun made a direct hit on the launch: it blew up like a mine.' He leaned forward and knocked his pipe against the grate.

'So we had only one hope. To get back through the town, out into open country, make our way as others had done, to Spain, and then to Gibraltar. But I couldn't think of anything except this man who'd told me to leave Jack. I hated him more than the enemy, with that kind of hatred you feel at a time of extreme exhaustion. No sense in it, perhaps; Jack was quickly unconscious and he died soon after. And yet—'

Dorothy plopped up from the sofa and began, 'Oh, but of course—'

'We tried to make our way back through the town, by the side of the river. We moved in the shadows. With our rubber-soled boots we made no sound. The stranger was a little ahead of me. I went behind him, hating him. And then the boy came, limping and lolloping by the river side.'

No movement from Dorothy now; the tragedy-queen's face looked bewildered, mournful and expectant.

Matthew said, 'I don't know where he came from, or what he was doing there. He was a simpleton, of course, a half-wit; not more than seventeen. He was very excited; he shouted that his name was Pierre; that he'd come to help us—'*Moi, Pierre, je vous aiderai!*' —he danced around us, when all we so desperately needed was silence and the chance to escape. He began pulling at the arm of the stranger ahead of me, insisting that he had come to help; I can see his face now very clearly: he was pale with tumbled fair hair, and there was a kind of silly love in his face, like a child who expects to be welcomed.' He looked now, Mary thought, like a tough dreamy apostle; the bearded face had a strange vision on it.

He said, 'I saw what happened then. The stranger turned with one savage movement. It wasn't just temper; it wasn't just fear: it was the violence of a man

66

who intends to kill. And he killed. With the old unarmed-combat stroke, upward, across the throat; then threw his body in the river. I saw the black water go over the bright hair, and then there was nothing; only one more amongst the dead.'

Mary heard again the thrumming of the wind; there was now perhaps the light clash of rain against the window.

'There were so many dead: young men with so much more to live for. And he would have died anyway, most likely; he was running about with all the safety of a rabbit on a high-road. And yet . . . *that* is the death I remember; and the hatred I still feel is for the man who killed him.'

'Evil sticks with one,' said Mary, placidly lighting a cigarette. 'It touches the stuff deep down; the stuff one keeps hidden.'

He gave a little grin. 'Sub-conscious mind, eh? You know all about it—'

'I wouldn't say all.' Mary was still placid.

Dorothy gave another little bounce and said, 'Oh, but she does; she's always talking of—'

Matthew went on as if he hadn't heard. 'The man beside me turned to meet my eye; he knew I'd seen it all. I couldn't see his face well, but his eyes seemed to smile. He said, "Take it easy, chum; what's one more stiff amongst so many?" I didn't have time to answer; it was then that I was hit. I felt the blow on the side of my forehead, as if a brick had caught me. I don't remember pain, only a sudden darkness coming up like water. I was on the ground. It was all fading out, the smell of high explosive, burning oil and blood. I could only see one thing clear: the blackened face of the strange man, leaning over me.' Matthew had taken his pipe from his mouth and was holding it tightly in his hands. 'He was saying—and it was the last thing I heard—"Take it easy. Take it easy, Araminta." '

After a little silence, Dorothy leaned forward and said, '*Who*, Matthew dear?'

'Araminta.' He repeated it slowly. 'Heard it? Know it as a name?'

'No, I don't think—'

'Heard the expression, "Take it easy, Araminta"?'

Mary sat frowning. Dorothy was burbling on in a nervous gabble: Heard take-it-easy of course, that was American wasn't it; people often said it; you heard it at the cinema, but Araminta, now; that was something she—

'Because I haven't heard it,' Matthew said. 'I haven't heard it in more than twenty years. Until yesterday.' He paused, and Mary caught in the fire's light the sudden anguish on his face. 'When Anita said it, running into the hall.'

Mary said, with a flash of sight, 'And she heard it from—'

'Precisely,' said Matthew. 'From the man she apparently intends to marry.'

Dorothy gave a bounce and a muted bark; Mary said, 'But—'

Matthew got to his feet and began pacing the room. 'Oh yes; the buts are enormous. *He* could have heard it anywhere; perhaps it's well-known: some American phrase that I've missed; something out of a film or a play. And yet . . . he's a man of my age, or thereabouts; he was in the war. He wasn't a Colonel then, of course . . . But when I heard her say it, I thought *Here it is. I've met it again as I always feared I would.*'

Silence. Dorothy made one or two nervous movements, then came to rest. Mary went on looking at him. This moment for her too seemed to be one of recognition, something she had been waiting for: her affection, curiosity and concern had come to an appointed place.

She said, 'This man—would you recognise him?'

'I don't know—I don't know. Our faces were blackened, remember. I think of him as a small man; anyway, shorter than myself . . . I didn't see him again. When I came to, it was morning, cold and misty, and I was laid out with the wounded and the dead and the dying on the floor of a kind of warehouse. We were piled into lorries and driven to the prison hospital at St. Faure. I don't know what happened to him. He may have escaped; got back to England . . . been one of the lucky ones.' His mouth turned down. 'He may have been killed. I used to lie in that dreary prison hospital, thinking of him, praying that he'd been killed. I liked to think of him dead.'

The words, Mary thought, were surprising in this room, the room of two maiden women who lived alone. They had a naked edge of anger like the sharpened edge of an axe. She saw that his hands were trembling.

Yes, this was the unknown thing about Matthew; this cherished hatred, this remembered pain.

'So many of them died,' he said. 'I used to imagine the ways in which he'd been killed. I saw the wound, in the chest, in the stomach, in the head. I was comforted to think of it.' (Almost a stranger's face now, Mary thought: fierce and dedicated. She felt a sudden cold apprehension.)

'I have to know.' His head was down; he was rubbing his forehead with his hands. 'Somehow I have to know.'

Mary said, 'Wait a little—'

'And let Anita marry him?'

'No—no. Try to find out a little more. What is it, after all? A phrase; a few words. Nothing.' She could feel, as she spoke, the threat rolling off, rolling away:

the relief was palpable. 'Something will happen; you'll see Anita again and your mind will be set at rest—'

Dorothy was up from the sofa; she had a hand on his arm. 'Oh, I'm sure she's right; I believe one's *shown* what to do—'

Mary saw the gleam in the black eyes, the shaking of the head. 'I don't think I shall be shown. I don't think the force of a kindly Providence has any part in this. I think this is of the devil.'

Dorothy took a step back, knocking over the coffee cup; the rain was louder now, like the rattle of beads against the glass.

Mary said, 'You know we're always here, Matthew? That if you need any help—?'

He was planning to go now; he gave some acknowledgement to this, but she thought it hadn't reached him; his mind was turning and pacing within its cage.

The door was opened on to the rainy dark; the bare trees plunged and cracked in the wind, and the rain prancing in the puddles gave the sense of a company about them. He ducked rapidly into the car, offering them thanks for the evening; but it was as if he had already gone.

Mary stood at the door while the buffeting weather blew against her face, watching the car gather speed in the dripping dark. Absurd to feel that he went towards disaster: he was only returning home to the house she knew so well, a place lonely yet benign, where no evil thing could happen.

Returned to the room, she emptied the ashtrays into the fire. Dorothy was billowing about, restless with alarm and curiosity; full of questions beginning, 'But do you think—' 'What can it possibly—' and 'Surely you don't believe—' To these Mary gave scant replies. She was pondering the story, trying to answer the questions in her own mind. So many years ago, yet this violence was still alive for him. She murmured, more to herself than to Dorothy, '*Why* should it have gone so deep?'

Dorothy said, 'Deep, dear?' but Mary went on, answering herself, 'One has to remember he was young, of course; always sensitive to cruelty and pain; great courage, but vulnerable beneath.'

'Oh, yes, I always think Matthew is the most—'

'And this was his first real engagement, the first true taste of war—'

'*War*,' said Dorothy: 'Oh dear I—' but Mary was turning away, absently taking up book and spectacles, preparing now for bed. She wanted to leave the thought of Matthew, but the memory of the evening persisted uncomfortably in her mind. She would be glad to sleep; to wake tomorrow, seeing the daylight again, with the unreasoning fear gone.

Matthew slammed the door of the car, and stood in the enveloping rain. He could see the darkened windows of his house: the silent, friendly place that could be turned, for the purposes of the game, into an enemy. Should he play the game tonight? The game of creeping up on the house, as if someone waited in ambush there; entering with care and silence, as he'd been taught to in war-time, long ago.

No, tonight he was not in the mood. He strode through the rain and went quickly into the house. Back in the room his earlier thoughts seemed to be waiting for him: there was his empty glass, the fire had burned low. He stood there moving one hand across his forehead: the headache was gone, leaving only a dim reminder, a little pulse without pain.

71

Had it been wise to talk, to tell the whole story, after so long? Perhaps he should have kept silent. Talk had roused a kind of fury in his thoughts: the memory of the raid was too lively, agitating, like a thirst that cannot be quenched. He moved restlessly about the room, hearing and not hearing the sounds of the river and the rain.

He paused by his desk. Comic drawings for birthday cards; sketches of dogs and small children: he pushed them away. The violence and death, so vividly before him, gave them an offensive triviality. He took a black pencil and began to sketch the images in his mind: the cliff, with Jack Forge wounded there; the river, carrying the boy's fallen body.

For a few moments he stared at the sketch, as if it were a puzzle he had to solve. The sequence of the raid was still running in his head, ending in the moment when he'd been hit, when the black face had leaned over him—

Of a sudden, he turned, sat down at the table; pulled a piece of writing paper towards him, and took his pen. He began: 'Dear Colonel Blessington . . .'

3

IN THE VIEW of Ivy Stone, this Meet-Your-Candidate reception was a grave mistake. She could not imagine why the Colonel permitted such a thing. His own idea, too. Nobody would have dreamed of asking him: the dubious function had been planned to happen in Spode House, which was owned by the Borough Council, and could be cheaply hired for weddings, poetry readings, group-therapy and folk dancing: 'A morgue of a place,' said the Colonel. 'They'll all feel much happier here.'

They would indeed. Who wouldn't?

She stood now, just inside the dining-room door; tall and dignified in her best black dress, the dignity threatened by a heavy cold. From the painful fog of it she watched the first out-riders, the True Tory ladies at work. 'We'll do everything', their leader, Mrs Vernon, had cried. Mrs Vernon was a large-nosed woman with a loud, organizing energy which rubbed Ivy on the raw. 'All the laying; and all the washing-up afterwards. And of course we'll *bring* everything.'

So the gracious high-ceilinged room was rapidly turning into the kind of horrid buffet demanded by the occasion. Out of interminable baskets they brought cups, plates, food and, worst of all, glasses. 'So sweet of the Colonel,' exclaimed Mrs Vernon; 'We never expected wine.' (Another example of his mysterious generosity; not that one could call it wine, Ivy told herself with a sniff. Two crates of the cheapest Spanish burgundy.) 'And they're all Woolworth glasses, so it doesn't matter a bit if they get knocked over.' Mrs Vernon's imagination—presumably—stopped short of the polished parquet and the Persian rugs. Depressed, Ivy turned away; she crossed the hall to inspect the drawing-room. Here two more ladies, introducing themselves as Miss Crutt and Miss Appleby, helped by a nameless young man with spots, had set about the furniture: there were some people, Miss Crutt said, who always liked to sit down for a speech. As she spoke she imperilled one of the Chinese lamps with her elbow, then stuck a Union Jack in a flower-vase.

The young man was now unfurling a poster, securing it with Scotch tape to the corners of the mantelpiece. It hung like a banner. At once the message VOTE FOR LEDYARD THE TRUE TORY began to puff up and sway, blown outwards by the heat from the electric panel behind it. Mrs Stone who had been expecting this development, said, 'I shouldn't put it there, sir.' She added, 'It might catch. That panel gets very hot.' Miss Appleby, a lean tall woman with spectacles, had the bright idea of switching off the electric point. 'You'll find the room gets very chilly,' Mrs Stone warned.

'Oh no. The central heating's quite enough—'

'Let them freeze, Ivy dear, if they want to.'

The voice of her employer at her back made Ivy Stone jump. Like a cat, she thought, the way he crept up on you. She had never known a man to walk so quietly. When she tried to analyse the 'funny feeling' the Colonel sometimes gave her, she found that this quiet walk was one of the factors. She confided the funny feeling to nobody. It came and went, a small unaccountable shadow.

Tonight it wasn't there at all. On the contrary, his appearance was magnificent, heartening in the extreme. Slight and graceful, he wore clothes so rare in these days that they gave her the effect of fancy-dress; tails, white tie and a white waistcoat; on the black coat the miniature medals completed the picture of an English gentleman, the genuine, half-forgotten breed. It was amusing, Ivy thought, in waspish vein, to note the impact of the Colonel upon Miss Appleby and Miss Crutt; they lit up like torches, they fluttered and twitched; then let out a rush of small half-finished sentences—'So good of you to—' 'Can't tell you how—' 'Everybody appreciates your—'

'Heavens, don't thank *me*. I haven't done a hand's turn. Only looked in to apologise for ratting on you.'

'Oh, but we perfectly—'

'Aiee-aa-aa-aa-chew-ew!' The gigantic sneeze caught Ivy unaware. Emerging ashamed from her handkerchief, she saw the sympathy in the Colonel's face. 'Ivy, your cold's *much* worse,' he said, ignoring the invasion of Mrs Vernon and the bossy Mr Anthony Price.

'No, sir, thank you; just about the same.'

'Worse,' he said; 'and I insist that you go to bed. Repeat *insist* . . .' Masterfully he drew her away, around the corner of the passage that led to the kitchen. His manner now was a mixture of firmness and solicitude. He really seemed to care about her cold. 'That's an order, Ivy dear—get it? Straight to bed. If I find you still up and about when I come back, I'll be very angry. There's a whole *staff* here tonight.'

'And who will lock up after them, I should like to know? *You're* going to bed early. Got to be up by seven, haven't you? Or so I understood you to say.'

'Doesn't matter. The lady helpers will be the last to

75

go. I'll ask Mrs Vernon to lock up; she can put the keys in through the letter box.'

'Can't bolt it from outside, can she?'

'The bolts,' said the Colonel, 'are an unnecessary precaution. Like wearing braces and a belt.'

'Well, how are we to be sure somebody won't open one of the big windows and then forget to close it?'

'I'll make Anthony Price O.C. windows. No nonsense now. Remember, it's an order. *Bed*. Promise?'

She nodded gloomily. It was easier to promise than to argue. She had no intention of keeping the promise; not with all these strangers coming to the house. Remembering his early start, she asked, 'Have you put out your things for me to pack?'

'All packed,' said the Colonel. 'Take one of those pills, like a good girl. And don't give me a thought in the morning. Stay in bed. My alarm clock's set. The car's ordered for seven-fifty, and I'll be having breakfast on the train.'

He was saying 'Promise?' again, resting his hand on her arm, gazing into her eyes: giving her, which was absurd, the look he gave to his succession of ladies across the dining-room table. Ivy had seen it often. Ten years a widow, she still possessed keen memories of what she termed All That. The Colonel, as the saying went, had a way with him. And knew it.

'Very well,' she said.

'Don't forget the pills, Ivy. They're damn good.' The Colonel was knowledgeable about pills of all kinds, a knowledge acquired on his world travels. In the drawer of her dressing-table there lay a whole collection of capsules, prescribed for her by the Colonel on one or another occasion and steadfastly shunned.

'All right, sir. Good night, sir.' She turned from him towards the kitchen. A deceiving gesture. Beyond the kitchen (a world of up-to-date excellence) was the short passage that led to her own bedsitting room and bathroom; lastly to the back door. Ivy went no further than the kitchen; here she waited until she heard the front door slam, followed by the faint sound of the Colonel's car moving away. Then she set off in search of that woman—the one she didn't like—what was her name? Vardon? Ventnor? Some name like that . . .

Yes, there she was beside the buffet. Ivy said, 'Just to remind you, madam, that the Colonel has made it clear that *Upstairs* is *Out of Bounds*.' Not displeasing to give orders to Mrs Vernon (that was it) who seemed to have taken command.

Mrs Vernon gave a cool nod, and said Naturally, no one would dream of setting a *foot*.

'Thank you, madam.' After which, Ivy herself mounted the white panelled staircase; one curving flight led to the sacred upper floor. An elegant looking-glass showed Ivy herself, pink-nosed, swimmy-eyed. She turned away from this, and went on up the stairs. The Colonel had left his study door standing open, a lamp still alight. The best room in the house, this so-called study; a long room with bookshelves going to the ceiling. Here the Colonel spent most of his time when alone, with his treasures around him; the T'ang figures behind glass, the Sheraton desk, the ancient globe, the pistols, the old duelling-swords. On the bookshelves, beside the leather-bound edition of the English poets, were stories of war-time exploits, the three-volume history of a regiment. It was very much a man's room, Ivy thought, as she had thought before; like most Englishwomen, no matter what age, she found the mere fact of a man strangely important. It was her employer's sex that gave her job its prestige.

As she crossed the floor to switch off the lamp, the

telephone on the desk began to ring. Ivy said, 'Colonel Blessington's residence.'

'Is he there?'

Unmistakable; that girl. That huge girl on the television; her name would come back in a minute. Ivy said, not without pleasure, 'No; I'm afraid he's just gone out.' (Gilroy, that was it.)

'Damn.' Miss Gilroy seemed to be thinking. 'I thought he said—Never mind. Perhaps you'd leave a message for him—tell him I'll ring tomorrow morning—'

'You won't find him here, I'm afraid.' Nothing could obscure the note of triumph in Ivy's voice. 'He's leaving early for Bristol—'

'For *Bristol*?' Miss Gilroy was clearly overthrown.

'On business,' said Ivy, still enjoying herself; 'the Colonel frequently goes to Bristol on business at the weekend—'

'But not *this* one—he never said—' Miss Gilroy seemed to take herself in hand. 'Oh, well. Thank you. It doesn't matter.'

Ivy put down the telephone. Getting in a State, poor girl, thought Ivy. Like others before her; by no means the first time she'd given news of the Colonel's absence to a stricken female voice: the Colonel took sudden decisions, went his own way. On the whole, Ivy thought, she was glad she wasn't nineteen and Miss Gilroy. She still stood in the room, listening to the swelling chatter of the party downstairs. Early chatter; the evening, Ivy thought, through the muffling blanket of her cold, had a long way to go.

Anthony Price looked at his watch. Nine-five. His peak of disenjoyment must still be some way ahead, but the climb was progressing, and included all expected features, plus one or two that were unforeseen: for example the cold, misty rain swirling across Heath Hill. It was one of those nights when North Royal could produce a fog out of its hat, as you might say. (It was generally agreed that the air of North Royal—being set so high—was the best in London. What was not admitted was the curious tendency of North Royal to produce its own fog out of season. So, now.)

The front door was open. The faithful and the curious, all in mackintoshes, seemed to bring some of the chill blur with them.

'*What* bad luck—' 'Most unusual for *us*—' 'March, mind you; more like November—' 'Umbrellas in the cloakroom, on your right.' 'Mr Ledyard, you won't remember me, but—'

The impression was already that of a multitude. A false impression, it owed itself to the presence of the converted, to the committee and the helpers. He was on patrol between the dining-room and drawing-room, counting heads ... Twenty-four in all. Extraordinary that twenty-four people could sound like forty-eight. The effect of the wine, perhaps. Also the effect of the wine, he decided, was the fact that he was vaguely looking out for that huge girl, with a half-hope that she might appear and liven the doomed evening.

He cleaved through the prattling voices: 'Beautiful rooms, aren't they; beautiful, beautiful rooms—' 'So good of Colonel Blessington—' 'What about a sardine on toast? Or one of these little—' 'I remember Minster House in old Lady Firmament's time—'

A young woman with a wide grin and a note-book, short hair and a shorter skirt, introduced herself as the North Royal Echo. 'Come to write it all up,' she said, looking over the tall room; '*what* a place; you could get my bedsitter into it eighteen times over ... anything interesting going to happen here tonight?'

Anthony gave her a long brooding look, and made for the hall where a shrill voice was saying, 'And your address, too, if you don't mind—it doesn't commit you to anything, we simply like to be able to keep in touch with anybody who's really interested—' Who on earth, thought Anthony, had put Winifred Crutt in charge of the visitors' book? For the toothy, tentative inescapable approach, there was nobody to beat Winifred.

'Wouldn't you like me to take that book off your hands?' Anthony asked her. She clasped it coyly against her chest, as if defending herself from assault, and said, 'Oh, no, thank you, Mr Price; I've just taken over from Miss Appleby while she goes and—' What Miss Appleby was doing was lost in the brisk voice of the elderly woman who had known the house in old Lady Firmament's time: 'I'd like to take Mrs Mitchell on a little tour before the business of the evening begins. The upstairs rooms, particularly the—'

'I'm sorry,' he said. 'Nobody upstairs, I'm afraid. The Colonel's special request.'

He left a little murmuring confusion behind him, while he turned to new arrivals. A positive crowd; at least six. Greeting them with a show of enthusiasm, he noticed that one of the number was the Pink Aunt.

'Now you haven't forgotten me!' she cried, unwrapping herself to reveal a shiny frock of mauve satin and a sparkling ornament, shaped like a crab. 'I'm Beryl Crawshaw, and we met in the High Street and had such an interesting talk afterwards—you told me all about the Colonel—'

'I think *you* told *me*,' Anthony said, but this didn't reach her; she was bringing forward a small bored man with a reddish face and a grey moustache and saying,

'This is my husband!' with a note of triumph, as if she'd won him at a fair. 'I've talked to him so much about the Colonel—we're hoping there'll be a chance of seeing him—' Mr Crawshaw didn't look as if he were hoping any such thing; he was peering anxiously about, Anthony perceived, in search of refreshment, and settling into even deeper gloom at the sight of the Spanish wine.

As Anthony made his way once more into the drawing-room, he found that the Pink Aunt persisted beside him: 'I've made up my mind, I'm going to be a helper; I'll stay and wash up; there must be a great deal to do, all those glasses; after all, I may not agree with everything the Party stands for, but one's got to come out on one side or the other, don't you agree?' If he did, she didn't wait to know, but galloped on: 'I've been thinking so much about the Colonel—all that dreadful glooming at Bowood, quite gone; a happy man now, you'd say, wouldn't you? I can't help hoping we'll get a glimpse of him before the evening's out; just to talk for a little while; so *much* water's flowed under the bridge, hasn't it? There must be so many things to say.'

Yes indeed, thought Anthony, perceiving that Beryl Crawshaw's resolve to wash up sprang less from the desire to help than from a vivid curiosity about the Colonel.

As he encouraged one of the new arrivals, a surprisingly pretty blonde, to form part of the audience in the drawing-room, Anthony was forced to admit that he wasn't free from such curiosity himself.

And much good would it do him. No more improbable image presented itself than that of the Colonel unburdening himself of his life story to the Pink Aunt.

He saw, with a deeper fall of heart, that Ledyard was about to begin.

*　　　*　　　*

Anita walked out of North Royal Tube Station as the clock struck ten. She met the drifting fog, said, 'Oh, wouldn't you know' and stood still to tie her scarf across her newly-perfected hair. There had been no fog in St. John's Wood. Only six minutes downhill walk lay ahead of her to Minster House, and she could have done it blindfold; she found the white barrier intimidating because she was already intimidated. Most of her courage had ebbed away in the Tube. She had been fighting ever since lunchtime. She had lost.

Harvey had asked her not to come here tonight. She could see him clearly across the dinner table: 'My darling, we shan't have a moment alone together; I'm going out and the Lord knows when I'll be back; you'll be bored to tears.' Vainly she had appealed to her own belief in the rightness of Harvey on all issues, including this one. Imploring, she had called upon her self-respect, her pride and her common sense. Halfway through her dressing, she had telephoned Minster House, with some thought that a final word from Harvey would tilt the scale.

And heard, instead, in Stonehenge's catarrh-muffled voice, about Bristol. Bristol. *This* week-end. Leaving early tomorrow morning. Without telling her. *Why?* Something here she had to know; the war was lost.

More emphatically lost when she remembered the name of Jane Rolf. Mrs Jane Rolf. '*Ow!*' cried Anita, and heard the '*Ow*', the genuine reflex of pain, echo in the white thick air. Again she saw Harvey across the dinner table: 'My beloved, there won't be a soul there who'd interest you—unless of course Jane turns up. But there's no certainty that she will.' A falling thud of her heart at the name: it had been spoken with amused, reminiscent affection; the secret and intimate pleasure with which men spoke of past loves. To her uncontrollable enquiry—'Who's Jane?'—he had given her the most satisfying answers: Mrs Jane Rolf was quite old; just a family friend on a visit from California. Harvey hadn't seen her for years; she used to be a friend of his sister, the sister who had died.

But.

Close to the house now, the lamp palely shining above the gate. Mystery and quiet; muffled footsteps going away into the fog . . . *I don't like this* Anita thought, and suddenly Matthew was in her mind; Matthew and 'Take it easy, Araminta.' The phrase that didn't matter, that couldn't mean anything, yet . . . She hadn't used it again; she hadn't spoken of it to Harvey. Matthew had said nothing more. Yet now she was much aware of him, of things undiscovered and threatening . . .

Relieved, she saw the front door was open; that here were lights and people; that she could come out of the drifting dark, leaving the fog and mystery outside.

'Cloakroom on the right,' said the toothy girl at the door. 'Then go straight in; plenty of room; Mr Ledyard's speaking; just remember to go in quietly.' Hardly a necessary instruction, Anita thought, beginning to lose her sense of doom; Mr Ledyard could predominate over any volume of noise. She shed her coat and her scarf in company with three scared-looking women, none of whom could conceivably be Mrs Jane Rolf. Sliding in behind them she found herself next to Anthony Price. She whispered 'Hullo' and he grunted. He was rather good-looking in his pompous Old Etonian way.

'Loyalty. Efficiency. Dynamism. Youth. Adventure. Reform. Devotion-to-Duty. Those are what I stand for,' Ledyard told the company, looking more than usually

pleased with himself. A delicate table before him shook
to the thump of his huge hand. 'If I may repeat the
words again you'll notice something about them. Not
only do I stand for them. They stand for me. L—
Loyalty, E—Efficiency, D—Dynamism, Y—Youth,
A—Adventure, R—Reform, D—Devotion-to-Duty.
L—e—d—y—a—r—d.'

Anthony Price winced sharply as though in pain; an
attractive blonde (Mrs Rolf? Oh God forbid, God
please forbid) called 'Bravo!'; a ragged sound of
clapping arose. Under cover of the sound, Anita laun-
ched her urgent quest—'Mr Price, who's the blonde
on the sofa?'

'Blonde? Oh, that one.' His sad blue eyes were almost
friendly. 'Think her name's Barlow.'

'Has Mrs Rolf come?'

'Sorry—couldn't hear.'

'Mrs Rolf?'

'Sorry couldn't say. Ought there to be a Mrs Rolf?'

'Oh no. No. I wondered, that's all.'

Ledyard was bowing. He was moving away from the
table. It couldn't be the end of the speech . . . it could.
It was. Unable to believe her good fortune, Anita asked,
'Is that really the end?'

'And about time too.'

'How long has he been talking?'

'At least three days.'

She laughed. She now decided that she liked Mr Price.
He looked a little as though he liked her. Mrs Vernon
was saying, perhaps with some failure in tact, 'Now
I think we're *all* ready for refreshments'; she went on to
announce that there'd be plenty of time for informal
discussion afterwards.

Anita spied upon the group that now formed around
the vast pillar of Ledyard. This included, she remarked,

a smaller, younger version of Ledyard himself: 'Junior,' Mr Price observed mournfully, answering her question; 'Rupert's son: Gilbert Ledyard; a second edition, as if one wasn't enough . . . Come and have a drink.'

'A drink would be dreamy.'

'Well, you won't want the wine.'

'I adore wine—'

Gloom came down upon Mr Price. 'Not this wine. Sure you wouldn't rather have whisky? Got some up on that shelf in the cloak-room—'

'I'll take your offer,' said the voice behind him; the only voice Anita wanted to hear. Harvey, unannounced, unheard, was standing in the doorway, Harvey in the full glory of tails and white tie. She was so pleased to see him that she forgot about Jane Rolf and Bristol; she forgot to worry about his being cross. He did not seem in the least cross. He looked at his most sparkly and satisfied. 'Hullo, ducky. So you decided to come after all. Beautiful, that dress. Excuse me while I make polite noises.' She stood by the door with Mr Price, watching Harvey go the rounds, gracefully and at speed. She did not realise how she looked while doing this until she heard Mr Price remark sadly, 'Love is a wonderful thing. Or so they say.' She had not blushed for a long time and it was irritating to blush now. She turned on him what she hoped was her Dowager Duchess manner. 'I beg your pardon?' said Anita.

'Nothing,' said Mr Price.

Harvey moving fluently out of the Ledyard orbit, took them each by the arm. 'One quick one—in my study —yes? The resources are all there.' They were halfway up the stairs when, a figure full of doom, Mrs Stone came coasting down the passage from the kitchen.

'I thought I made it quite clear . . . *oh.*' It was interesting to see that Mrs Stone too could blush. Her forehead and her cheeks now matched her poor nose. 'I'm sorry, sir. You're back early—'

'Didn't I tell you to go to bed?' Harvey was smiling, but the voice had a command in it somewhere.

'Yes, well, I'm going now, sir.'

'No nonsense?'

'No, sir. Good night.'

Harvey led the way into his study; the sacred place; site of all happiness. Too sad that Mr Price must be here too. Harvey looked charmingly guilty, opening a wall cabinet below the bookshelves. 'Ought to have invited Ledyard, I suppose, but—'

'God forbid,' said Mr Price.

Harvey looked amused; like a magician he was conjuring a bottle, a decanter, glasses, a syphon and an ice-bucket from the cabinet, which Anita had never seen before. It was a little disquieting, she did not know why.

'Well, it all seems to be going a fair treat, as they say. Burgundy for you, my darling—am I wrong? I am not.' He filled her glass from the decanter. 'Whisky, Tony? Say when.'

'Doom, death and damnation,' said Mr Price, stretching out his hand for the glass.

'Come, come. According to Miss Appleby there's a most generous response to the silver collection.'

'You know it stinks. All of it.' Mr Price came to sit on the sofa beside Anita. Not what she wanted. Harvey took the armchair. She was almost consoled by the effect of the lamplight on his head, on the smooth-skinned, lively face and the beautiful hand holding the glass—

She blinked. Yes, it was true. Harvey, teetotal Harvey, had furnished himself with a whisky and soda. Disturbed by this, she lost the next exchanges. When she came back to the talk, Mr Price was saying, 'The only answer is for Ledyard to follow his predecessor to the Bahamas. Or even,' he added darkly, 'further.'

'Perhaps he will. I believe he has high blood pressure.'

'Not the Bahamas, then; somewhere cool, like the Antarctic ... In which happy event you'd let yourself be nominated?'

Harvey, amused, sat back with his legs crossed; one slender foot swung. 'I'm making no promises.'

'We can't go on like this. We're a laughing-stock already.'

If only Mr Price would stop arguing; would finish his drink and go. Then the thing might begin to happen in this room. 'The thing' was the most that Anita's vocabulary could achieve. Down on a lower, cruder level there was her own probing curiosity. 'This can't be all he ever does with anybody ...' The gentleness of his kisses; the controlled caress: never more than this ...

And there would be nothing more tonight; the time was half past ten, and Harvey must go to bed.

(He was no different, now that he had drunk the whisky; his eyes were perhaps a little larger and shinier.) But why the whisky? Suddenly tonight? One wanted to know because one wanted to know all there was to know.

And now they were all standing up; Mr Price was offering to see her to the Tube Station; Harvey was encouraging this, even making it sound as if he wanted her to go: 'Take her away, Anthony, past her bed-time; and there's nothing more for her here.' And she didn't know why he was going to Bristol, nor where he was staying; there was a sudden darkness coming down. Anthony Price was saying to Harvey, 'Very well; see you for lunch on Monday.' He went on ahead downstairs. Anita felt the long hand grasp hers, the forefinger touching the middle of her palm, stroking it.

She said, 'I didn't know you were going away—'

87

'Just a business trip.'

'You never told me—'

'Only knew this morning. Something cropped up.' Their voices were low, as if Mr Price could still hear them. 'I'll call you Sunday night, or Monday morning. We'll have dinner on Monday.' There was a quick embrace, and then standing away from each other. He said, 'Sleep well, my darling.' He pressed her hand, and then she turned away from him, going slowly downstairs, into a clatter of voices:

'*I* think it's clearing, just a little . . .' 'Such an inspiring speech—' 'If you'll just sign your name—*and* your address . . .'

It was only a little cheering to see Anthony Price waiting for her, his expression of civilised gloom lightening as she came towards him.

It wasn't true the fog was clearing; the trees were drowned and lost; the mystery was still there. As she walked with Mr Price up the hill she heard sharp, hurrying footsteps behind them. Turning, she saw the woman Mr Price had called without explanation the Pink Aunt, with a small unwilling man coming more slowly behind her.

'*Do* wait for us,' the Pink Aunt said; Mr Price's gloom, Anita perceived, was back again. 'You're Anita Gilroy, aren't you? Yes, I thought you were; I've seen you so often; watched every word of *Salvation Road;* not that one believes any of it, of course, but somehow one has to go on, like eating chocolates . . . I was *so* disappointed tonight, not seeing more of the Colonel; he spoke a word to me in the drawing-room, said he was looking forward to having a long, long chat—and then I never saw him again. So I decided to come away.'

The incline of the hill had by now robbed her of breath; Anthony Price said that the Colonel had taken a night-cap, then gone to bed early—

'A night-cap?' Her breath was back; her voice rang crisply through the foggy dark. '*That* sounds more like it; remember he only drank ginger ale in the pub, and that was a change from the old days, my goodness, yes . . .'

Anita, walking solidly in silence, found she wasn't enjoying this; the blankness of Harvey going to Bristol was made no better by this silly woman having memories of him that she couldn't share. She still didn't know what this woman had said to make Harvey reply, 'That's all over now, thank God.' This question, with other questions, stayed in her mind.

'Of course you might say it was a little rude, his disappearing like that after sounding so friendly; but I'm sure he didn't intend it, and anyway there'll be plenty more chances of seeing him; I've signed on as a helper; said I'd do anything—head cook and bottle washer; got used to doing dull jobs in the war—'

Nor did Anita want to hear any more about the war; it was something again she couldn't share; she was glad when, as they reached the Tube Station, Anthony Price came to a stop, holding her firmly by the arm. He was, he told the Pink Aunt, going to have a cup of coffee and a sandwich; he'd been too busy to eat—yes, it had been a splendid evening; a pleasure, he added sombrely, for him too.

Anita faced him across the small formica-topped table. Dim light; muffled music; scarlet chairs and what appeared to be a flamingo in travail painted on the wall. She felt grateful to be relieved of the Pink Aunt, and told him so; he gave a wry smile and said, 'Well, something had to be done.'

Was he beginning to look at her as other young men

89

looked at her? No; not quite; after a brief stare, he leaned back with a sigh, as if abandoning hope. Had her mind not been so full of Harvey, she would have been sad for him.

He glanced at his watch. 'No need to go back yet,' he said.

'Go *back*?'

He gave the wry smile again. 'I have to lock the windows.'

'Won't Mrs Vernon . . .?'

'No: my job. Orders from the Colonel.' He sighed. 'Can't say I'm anxious to face it all again.'

She made a sound of sympathy. The confused evening with the eager worthy women and the windy booming of Ledyard was fading from her mind, leaving only one thought there; an uncomfortable thought with spiky edges: 'When is a printing-press not a printing-press?'

She looked sadly at Anthony Price over her coffee cup; not possible, of course, to ask him; against all her principles . . . He was, apparantly, still thinking about the True Tories. He stared at his cup and muttered, '*Ledyard*. Things can't go on like this. Something will have to happen; quickly too. There isn't much time.'

Sitting there with him in the café on the hill, she thought the words sounded desperate . . . Absurd. The True Tories were a harmless nonsense, prattling away still in the rooms of Minster House; there wasn't any danger there.

But when they had left the café and Mr Price stood, hat in hand, outside the lift gates in the Tube Station, she thought he had the doomed look of one set for the Old Bailey or the Salt Mines. As the lift sank down, she thought of him, on his way back to the party. In the midst of her concern about the printing-press, she had time to feel sorry for him.

4

JANE ROLF turned up the lamp on the Sheraton desk and
stood looking about her, cataloguing the detail of Harvey
Blessington's study with a certain detached amusement.
Forbidden ground. By the Colonel's special request.
She did not intend to linger here; there was no need. She
let her eyes dwell affectionately upon the old swords
(Jane liked swords) and for a moment on the shelf of
military books. To these she gave the amused indulgent
glance with which women look upon the violent pursuits
of men. Then she switched off the lamp. Coming down
the stairs she caught up with her own reflection in the
Empire looking-glass that hung in the hall just above
the last curving step. The reflection pleased her; the
short, springy fair hair; the light, long-lashed eyes; the
neat composition of the face, with its smooth bronze
make-up, emphasizing the natural tan. Jane tanned
easily and becomingly. For years, between tanning
seasons, she had devoted herself to getting the same effect
out of a bottle. The light brown tweed dress matched
the make-up. Over it she wore a short jacket of pale
beaver lamb. This had not been confined to Colonel
Blessington's cloakroom.

'Excuse me . . .' That lean spectacled type barred her
way; the one who carried the book, Miss Appleby.

'Hi,' said Jane lazily. 'Just taking a peek upstairs.'

'Oh, of course—I mean—Well, people aren't really supposed—but I'm sure ... You haven't signed the book yet, have you? I know it's annoying to be asked twice, but you see Miss Crutt took it on for a shift while I was having my coffee so I ...' Seldom had so much been said about so little, thought Jane, taking the proffered pen.

'What a lovely perfume you're wearing,' said Miss Appleby, giving small but enthusiastic sniffs. 'Would I be rude to ask what it is?'

'Arpège. Lanvin.' Jane made her usual illegible signature. She saw Miss Appleby peering at it. 'And the address too, please, if you don't mind. It doesn't commit you to—'

'My American address? Or my London address? I'm only over here for a little while.'

This produced a rapid sequence of ohs, wells, perhapses and if-you-don't minds; these continuing while Jane wrote Squiggle Pacific Avenue San Francisco, and under it Squiggle Hotel W.1. From the kitchen she could hear the clashing tumult incurred by the helpers at work on dirty plates and glasses; the dining-room door stood open; there was still a number of people grouped at the buffet; still a small hard core drinking in the drawing-room. She had a glimpse of the huge purple Ledyard, holding court.

'I want out and fast,' Jane said to herself, while Miss Appleby took a surprising turn for the coherent. 'I *do* hope you met Colonel Blessington. He would have stayed with us longer only he had an early start tomorrow.'

'He told me. We're very old friends. Good night, and thanks a lot.' She added a few adjectives as she went, among them 'meaningful' and 'worthwhile'. Jane, having no interest whatever in politics, knew none the less what was expected of her. She was on the verge of a laugh now.

The various doorkeepers had all gone off duty. So she opened the front door, holding it politely for two solemn little bundled-up women; one saying to the other, 'I can see Mr Ledyard as the future Prime Minister'; and the other replying, 'I wouldn't go as far as that . . . Sounds like our taxi dear.' They scuttled down to the gate. Jane pulled her head scarf from her pocket and tied it on.

The air was still opaque with mist. Outside the gate she found an immediate road-block; a car was parked beside the pavement; the two little women and several other customers had stopped for a prattle, which seemed to be concerned with refusing a lift in the car; an identifiably British chorus of decision to do the less comfortable thing.

'No, thank you; I'm only just round the corner;' 'No, thank you; I really like the walk;' 'It's quite all right, we've ordered a taxi . . .'

'Excuse me,' Jane said to the obstructing backs. The man at the wheel of the car poked his head out: Gilbert Ledyard. She got a glimpse of a smaller, less purple reproduction of Rupert. 'What about this lady? Can I give you a lift, madam?' The same voice, a few decibels quieter.

'I'm okay, thank you very much.'

She broke away while he was still speaking: He knew an American accent when he heard one; always charmed to meet Americans—

Rude not to wait for the rest of it, but she couldn't afford the politeness. She did not take the right turn into Heath Square; she turned to walk down the hill. As she did so she saw a figure emerge from the Square; a bowler-hatted figure, going at a brisk pace towards the house: Anthony Price. She stood still in the shadow of the wall till he had passed in under the porch. She smiled to herself. Luck, as usual, was with her. Then she went on, rapidly down the hill. Here the fog was lifting a little: the lamps shone clear. Which was Gilbert Ledyard's way home? If he passed her it might be tricky. But here, again, was fortune; a taxi crawling on the uphill gradient. No light in its forehead; the flag was down. Jane stepped into the road. 'Hey—I'm your pick-up,' she called to the driver.

The driver was a young man; he put on his brakes and grinned widely. 'My pick-up, lady? Fancy that.'

Jane smiled back. She saw him appraising her; in this poor misty light he probably took her for somebody of his own age. 'No. 66 you called from?' he was asking.

'That's right.'

(Tough on the two little women. They could always call another.)

'And you're going to St. John's Wood, you said?'

'No. Chelsea.'

'*Chelsea.*' He didn't seem to like the idea. 'Nobody said anything about Chelsea. Whereabouts in Chelsea?'

'Shepherd Street.'

'Never heard of it.'

'It's a turning out of the King's Road.' Jane climbed into the cab. The driver shut off his engine: he pulled back the glass panel.

'Just a minute. I wasn't counting on going that far. Beyond the five-mile limit, you'll have to—'

'Never mind.'

'It'll cost you—'

'You'll be paid. Handsomely.'

He said nothing. He started up his engine and made a savage, ill-tempered turn, narrowly missing Gilbert

Ledyard's car as it proceeded downhill. Jane leaned forward to shut the glass panel. The driver's sulks were infinitely preferable to a long flirtatious chat. She settled herself comfortably in the left-hand corner, alone with her private exhilaration. It was, sometimes, exhilarating to be Jane Rolf. There was a tang to this moment; there was the sense of escape into solitude. Blissfully she let the matters at Minster House, the True Tories, the striving girl with the name-and-address book, Mr Ledyard and the whole dull gathering, float away out of her mind.

Was this the state called euphoria? More than a casual student of words, Jane examined the word; while the taxi, racing, bouncing, taking a chance at every amber light, carried her perilously away from North Royal, and from North Royal's fog. She decided that euphoria was wrong: it suggested a vague, all-embracing anaesthetized happiness; a kind of pink and gold mist. It failed to describe her own sharp, immediate sensations, of being broad awake, keenly alive, all-of-a-piece; herself quite alone in the world, filled with power. Light-hearted power; delicate, individual power; more precious than any similar emotion felt by Dictators, Presidents, Field Marshals or industrial tycoons. More precious and much more important. Remembering the artificial aid to this highly arrogant conclusion, Jane stifled a laugh. The aid was a small blue pill. She could, she thought, have got through the evening without it: its effect would last for half the night. All the better. The pill was a friend. Untroubled by the behaviour of the angry young man at his wheel, she found herself back in the past. They were bright pictures that came into her head. The harmless but useful little drug always lit up her memories. She saw the young girl Jane riding her favourite Palomino on her family ranch. Beautiful

95

with a boyish beauty, that young girl; strong and happily wicked by the crazy grown-up standards—until they, the crazy grown-ups, put an end to all the fun. Only a temporary end. She had escaped them, as she had escaped ever since. Escape was her speciality. The bright pictures were moving her on, into danger, because danger was forever delightful. You felt no fear. You would always win—even this time, you would win—

The taxi driver slammed back the glass panel, shouting, 'Where's this street now?'

Abruptly awoken, Jane saw that they had reached King's Road, Chelsea. 'Well, Bully for you,' she said.

'What's that?'

'I said Bully for you. You were just as likely to hit a lamp-post head on.'

'Is that meant to be sarcastic?'

'No.'

'Well, where's this place?'

'You can put me down right here.'

'What was the name of the street again?'

'I'm getting off here.'

Since the traffic light was red against him, he couldn't argue. The meter registered twelve shillings. From her large, luscious pigskin bag, Jane took her large, luscious pigskin wallet. She handed him two pound notes. 'Good night,' she said, 'and try to drive more sensibly on your way home.' She walked on, debating the number of risks taken between North Royal and Chelsea; the signing of the book, the stealing of the taxi, the Chelsea address—though she had been careful not to give the driver the right address, the district—in certain circumstances—might point the way. She had laid a trail. But the risks were a part of the fun, always. One couldn't help taking them; more, one created them, just for the hell of it. On balance, she knew she was safe. Breathing a milder and clearer air than the air of North Royal, she walked on, turned to her left down Church Street, took the first on her left again and saw lights in the windows of the cock-eyed house at the corner. Miss Deerhurst, then, was still up and about. No matter. Not unexpected; the time, after all, was only a quarter to twelve.

Miss Deerhurst was a Character. This, Jane had realized before they met; on reading her advertisement in the Sunday *Observer*: 'Nowhere to park your car?' the advertisement asked: 'I have a lock-up garage to let, with tiny Chelsea Cottage attached if required.' It was in no sense a cottage; it was half a house at the end of a row; attenuated rather than tiny; tall and thin (like its owner). Semi-detached on one side; sliced off on the other side by a bomb. The assistance of an architect who had begun to construct an adjoining studio and then gone bankrupt resulted in the garage.

Here she was, the tall grenadier, wrapped in a cloak, flinging her front door open to the night, calling, 'Hullo, Stranger; I was wondering where you'd got to.'

'I got to Paris,' said Jane. 'I meant to send you a postcard.'

'How sweet of you.' Miss Deerhurst sounded as gracious as though she had received the postcard. 'I hope you had a lovely time, I'm sure you did. You look so happy. So *well. Très flatteux*, that little fur jacket. Terribly cold, isn't it? Do come and have a nightcap. I was just going to have mine.'

'Bless you; I think I mustn't. I'm a touch late.'

'Don't tell me you're off somewhere now—in the motor?' Miss Deerhurst's vintage could be calculated by her apparent ignorance of the word 'car'. 'But of course you must be—or you wouldn't be here at all.

How stupid one is. Not a long drive, I hope? Rather a beastly night.'

'Quite a short drive. Some rather lovely friends of mine have a house on Chiswick Mall. On the river.' She pointed south. 'Theatre friends, so it's a late party. I'll be staying with them through next week,' Jane added. 'Do go in, Miss Deerhurst, *please*. It's no night for standing around.'

'No. The contrary. Well—hope it's a good party.' She raised one arm in a salute that had all the angular stiffness of a railway-signal going up. She shut the door, then lunged round it again to call, 'Got your key? Well —drive carefully, won't you?' The door slammed again.

Nice old Lesbian, really.

Jane opened the garage doors. The car was a glittering black Millaux, last year's model; bought at second-hand, it was a bargain. Beautiful lines, reliable engine, only six thousand miles on the clock. She threw her bag and gloves into the front seat; she found her torch in the dashboard compartment. She strolled back to unlock the boot. Rapidly she played the beam over the contents, checking each item. All in order. She took out the so-called Beauty Case, a luxurious relic from California; white rawhide. This would go beside her in the passenger's seat. Certain other necessary things could stay where they were for the moment.

Jane locked the boot again. She switched on, backed out of the garage and shut the doors after her. She sat for a few minutes at the wheel, letting the engine warm up. The lower light in the cock-eyed house was off. Miss Deerhurst's upper window still awake. Jane leaned out, waved and blew a kiss up to the window. Then she drove away; turning to the right, and to the right again at the corner of Church Street. She shot along the King's Road. She headed North once more, by the precise route the taxi driver had taken; the difference being that she drove, as always, with care and skill.

Ivy Stone's dream was a tiring and tangled affair: there was a party going on. The Colonel had planted a little row of cypress trees along the drawing-room floor; she herself, wearing only the top half of a Bikini was serving coffee at speed because she was due to catch her aeroplane in a few minutes and hadn't yet had time to pack. Oh dear . . . That impatient ring at the door meant the aeroplane was outside already. Need it go on ringing?

Mrs Stone sat up. Her hand groped towards the alarm clock on her bedside-table. She turned it off; she turned on the lamp. Seven-fifteen. Not only did she feel extremely worried about something as yet unidentifiable; she felt drunk. Why? Her cold had never had this effect before. Very peculiar. It took her some time, weaving from bed to bathroom, doing her hair and dressing, to remember that she had—at last—succumbed to one of the Colonel's pills. Presumably it was still operating. Her own fault. She had taken it at one o'clock this morning, after an expedition to make sure the windows and doors were locked, the keys put back through the letter box, and the True Tories gone. Finding all in order, Ivy had bolted the front door and returned to bed, and a wakefulness that had driven her at last to the pill.

Idiotic to make oneself feel like this when one should be brisk and busy. Groggily she laid the Colonel's tray. She put the kettle on and forgot to light the gas ring under it. She went back and lit the gas. She wove her way to the front door. Her hands were clumsy with the bolts, clumsy with the key. She opened upon a dark, wet morning. She picked the papers off the lowest of

99

the front steps where the wretched little boy from the newsagents always flung them, being too lazy to go further. In the wet too. They were damp already.

'What am I worrying about? What's the matter? I'll remember in a minute . . .'

There was time only for a sip of her own tea before she embarked on the journey upstairs. Ivy had never dropped a tray in her life; nor did she let it give as much as a wobble now. It was a slow steady assault; she fought her way up, rigid and precarious; the newspapers clamped under her left arm. She kept her eyes fixed on the teapot, the toast-rack, daring them to move. Relieved to reach the landing without disaster, she set the tray down on the carved chest outside the Colonel's door. She knocked.

No reply meant that he was still in the bathroom. Wasn't he cutting it a little fine? With the car ordered for seven-fifty sharp? After the third knock Ivy picked up the tray and marched in. Quite safe to do this. The Colonel's modest, gentlemanly manners would never let her catch him in his shirt-tails.

'Good—er . . .'

The bed was empty, the bedclothes flung back. The bathroom door stood wide open. Nobody here.

Still in her daze, Ivy looked around the room; a square, high-ceilinged room, panelled in white, curtained and carpeted in green. When her eyes came to the dressing-table (what was known as a Good Piece— one of those tall dark inadequate dressing-tables favoured by the gentlemen) she saw the note. He had propped it up. She was looking straight at a standing white envelope with the word 'Ivy' printed on it.

'I'm off, ducky', the note began, after his frivolous fashion. 'Woke up ahead of the alarm-clock, find there's a seven-fifteen, so shall catch it. Please take care of that cold. And take Sunday off, as usual. If I get an afternoon train back, I'll dine at the club. If I have to stay over till Monday morning, I should be home by noon latest. Have luncheon-date with Mr Price. As to the evening, please get dinner menu from Ring-For-Your-Supper and order for two. Scampi vital—' (That meant Miss Gilroy)—'Otherwise I leave choice to you. All messages can wait. Just tell anyone who wants me that I'm in Bristol on business this week-end. Thank you kindly. Hope to find you quite restored. H.B.'

Ivy's reaction of grievance, seldom inert for long, was immediate. He could—couldn't he?—have left the note on the hall-table, thus saving her the trouble of the tray . . . Ah. But then of course he wasn't expecting the tray; he had told her to stay in bed. She glanced at the note again; something odd about the handwriting— certainly the Colonel's, but it looked—to her muzzy wits—slapdash, as though he had written it in a bad temper. Written in a hurry, she reminded herself. She picked up the A.B.C. timetable; he had used it to prop the note. She took this back to its place on the shelf in his study. She stood there a moment, looking around to make sure that none of those stupid women on their wholly illegal visits had been meddling. There was no sign that they had. But for a very faint smell of scent, still on the air, there might have been no trespassers.

Ivy returned to the Colonel's room for the tray. The unidentified worry went with her. 'What was it? What is it? It'll come. Fast enough. What I need's a good strong cup of tea. I will say for him, he's tidy. Tidiest gentleman I ever worked for. When they go off in a hurry one usually finds things all over the place. Towel on the bathroom floor, though; bound to be: and his pyjamas.' She looked round the door. She was wrong. No towel on the floor. The pyjamas, after investigation, were in the white whicker box that held the dirty clothes, or soiled linen, as Ivy preferred to think of it. Not a razor nor a sponge out of place.

Ivy, with the Colonel's tray in her hands, the newspapers under her arm, began the return journey downstairs. She was still foggily pondering the tidiness of the bathroom; the cupboards not only shut, but locked . . . Why not? He was always a great one for locking up—

Locking up. Ivy, rounding the banister rail, stood abruptly still, staring at the front door. The tray gave a sudden wild lurch; she just managed to save it, though the toast-rack went flying and the newspapers slipped out from under her arm. She trod on the toast.

'*That door was bolted.* I unbolted it myself—can't be more than fifteen minutes ago. How did *he* get out?'

She felt more drunk than ever.

'By the back door, then. He went by the back door.'

'But why on earth should he do a thing like that?'

She tried to imagine him tiptoeing past her room, sliding out cautiously into the narrow alley-way, carrying his suitcase, making his way round to the front of the house and the gate. Why? What would be the point? With the tray safely lodged beside the sink, Ivy poured herself a cup of tea. She gulped it thirstily before she went to investigate.

The back door was unlocked. And now, as she stood facing it, the worry came lifting clear of the fog. Her last thought, before the pills finally ensnared her: I don't believe I ever locked the back door. But—*surely*—she had unlocked it herself this morning? It was such an accustomed exercise; one did it every day without thinking, even when one wasn't all muzzy like this . . . Well, she couldn't have done. The Colonel must for some unfathomable reason have gone that way. And her memory of unlocking it herself this morning was just an echo of all the other mornings.

She still felt dopey. Her mouth was still dry and there was a buzzing in her ears. 'I know one thing, that's the last time I touch one of his precious pills . . . tell him so, as soon as he gets back. Lucky it's an easy day.' For a minute she reviewed the notion of returning to bed.

'I'll give him pills,' thought Ivy.

Why the back door? What was he up to? Here it was again, that old shadow of mistrust: the thing she had never confided to anybody.

The front door bell ringing loud and long revived her silly dream about the aeroplane. And that Bikini . . . really. Dreams . . . She went to answer the door.

The policeman standing on the step said, 'Good morning, ma'am. Colonel Blessington's house? I'd like a word with the Colonel, if you please.'

5

It was an enormous jig-saw; two thousand pieces: a parade of fishing boats in harbour, a frieze of cottages above the harbour, a vast width of sky above the cottages. As usual, Matthew had left the sky till the end. Only a dozen pieces remained; pale, tricky customers, all shaped more or less alike. Here, now—surely . . . *no*, fool, you know that one doesn't fit, you've tried it twice before.

He straightened himself, rubbing his forehead. Today the pain was diffuse, threatening rather than present. He looked at his watch. Four-fifteen; he had meant to give ten minutes to the puzzle between lunch and work. The damned thing was a hypnotist. More; it had acquired a double meaning. Built into the coloured mosaic he could trace another pattern, a thought-pattern, eight days long. This was the eighth day since Anita had left. He had begun the jig-saw the day after. Finished, broken up, jumbled and replaced in its box, the no-more puzzle would still leave the thought-pattern. It pursued its relentless way, coming up with the same answer each time: there was no evidence. There was only one small, authentic mystery: 'Take it easy, Araminta.'

That—and the dark undertones to the present; the tiger crouching inside, the black river running. But you couldn't call your own obsessions evidence.

With a last wistful look at the teasing gap in the sky, Matthew turned away from the jig-saw table, and moved to his desk. Here was the half-finished plan of a crossword puzzle; the sketch for a birthday card, showing a man with a bucket and brush slapping a poster on to a wall: the poster read 'Happy Birthday to You.' Ordinary, uninspired; he crumpled the sketch and threw it in the waste-paper basket: this had been a day of broken concentration, things begun that died on him . . . Only one triumph, a short poem completed, a little rocket of gaiety breaking through the curtain of thought. Inspired by much chatter in the paper this morning about narcotics and the young; triggered off by the squalid ritual of emptying tea-leaves and potato peelings into the dustbin:

Garbage, garbage, give me your answer do
I'm at the Phenobarb-age—am I rotting as fast as you?
My *mens* is far from *sana*
Without my marijuana
But LSD
Is the stuff for me
On my psyche that's built for two.

Pleased with this, he was momentarily diverted; perhaps there was a lightness in the day, so far undiscovered; perhaps he had mistaken it . . . But then, pushing the poem aside, he saw the rough draft of the message, his own message, written and posted six days ago. His instinct was to cover it again; he was now ashamed of it. He could see Colonel Blessington reading it with astonished bewilderment, throwing it aside and writing him off as a lunatic. He wished he'd done nothing; he wished he'd let it alone. And yet . . .

The scribbled words drew his eye; against his will he read them again:

How many miles to midnight
And how many miles to the moon
How many leagues to the top of the cliff
And the light that comes too soon?

How far down to the river
And the one no longer alive?
Do you still take it easy, Araminta?
And how many pills make five?

Written on headed notepaper, signed with his name.
Crazy thing to do. Crazy way to do it. Yet all the
formal letters, beginning 'I have heard your name from
my daughter, and wonder if by any chance—' had
seemed pompous and alien, and he had turned to his
natural form, the oblique approach of the crossword
clue. The last line he'd picked at random, remembering
that Anita had said, 'He takes pills to make him sleep,
but you have to do *something* . . .' Posted six days ago.
No answer; none would come. Colonel Blessington
would find the odd phrases meaningless; might or
might not show them to Anita. He would conclude,
in any case, that her father was some way out of his
mind.

Unless of course—

But the alternative revived the thought-pattern, and
he wanted to be free of that; the room was too full of
thinking. Here on the desk was the black-lined sketch
he had drawn of Jack Forge's body on the cliff; the body
of the boy in the river. He was glad when the door
butted open and Mrs Oakley, tying a woolly hood under
her chin, said, 'I'm off now, luv. Kitchen floor's done;
all nice and tidy for the week-end. Bus'll be passing in
five minutes.'

'I'll drive you home—'

'Gracious—no need for that, Mr Matthew—' Mrs Oakley had the active seventy-year-old's reluctance to be given any sort of physical aid.

'Yes, there is; I want to get out—I'll take a walk—'

'Can't pretend you've been working; you've been wasting your time on that great silly puzzle—'

He grinned, pulling on his windcheater; Gertrude Oakley, who'd known him all his life, could still make him feel like a boy who'd broken the rules.

Coming through the hall, he stared at the telephone with a clear picture of Anita stooped above it and all the coats draping her haunches. Very vivid that picture; prologue to—

No, he was going to turn away from that, switch it off in his mind. Out, shut the door on it, as if the house contained it, and the thought-pattern could not escape from there.

He followed Mrs Oakley to the cobbled path where the car stood. 'Car wants a wash,' she told him in the same voice she'd used to tell him to scrub behind his ears. 'And is about to get one,' said Matthew, with a glance upwards.

No rain yet; but the heavy clouds massing; to the west a cloud break spilling a wild light. 'Not too fast down the hill, luv,' Mrs Oakley cautioned him—'and slow down when we come to the bus-stop. I'll ask Sally to tell George not to wait for me.'

Sally in the shop would call to George at the wheel of the bus; familiar, these small things, even heartening, but far today, as though he looked at them through the wrong end of a telescope. He wasn't hearing Mrs Oakley's talk; he was alone. He drove fast up the river-road, past the church, past Squaretrees, Mary and Dorothy's house, on and up towards the reservoir. The clouds hung low; the tops of the brown moors were hidden. Though Mrs Oakley mistrusted the short cut, the narrow rutty road that climbed away from the river, he took that way.

'Careful,' she said, as he turned out of the river-road, 'there's a car behind you.'

'I can see.'

'Well, he didn't give you much time to turn. Right on your bumper, he was. Who would that be, now?'

He grinned; a typical village reaction . . . Mrs Oakley went on peering out, letting down the window, the car being by now some way along the river-road and quite invisible. The monologue continued until she had decided that it must be 'one of them Water Board chaps' off to inspect the dam. Much more rain, said Mrs Oakley, and there'd be flooding.

'You're always sad in this weather,' she told him; 'you don't like to wait for the spring. Your father didn't either.'

'I'm not sad.' But he was. In memory there was the bright vigorous morning, eight days ago. Tramping up through the bracken with Anita; blue skies and an alpine wind, the grey mournful sheet of the reservoir bright as a mountain lake on that lost morning.

The road mounted, Mrs Oakley saying 'Careful' at every bend, the valley dropping away. The Oakley farmhouse was perched high; when she took the bus she had to walk up this gradient: he could see her climbing with the butting belligerency of the old who refuse to be done down by slopes.

'See you Monday—'

'Gracious,' he said, 'it's Friday; have I paid you?'

'You're asleep today; gave it me before I went to the shop—remember? And thank you for the ride. Careful going down.'

He speeded up with a roar. Not that he was in any hurry to get home, to open the door again on the explosive thoughts within. The dying, steel-coloured afternoon with its drifts of storm-light was better company out here; he would walk for a time, letting the windy spaces of wild ground ease the pressure in his skull . . .

Now there seemed a voice in his head, giving him orders: turn right at the river-road, away from home; park the car by the roadside; climb up to the dam itself . . . And now he was standing halfway across the high-walled metal span, leaning out like a gargoyle, looking down at the spread rampart of stone covered with its shining, boiling swirl of water. Another hypnotist, the slanted skid-surface of the water, flowing down, down, down.

Footsteps, coming close? . . . No; nobody up here. The same old footsteps in his head, part of the haunting of the past; someone walking close behind him . . . Nobody here. He stiffened, but he wouldn't turn, he knew this nightmare too well; the war nightmare, another legacy of the raid. Shrug it off; put it out of mind.

Down, down, down. He could get this feeling on the bridge at home looking down the waterfall.

'Not too long,' a voice was telling him; 'get that walk in before the rain comes.'

Pulling himself away—as wistfully as from the puzzle—Matthew saw, in mild astonishment, that the following feet had been no nightmare. Somebody had in fact passed him and was now walking off the dam; he saw the back of a head and a buff-coloured pair of shoulders disappearing down the steps. A moment later there came the sound of a car starting up. Mrs Oakley's Water Board chap, no doubt.

He laughed, disproportionately relieved, and set out upon his walk.

'A walk!' exclaimed Aunt Dorothy, taking his drenched windbreaker; 'on an evening like this; you must be crazy!'

'Not at all,' said Aunt Mary, coming into the hall; 'if one only went for walks up here when it was fine one would die of immobility . . . Come here by the fire. Take your shoes off; we don't mind your socks.'

He went into the small welcoming room. After the wild weather his skin glowed from the warmth; Mary poured him a whisky; he sat cradling it by the fire.

'We've missed you,' Mary said; 'we haven't seen you since—'

'I've been busy,' he said. He didn't want to talk about the last time; he didn't want them to revive the insistent question in his mind. Mary, he judged, had picked this out of the air; she had a shrewd ability to tap his thought, but Dorothy was leaning forward with the wide-eyed moon face full of concern, saying, 'We wondered if you'd heard from Anita—'

He laughed and shook his head; took a gulp of whisky. 'Bread-and-butter letter; four lines of it; no more.'

'The young don't write,' said Mary placidly. 'They see it as an old-fashioned exercise, like sewing samplers. Tape, telephone or carrier pigeon—anything rather than put pen to paper.'

Matthew laughed. 'And none of those could be easily tied with blue ribbon and put away in a drawer; love-letters have gone overboard, I suppose, with all the other things. Leaving us a stream-lined, mechanical world. Not sure that I like it.' But his humour was mending; glow from the fire, glow from the whisky; he felt an upward surge of heart, a loosening of the obsessional thought. 'Anita does her best; she has a conscience, poor darling, and occasionally I prod it. Lone widowed father, brooding on the moors.' He thought Mary was looking at him as if she didn't quite trust his gaiety; he lifted his glass to her and drank again.

'All the same,' she said, 'you spend too much time by yourself. We used to see far more of you. You're turning into a hermit.'

He shook his head. 'I always was. Long walks by myself from an early age. Always coming home to find mother in hysterics because nobody knew where I was.'

Dorothy bounced towards him with a tin of little biscuits. 'Mrs Oakley thinks you ought to—' His sudden shout of laughter left her startled, holding the tin in mid-air.

'Nanny's-eye-view,' he said. 'Village gossip. What does dear old Oakley think I ought to do? Join a boys' club? Take up folk-dancing?' He didn't quite know why he was finding it so funny. Dorothy withdrew the tin; Mary was looking at him with speculative concern.

'She thinks,' Dorothy was saying, 'that you ought to have someone to stay. She says she doesn't like to think of you alone in that house at night—'

'Oh . . .' He was still laughing. 'I like the house at night. It's . . . companionable; no trouble. And as for marauders, I had a commando's training, remember.' But that, for a second, brought back the poisoned memory; he felt the laughter slip, the sudden haunting in his head. Unasked for, the lines of the message came back: *How many miles to midnight* . . . The days of waiting and no answer; the question unsolved. For a moment he was lost to the room, enclosed within the old thought-pattern. 'Dear Colonel' Blessington . . . He drank from his glass, aware now of Mary's eye on him. He drank further, and felt the glow return.

'Here's a promise,' he said. 'When Anita next comes, we'll have a party—ask all the village—get old Oakley to make some of those murderous little things on plates—' He was, he found, falling in love with the idea: he could see his room robbed of space and silence, full of the familiar Yorkshire voices, with Anita the focus of it all, vivid and gleaming with the shine of youth. It was almost real; in this picture there was no shadow behind her.

Dorothy was letting out little coos of approval; Mary said, 'That would be nice,' but she looked as if she were remembering that Anita came seldom to the valley.

He drained his glass; got to his feet. 'Oh, don't go yet!' Dorothy was crying; 'stay to dinner; we'd love you to stay.'

He shook his head. His mood still surged upward; he was ready for the house again, ready for work; new lines for a poem were ticking through his head; the pale scalloped pieces of the jig-saw teased his mind. The familiar footsteps that had proved to be not a nightmare after all, but a solid person who had driven off in a car; the moorland walk; the whisky by the fire had all set him on course again: there was nothing to fear in the house.

In the hall he pulled on his still sodden shoes, the half-dried windbreaker. Mary's calm, intelligent face was given to him; he thought, in the midst of his hurry to be off, that it was the least self-concerned face he had ever seen. She said, 'You're quite sure you're all right?'

He pulled up the zip of the windbreaker. 'Of course I'm all right.'

'You worry me—just a little.'

'Bless you,' he said; 'I don't worry me.'

Out of the house. And however kind they were, the small relief at going; at being on his own again. Wind and darkness now but no rain; ragged, streaming clouds, the colour of smoke on the evening sky.

Still aglow, he drove along the valley road at a speed that would have troubled Mrs Oakley; he charged the hill with his foot hard down; safe enough, no lights up ahead; he slid under the buttressed wall of his own garden and wrenched the wheel to make a perilous entry, grazing the near gate-post. This for some reason amused him. He walked across the flagstones; he could see the waterfall darkly shining; the trees rocking with the wind's tumult; a wild night, a night to be welcomed and he didn't know why. Now he was ready for the game: the game of creeping up on the house, rushing it. Which way tonight? He took the steps leading to the garden door; the door which was unlocked. He moved noiselessly. (And he didn't hate the house; its squat rambling shape had always been there; it was only an imagined enemy, just the rule of the game.) He mounted slowly and gave the door a soft nudge with his shoulder and dodged into the hall.

An especial quiet was, no doubt, the gift of the descending dark. He stood for a moment, hearing his own breath, nothing more. Then he moved, still silent, towards the living-room.

He went in. He moved rapidly across the long dark room, the blind man knowing his way; the last stage of the game. It was over when he put his hand to the lamp on the table; he knew just where the lamp was. His hand found the edge of its shade, his hand slipped under the shade to press the cross-bar switch—

His hand drew back. The switch and the bulb were warm, as though he had only just put out the lamp.

Slowly, slowly now. Nothing to this. Your hand's

cold, the bulb feels warm against your cold hand, that's the answer. But he didn't believe the answer. He was on his toes as he pressed the switch, his whole body turning, on guard, facing down the long room—his hand coming quickly away as the lamp-light shone out, hand into a fist, both hands into fists; ready.

Nobody here. You could be sure of that, you would know. You did not need to turn up the other lights. These solids and half solids, spaces and shadows, the hunch of the chairs—you knew them all. The room was here, a friendly enemy was here, nobody else. He pulled a box of matches out of his pocket and crouched, putting a match to the fire. The paper flared beneath the kindling, flame poured up the space between the pyramid of logs; he waited to hear the reassuring crackle before he pounced upon the jig-saw—

He stood still.

The jig-saw was done. The gap in the sky was filled. Not one of those pale teasing customers lay where he had left them. On the table under the lamplight was the complete mosaic, a finished masterpiece.

'I'm not imagining this.' He said it aloud.

At last, then, somebody here . . .

Where?

Fascinated, he began to prowl. The innocence of this room was still palpable; no need to pluck open a cupboard, twitch the fold of a curtain. Upstairs? Downstairs? Lurking in the cellar? The kitchen first. He was halfway there when his ears caught the sound beyond the window; it was the sound of light footsteps walking, just on the other side of the garden door.

Light footsteps . . . He paused, to make sure of that; the sense of wonder was still with him as he pulled back the curtain from the garden door, and plucked the door open.

'Come on in.' The words spoke themselves; the harsh, one-toned voice was not suited to the words. So, one would say 'Get out'; or 'What the hell are you up to?' But the voice said 'Come on in.'

'Thank you.'

A woman, smiling at him. A woman who wore slacks and a short fur coat, moving delicately past him, finding nothing odd, it seemed, about a man who said Come on in, and still stood blocking the door. She dodged by his elbow; a smell of scent blew past, heavy in his nostrils. There was the scent, the short springy hair and the face of a beautifully-painted boy. Not young, though her body was young. It seemed to him he had been waiting for her. This surprised him. He had come forward to meet an enemy.

'Sorry about your jig-saw,' she said. 'Unforgiveable, but I couldn't resist it.' The voice was husky American. She began to shrug off her jacket, then changed her mind. 'Cold,' she said.

'It'll warm up in a minute. I only just lit the fire. You'd better sit here.'

She did not move towards the chair. She stood where she was, hands in her pockets, saying, 'Sure?'

'Quite sure. Would you like a drink?'

'No thanks. Are you always so kind?'

'What d'you mean—kind?'

She moved towards the fire. 'I understood that an Englishman's home was his castle ... Even where I come from, you don't do this without letting yourself in for trouble.'

'Do what? Finish other people's jig-saws? A sin— agreed. You must have a genius for them—that sky.'

'Puzzles amuse me.' She sat down in his own particular chair. 'Housebreaking—aren't I?'

'I suppose you are. But you see,' Matthew said, 'I was expecting you.' He placed himself in the opposite chair. He saw the golden-brown figure now sitting very still, the green eyes widening; he thought she looked half-amused, half-angry. The eyes had some quality that puzzled him ... were the lashes false, perhaps? The make-up was heavy but skilful; the make-up of a woman wishing to look younger than she was.

'You *were*?'

'Let us say I was expecting somebody.'

'Okay, let's say that.' She was still watchful, on her guard.

'In one sense, I always am. It's a game lonely people play.' He paused, filling his pipe. 'I keep an eye out for strangers.'

'That sounds ominous.'

'It is.'

'Then I guess the sooner I cease to be a stranger the better. My name is Rolf: Jane Rolf.'

'Mine's Gilroy: Matthew Gilroy.'

'I know it.'

'How?'

'Your letters on the hall table.'

'Ah. Making a thorough investigation, were you?'

She laughed. He laughed with her, but his eyes going over the room caught sight of his desk: were the papers there just as he had left them? He wasn't sure.

She seemed unconcerned. 'I *can* explain,' she assured him. 'I came here a long time ago—to this village, one summer, before the war. I was a kid; we were touring around. It gave me a funny feeling, Garfedale; not love, exactly, but it was a place I had to remember. Yorkshire stuck around ... haunted me. Unlike any other place I ever saw.'

'Ours is a great wild country, Browning. Oh those high desolate moors, Mrs Gaskell,' said Matthew.

'I remember,' she said; 'we got out of the car down by the river and looked up—towards this house. I didn't see the house at first. I saw the grove of ash trees and that spectacular waterfall. And then, second blink—or third blink—the house, half in, half out of the trees—all grey-green stone and the little bridge. I wanted to climb up to it and explore. My mother said no. We drove on up Garfedale to the reservoir. First thing I did when I got here this afternoon was to take the same road. The valley hasn't changed or the village. All exactly as I knew it—that other me.'

'Other you? Ha,' said Matthew. 'We think the same way there.'

'Well, that's what fascinated me. Fascinated me so much I had to turn round, to come up here and—collect the house, d'you understand? Kept telling myself how damn silly and to get back to Ripon before dark ... but I couldn't. And when I found the door open—'

It was his turn to interrupt. 'Did you walk across the dam?'

She frowned. 'Across the *bridge*—yes—you heard me, didn't you?'

'I mean the dam—up at the reservoir?'

'Oh ... yes, I walked across.'

'And have you a black car?'

'I do have, yes. Why? What is this?'

Matthew didn't answer. He went on grinning at her, and she looked back at him unsmiling, eyebrows lifted.

'So you're simply revisiting the glimpses of the moon,' he said.

'Are you a writer?'

'Because I talk in quotations? That's just a British vice, as Evelyn Waugh pointed out.'

'Not only British. I can quote when I want to. I quote when I'm driving fast. Got quite a library back home, all your big boys—Shakespeare, Milton, Keats . . . *Are you a writer?*'

He shrugged. 'Kind of odd-job man. Odds and ends of verse; crossword puzzle clues . . . Have you dined? I'm getting hungry.'

'I ate a high-tea at a roadhouse kind of hotel just outside Borrowgate. Enough to feed six of me. But may I cook for you?'

He broke into laughter. 'As a penance? No, not tonight, thank you. I plan to carve a chunk off the cold ham. Other nights I cook with great efficiency.'

'You live quite alone?'

'Oh yes. I've an intermittent biddy—local biddy— who does the cleaning and nannies me. Unnatural for anybody to live alone, in her view.'

'I'm alone,' said Jane Rolf grimly. 'Only one person in my life I ever loved and they took him away. Tough.' All the same she smiled into the firelight.

'You might say that applies to me,' Matthew told her as he went towards the kitchen. 'Only not quite, I suppose; no wife, but I have a daughter: a beloved and engaging child . . . Stay where you are.'

'Sure?'

'Sure.'

Seldom, he thought, slicing the ham, mixing the mustard, had he felt so much at ease with a woman. This person might have been here a long, long time. When he came back, carrying the tray, she was loping around, hands in pockets, looking at the bookshelves.

'Always want to know what people read. I must leave you—'

'No—no, stay. Sure you won't have a drink?'

'Oh—small one, maybe. I'll help myself. For you?'

'Not for me.' The time for drink was past; now there was a lift in the air. He watched the gold-brown figure come back to lean on the mantelpiece.

'Where's your car?' he asked, suddenly.

'Down below. Outside the pub. Safe. I locked it.'

'You walked up to the gate?'

'I like to walk.'

'Here for long?'

'D'you mean England or Garfedale? I'll stay tonight at Ripon and then—oh, I don't know—on to Scotland, maybe. I've just turned myself loose for a while.' Her glance went lazily over the room. 'Were you ever in America?'

The question sounded casual; was he wrong in divining some importance behind it? He said, 'Once.'

'When?'

'Fifty-three.'

'Doing what?'

'You might say, making a discovery.'

He had all of her attention. 'What kind?'

'Ancient things. Forgotten things. Hunting for the bones of men long dead.'

'Well now,' said Jane Rolf.

'Heard of a man called Wallader? Sir Herbert Wallader?'

'I don't think so.'

'He's an archaeologist. He took me along with him on an expedition. My job once was reading cyphers—Yes?'

'Nothing,' said Jane Rolf. 'Go on.'

'He said I could help him by solving the cyphers of the bones. Tracing the movement of Siberian man through the Bering Strait and down the West Coast of America.'

'Must have been quite a trip.'

'Full of interest. You find things you never expected.'

'I'll bet. Did you never go back?'

'No.'

'You didn't fall for America?'

'I'm afraid not. I'm sorry.'

'Okay, I'm no patriot,' said Jane Rolf.

'What are you?' he asked lazily.

She was quiet, turning the glass in her hand. 'Just a person who takes chances, you might say.' She raised the glass to him and drank. She was now so palpably inviting another question that he could think of nothing to ask her. There was the feeling of a duel in this silence, each daring the other to end it, throughout the meeting of their eyes.

'You might also call me a cliché,' Jane Rolf said, twirling the glass. 'The rich rootless lady from the New World.' She looked at her watch. 'And now,' she said, 'I must hightail it for Ripon.'

A sharp thrust in his mind was crying No. He pushed the tray aside and stood up, comfortable with the words. 'I'd like to see you again.'

'You would?' He saw the eyes with the gold glint receive the message.

'Tomorrow?' said Matthew. 'Come to lunch.'

'I wouldn't want to give trouble to the—what was it you called her—biddy?'

'She doesn't operate over the week-end. It'll be my cooking.'

'May I call you in the morning? I never make plans.'

'As you wish.'

'I don't decide to do things. I just do them.' She turned up the collar of her jacket.

He let the affectation go, thinking, 'All the same, you'll come,' as he led her to the front door. Here again was the tumultuous dark; the branches adrift and swimming in the current of the wind. 'Let me drive you down the hill.' She was pulling on a pair of leather gloves. The green eyes caught a shine of light from the hall. 'Told you—I like to walk.'

The words came into his mind as he stood there: *she came with a cat's soft tread* . . .

He said, 'Good night, Mrs Rolf. I'll hope to hear from you in the morning.'

'You will. We have—or had once—a friend in common, I believe—'

'A friend?'

'Name of Blessington,' said Jane Rolf. 'Good night, Mr Gilroy.'

6

'I'D LIKE a word with the Colonel, if you please.'

Ivy Stone had no particular respect for policemen. They looked about twelve years old, these days. But the uniform still carried its immediate, enjoyable message of drama. She smiled at the twelve-year-old, saying, 'I'm afraid you've just missed him. Gone for the week-end,' her thoughts shooting away on their wild search: Murder? Rape? Embezzlement? Some ridiculous woman killing herself for love of the Colonel and leaving a note? Ivy's imagination in this kind was strong; her listening-capacities as weak as usual. She awoke halfway through the twelve-year-old's explanation.

An accident . . . To a friend of the Colonel's, a friend who had—the police understood—visited this house last night. Gentleman found at five o'clock this morning: lying in Mansell Passage at the foot of the steps. Not seen before because of the fog. Taken to North Royal Hospital. The name and the words 'Next of Kin' forced their way through Ivy's natural barriers. The effect was all the more stunning.

'Not Mr *Ledyard*? Mr Rupert Ledyard?'

The twelve-year-old said he was afraid so; adding that she had better sit down.

'Murdered? Don't tell me.' (She meant 'Tell me' but that was how it came out.)

No suspicion of Foul Play, the twelve-year-old assured her; by this time in the drawing-room. The gentleman had succumbed, no doubt at all. But the doctor on duty, Dr Padgett, who wasn't one to make mistakes, had diagnosed a 'cerrible heemeridge'. No fracture in the cranium, no bruising to speak of. The deceased had obviously collapsed while climbing the steps.

Huddled there in the fog all night; Ivy saw him—that great big man lying still.

This called for a cup of tea.

Shock, sorrow and thrill collided: there was also the smallest pinch of disappointment: her own absence from the final scenes last night. ('*I let him out of the front door, laughing and joking, he was, full of beans as well as you or I. Good night, Mrs Stone, he said, it's been a wonderful evening.*') Alas for the truth. In a voice whose tremor did not displease her, she began to explain the nature of the party. The twelve-year-old, maddeningly, knew all about it. Not only had a leaflet been found in the deceased's pocket, but the son of the deceased, when telephoned an hour ago, had given full information.

'Oh the poor boy, waiting up all that time—remember him so well at the party, just like his father—frantic he must have been—'

Young Mr Gilbert Ledyard had left the party and gone to bed early. The telephone-call from the hospital was his first intimation that—

'Gracious what a terrible shock.'

Young Mr Ledyard had been expecting something of the sort. His father had suffered from high blood-pressure for a very—

'*My* blood-pressure's much too low, my doctor was saying only last week that—'

It was presumed, said the twelve-year-old, that—as

guest of honour—Mr Ledyard would hardly have left
the house alone. Someone had—surely—accompanied
him? Since she herself couldn't know (a wound casually
inflicted) the Colonel was the most likely person to—

'Not him. He was in bed long before the party
ended.'

'In *bed*?'

She had scored a point. The twelve-year-old was
temporarily prepared to listen.

'What with his early start for Bristol and not being
the host, not really the host, just having lent the
house for the proceedings, oh he went the rounds,
talked to them all and said good-night; it wasn't as
though—'

She was again cut off. Anybody likely to have
gone with Mr Ledyard? Some of the committee
perhaps?

'What a dreadful thing to happen with the election—
one just can't believe it. Ah, *ah*, I see what you're
getting at—one of those silly women. I shouldn't be at
all surprised.'

'Pardon?'

'One of those silly women, that little Miss—there, the
name's gone, she'd have lost her head when it happened,
run off and left him . . . well, even if that isn't what
you're suggesting, it's what I'm suggesting. If you'd had
my experience with silly women. I know who could tell
you. *He* knows them all.'

'Who would that be?'

'Mr—Mr—the young one, blue eyes, in advertising
or something; he was in charge. I don't mean the
refreshments or anything like that, he's more the
organizer. Quite a young man, bit of a busybody, little
name. Like Bright. Only not Bright. I'll get it in a
minute.'

The twelve-year-old mournfully agreed that she should take her time.

To Anita Gilroy, television was a friendly, knockabout affair. Sound radio, on the other hand, scared her to death. She was scared now. The rehearsal had found her more or less dumb: this, the live performance, found her even dumber. Seated at a table in surroundings of antiseptic elegance, she was discussing legalized abortion with Miss Beulah Maxwell, ace reporter of the *Daily Blast* and the high-ranking novelist, Fleur Seltz. At least, she was supposed to be discussing it. In fact, Miss Maxwell and Mrs Seltz were clashing head-on.

They had met an insuperable road-block in the matter of tolerance. To be truly tolerant one must, Mrs Seltz insisted, be tolerant of intolerance. Miss Maxwell loudly disagreed. She was all for absolutely everybody doing absolutely everything. Her appearance, that of a Girl Guide, was contradicted by her ferocious broad-mindedness. The small, gravely beautiful and pedantic-ally-spoken Mrs Seltz punctured her like a picador. (Surely no end of a time-waster, this tolerance lark . . . and why, Anita wondered, had these two been chosen to deal with abortion? Mrs Seltz must be long past the necessity. For the Girl Guide, despite her spanking approach to sex, the necessity had not yet arisen. Miss Maxwell, like Anita, was a virgin. Anita could bet on it.)

'If we might get back—' the chairwoman's light, cheerful voice blew across the dialogue, a directing feather.

They got back.

'I find your suggestion that an abortionist should be located in every shopping-centre—as it might be the

Express Dairy—not only immoral but vulgar and ridiculous.'

'You're twisting my words.'

Anita glanced towards the control-room, visible through the glass panel behind Miss Maxwell's head. She could see the producer, a jolly, red-haired girl, signal her anxiously. She must say something.

'—A frank, practical approach to what should be seen as a Community Service.'

'—You said Shopping Centre, did you not?'

'As a figure of speech.'

Anita's thoughts moved over to Harvey: far away by now. Three o'clock. He had arrived; he had eaten his lunch; he was there in Bristol (a town of which Anita had no clear image beyond ships and the start of *Treasure Island*); lost to her among his own mysteries. She saw him at ease, content without her, not missing her at all. She gave a huge sigh.

'Advertising? You cannot be serious,' said Mrs Seltz.

'I'm dead serious. Why not?'

'To envisage a society which permits abortionists to advertise is—if I may quote the modern philosopher Solvey Ruttenheim with whose works you are certainly—'

'Excuse me.' The directing feather blew again. 'Our time's *almost* up. Might we have a word from Miss Gilroy?'

Among Anita's troubles was the fact that she could never quite believe in the transmitting abilities of the microphone. To her its neat black shape looked as quietly inscrutable, as unlikely to relay sound upon the air, as a shoe or a clothes-brush. Stifling her scepticism, she leaned towards it. 'I don't think I'm really qualified to talk,' she said and paused, assembling her thoughts. (I don't believe one *can* talk, until one starts having a baby oneself. Which is a thing I particularly look forward to ... Harvey's baby ... so I don't suppose I will even then, if you see what I mean. Oh, dear, that won't do.)

'*Because*—' she said, pulling herself together. Beside her elbow the little green lamp began to wink in an agitated way and the chairwoman spoke smoothly to the clothes-brush: 'Well, it's been a most absorbing discussion and I'm sorry that's all we have time for. Thank you, Mrs Fleur Seltz, Miss Beulah Maxwell and Miss Anita Gilroy.'

All three participants now tiptoed away through the swing door while a piping newcomer began to give her recipes for safe mushroom cookery. 'Didn't half make a pig's ear of that,' Anita told herself reproachfully. Mrs Seltz and Miss Maxwell were back in a flash at tolerance-of-intolerance: she followed them into the control room, meekly awaiting the wrath of the red-haired producer, who hissed 'Somebody waiting to see you. Very urgent and important, *he* says;' nods and becks and wreathed smiles.

Harvey. Nobody else. Harvey having decided against Bristol. Couldn't be ... *Must* be.

'Where?'

'In the corridor. I asked him if he'd like to listen, but he said he didn't approve of abortion.'

'*That's* my boy ...' Anita grabbed her coat, fur hat, and gloves; she made a precautionary face at her face in the glass; it was all right; she had dealt with it just before the discussion began. She went swooping.

Not Harvey. (Naturally not. One of those wishful-thinks.) But why Mr Anthony Price should have any-thing urgent or important to tell her she could not imagine. As the smack-down of disappointment sub-sided, she noted that she still found him appealing. So

oddly neat, clean and masculine; far from today's
young men. He was—obviously—in a state. He
dropped his bowler hat and it bowled. Anita fielded it
with her foot.

'Thanks so much.' He picked it up. 'I'm awfully sorry
to come charging in on you like this.'

'Not to worry.'

'I rang you at your home number. Then I remembered you were on this programme so I looked it up in
the *Radio Times* and seized a taxi. I wouldn't have—
only the most ghastly thing's happened—'

Harvey . . . The world slowed up, stopped.

'Harvey?' She was barking like a sea-lion, she
thought. 'Tell me—what?'

'All right, all right.' A gentle hand patted her
shoulder. 'Not to him. But I have got to get hold of him
quickly.'

Anita's world went on its way again. Contentedly she
pictured it spinning, after the manner of Mr Price's hat.
Borne upon the sweet, drowsy airs of relief came the
voice of the young man saying, 'I feel like a murderer.'

'Do you, now? Why do you?'

'Just how do we get out of here?'

'We keep on walking. In about a mile there's a lift.
Why a murderer?'

'Poor old Ledyard.'

'Poor old *Ledyard*?'

'Yes, indeed. Would you believe it? On his way home
from the party. A stroke.'

'Golly Moses . . .' Anita thought about it; the sense
of wonder was enormous: somebody there and then
somebody not there. Last night the great, jovial figure in
Harvey's room, the roaring voice; that fearful joke about
his own name . . . 'The only way is for Ledyard to follow
his predecessor to the Bahamas. *Or even further*,' she

remembered, and now looked hard at Mr Price. 'Got your wish, didn't you?' she murmured. 'Oh, sorry . . . And I really *am* sorry,' she went on. 'Not that I knew him well or anything, but it makes one feel sad all over. Doesn't it? He's the first dead person I've ever met, except my mother, and that was when I was two. This is the lift.'

'I see it is,' said Mr Price in a dirge-like tone.

'Press G. We're on L.G.'

'What does that mean?'

'Lower Ground. We want Ground.'

The door slid. They were enclosed, in a sinister artificial light, travelling fast.

'Hope you won't mind telling me where I can get hold of Blessington. If it seems like an impertinence—'

'Oh, *hell*, it's going all the way to the top. We'll have to come down again. Not an impertinence. But you see—'

Mr Price had taken a turn for the talkative. '. . . Thrown the whole campaign . . . Blessington must stand . . . Can't be too late to nominate him—emergency-clause—must issue a statement . . . committee women all crying and choosing a wreath—where are we?'

'Going up. Like I said, we'll come down. Sorry I can't help. Stonehenge can give you Harvey's number in Bristol.'

'Contrariwise, she can't.'

'Why not? Here we are; well that's something.' The door slid open to reveal nobody on the top floor. 'How peculiar. Press G. quick. Otherwise we'll be stopped by some clot halfway.'

'Damn—I've pressed L.G. Does it matter?'

'Not really. We'll come up again. What's Stonehenge playing at?'

'She doesn't know the number *or* the address.'

'She's bonkers,' said Anita, 'probably shock.' The lift stopped at the third floor to admit a uniformed messenger.

'Says he's never given it to her yet.'

'Repeat, bonkers,' said Anita; the messenger pressed the top button and they were carried aloft again.

'We were going down.'

'Oh, sorry.'

'Harvey keeps going to Bristol. It's a regular thing. She *must* know—'

'She says not.'

'Here we are,' said the messenger.

'Good,' said Mr Price, making to stride out. Anita seized his arm. 'Top,' she explained. 'Press G. again. Better keep your thumb on it. Well, she's the only person to tackle.'

'I've tackled her. Till I was blue in the face. She hung up on me. Said she couldn't help me and that was that.'

'Well, nor can I.'

'Why not?'

'Because I don't know.'

Mr Price stared. '*You* don't know?'

'That's what I keep telling you, don't I? Look out, it's going to be three again. Keep on pressing.'

The lift wavered, stuck, and then moved down at the speed of light.

'Do people ever become seasick in these things? But you *must* know,' said Mr Price. 'I mean—didn't you ask him?'

'L.G.,' said Anita. 'Out—before it shuts—quick.' She dragged him through the closing door. 'Naturally I didn't ask him. If he'd wanted me to know he'd have told me.'

Mr Price appeared to consider this profoundly before asking, 'What do we do now?'

'About Harvey?'

'I meant about getting out?'

'Walk up the stairs. Only one flight.'

Mr Price stayed where he was, gazing at her. It was a very blue gaze. His shirt, she noticed, matched his eyes.

'Most remarkable,' he said.

'What is?'

'You didn't ask him. *If he'd wanted you to know he'd have told you.*'

'Yes—well. Is there anything remarkable about that?'

'Isn't there just?' said Mr Price cryptically. 'All the girls in *my* life—' he stopped.

'Are there many?'

'End to end,' said Mr Price, 'I daresay they'd reach a moderate distance. But they're not what I'm talking about. You're the cypher that foxes me.' She turned for the stairs. Mr Price caught up with her. 'You're clearly in love with the bloke. Yet you abstain from asking where he spends the week-end simply because—'

'He prefers it that way,' said Anita. 'End message. And you're implying Harvey's off on a date with a dish, when it's only a printing-press.' (Oh, please God, only a printing-press.)

'I know it's *a* printing-press. That's all I do know.'

'Isn't it called Blessington? Being a family business I'd have thought—'

'You'd be wrong. It's called something else. And the name escapes Stonehenge so far—like all the other names she's had a go at since I've had the pleasure of her acquaintance.'

'Oh, she's hopeless that way.'

'Egocentricity—carried to its furthest point.'

'How clever you are to know things like that. I'd have thought it was because she was deaf . . . Isn't the name on the leaflet? They printed it—'

'Not a trace,' said Mr Price.

'I thought printers always—'

'Well, this one didn't.'

They had reached the entrance hall. Mr Price stared about him, murmuring, 'Yes, the dear old place looks just the same.'

'If you ask me,' said Anita, having given the matter some thought, 'Stonehenge is holding out on you.'

'Why should she?'

'She doesn't want Harvey to be bothered with all this till he gets back. That's my guess.' She put on her fur hat, still thinking furiously. 'Not with me, though,' she said, 'she won't hold out on me. She's too sorry for me.'

'Sorry for you?'

'I wear my heart on my sleeve. And she's convinced he's Leading Me On—it's written all over her face.' The young man looked shocked. 'Are you going back to your Public Relations?' she asked him.

'Where are *you* going?'

'Up to the house. To wheedle Stonehenge. Ring you as soon as she's parted with her secret—how's that? Take me about half an hour. I have to change at Tottenham Court Road.'

'Would you be so kind as to call us a taxi?' Mr Price said to the commissionaire.

'Excuse me, but your presence won't exactly help.'

'Never mind.'

'My hunch may be a bad one, too.'

'Let's find out, shall we?'

'I've only got ten shillings,' she cried in desperation.

'I'm loaded,' said Mr Price.

'It's possible,' Mr Price said to Stonehenge, when she had, with reluctance, allowed them into the drawing-room, 'that someone may telephone me here. I've left a message at the Committee Rooms, telling them where I am.'

Stonehenge met this with guarded disapproval. ('Committee Rooms', Anita thought, sounded oddly grand for what had proved to be the semi-basement room of Mrs Vernon's flat in Worsely Gardens, North Royal.)

'I can't really see,' said Stonehenge, 'what all this has got to do with the Colonel. People bothering him. First a policeman. And—'

'And now us,' said Mr Price, who seemed to be a match for Stonehenge. 'I apologise. But it is really essential that we get in touch with him. Since the—um —unfortunate death of Mr Ledyard, there is only one person to stand as candidate for the True Tories—'

'Candidate?' said Stonehenge.

'The Colonel,' said Mr Price.

Anita, watching Stonehenge, saw her desire to protect the Colonel at war with the beginnings of reverence for Mr Price. 'Well . . . but . . . I've already *told* you, sir. I don't *know.*'

Don't you? thought Anita. Perhaps you don't: but one thing's clear: You're frightened. Why?

The defensive, explanatory voice went on: 'First time he said he'd leave it for me on the pad beside the telephone. When he came back I said you didn't do that, I said and he said No, I didn't, did I? he said and laughed the way he does. Second time he said 'You know the number,' and when I said I didn't he said well he said it's written down where it always is. But having no call to use it I didn't look and this time he didn't say anything at all . . .'

'But the name of the firm must be *some*where,' Anita said. 'It can't be all that difficult to find—'

'If you think I'm going to go snooping among the Colonel's papers, you're very much mistaken. The last thing he likes is poking and prying. Most particular. And why not? He's a right to his privacy, hasn't he? The things up there under lock and key—you've no idea.'

Receiving a picture of Harvey's wardrobe crammed with skeletons, Anita suppressed a giggle. 'We're not asking you to pry, Mrs Stone. We're only asking you to help us, because we're worried stiff.'

'Worried for who, I should like to know?'

'Well, for the Colonel, of course. Imagine what a shock—to read about it in Bristol—all by himself.'

She had, she thought, scored a point, and was about to pursue it when the doorbell rang. Stonehenge went to answer it.

'Odd,' said Anita, while a feminine voice came from the hall.

'What's odd?' said Mr Price.

'I never realised it before. She's frightened of Harvey.'

'Frightened?'

'Scared to death.'

'?' said Mr Price with his eyebrows.

'.' said Anita with her chin.

Stonehenge was once more in the room, her face sunk back into lines of resistance. She was followed by Miss Appleby, whose lean spectacled face shone with the delight of the understudy called on to play the lead.

She began to talk fast, while Stonehenge disappeared grudgingly into the kitchen, apparently to put a kettle on.

Miss Appleby was very sorry, she hoped she wasn't

intruding; they'd told her Mr Price was here, and it was *she* who had been the last to see Mr Ledyard alive: she'd left the house with him and parted from him at the corner of Mansell Passage: 'Oh dear,' said Miss Appleby, 'he said good*bye*; it all seems so . . .'

'Doesn't it,' said Mr Price.

Miss Appleby went on. She'd been with the Police. For half an hour. Answering questions. (Stonehenge, back in the room with an unenthusiastic offering of biscuits, was listening to this with a mixture of gloom and envy.) But now, Miss Appleby said, thanks to all she'd told them, the Police were satisfied. She thought Mr Price ought to know. Nervously she took a biscuit, and then on second thoughts, put it back. Stonehenge disappeared again.

Mr Price said he was glad to know: however, it did nothing to help him make contact with the Colonel.

'Oh dear,' said Miss Appleby. 'Friday afternoon. Bristol, he said, didn't he. The printing-press—'

Mr Price explained with dubious patience about the printing-press.

Miss Appleby blinked two or three times, then cried, 'The invoice! For the leaflets! The name'd be on—'

'They haven't sent the bill in,' said Mr Price.

'But—' began Miss Appleby, when both the doorbell and the telephone rang at once.

'I'll take the door,' said Mr Price, while Anita forestalled Miss Appleby at the telephone.

'North Royal 2147? Can Colonel Blessington take a personal call from Bristol?' asked the operator's voice.

'Well no, he can't. He's *in* Bristol.'

'He's—just a minute, please.'

Bewildered, Anita waited.

It was a very long minute: it stretched out, giving Mr Price time to return, reluctantly ushering in Miss

North Royal Echo. Who had, Anita gathered, already been to the Committee Rooms and had just heard the news; what a dreadful thing, what plans for the True Tories, go to press today, just a paragraph if the Colonel wasn't here perhaps Mr Price or Miss Appleby could—

Mr Price replying briskly that Miss Appleby could, put them together on the sofa and leaned over Anita's chair.

'Somebody for Harvey,' she said. 'Calling from Bristol. I said he was *there*. Can't make out what's going on.'

'Hullo.' Another voice this time, a young one, familiar—where had she heard it before? . . . Here with Harvey, just over a week ago; Quentin, the petulant queer, scattering leaflets in the hall. 'Who is that?' he asked.

'Anita Gilroy. I was with Harvey when you turned up in the hall.'

'Oh.' He didn't sound pleased about this. 'I just terribly want to speak to the Colonel. Isn't he there?'

'Well, no, he wouldn't be, would he?'

'I don't see why not—'

'How can he possibly—?'

'I suppose he doesn't want to talk to me. You might just tell him I'm sorry. Most frightfully sorry. I know I broke the rules. And I shouldn't have lost my temper—please tell him that. Some idiotic operator said he was in Bristol.'

'So he is. At the printers.'

'*I'm* at the printers, Miss Gilroy.'

'In Bristol?'

'Well of course in Bristol.'

Anita blinked.

'Hullo?' said Quentin.

'But Harvey's there,' she said.

'Where?'

'In *Bristol*. He went down on the early train this morning. He was going straight to whatever its name is —what *is* its name?'

'What's what's name?'

'Where you are?'

'Oh heavens, the Lovell Press,' said the peevish exasperated voice. 'And it's no good your telling me the Colonel's here, because he isn't. I've been here since nine o'clock and I haven't set eyes on him.'

For the second time in the afternoon Anita's world slowed up and stopped.

It started again, most hideously, with a name. The name arrived instantly, like a dart from a blow-pipe: the name of Jane Rolf. While Miss Appleby cried, '*Not* in Bristol!' and Stonehenge returned, setting a tea tray down with a valedictory thud as if it were a tombstone, Anita explored the tormenting possibilities of the name. Harvey wasn't in Bristol. Harvey had lied to her. Harvey had some reason for lying. And a man's reason for lying to the woman he says he loves—

Anita tried to push the name away. She tried to listen while Mr Price with increased desperation pursued his questioning of Stonehenge: Had she *no* idea where the Colonel could be? If he didn't go to Bristol, where did he go? Weren't there friends he stayed with, someone who might possibly . . .

Anita stopped listening. It was no good. The little dread, once admitted, grew stronger; she was stuck with it now, until she saw Harvey again.

7

Jane Rolf awoke from a dead-quiet sleep; awoke and remembered. This large cold room was her bedroom in the hotel at Ripon. Today was the day. Saturday, March the eleventh. She felt well, rested, eager. Time, a quarter to eight. She had ordered breakfast for eight o'clock. Waiting, she ran a bath and fed shillings into the electric fire. They had given her a ground-floor room; drawing back the curtains she saw the bare garden, wide as a park and stretching to the fields and the rising moorland under a hazardous sky; long purple clouds split by vivid, wrathful sunshine; more rain on the way.

Plans to make, and a careful task of repacking. A certain repacking also in her mind, born of yesterday's visit to Matthew Gilroy's house. Lying in the hot scented bath, she observed the visit from beginning to end. She lingered particularly on the quarter of an hour she had spent alone in the house, before Matthew Gilroy arrived. The sum of this was to move her quickly on, out of her bath, into her warm angora dressing-gown; sitting before the looking-glass, making up her face with the rapid skill of one whose thoughts are elsewhere.

'Come in,' she said to the knock on the door.

(He said, 'Come on in.' Is he what I expected? No, because no one is.)

'Door, he is locked,' said a plaintive accented voice outside.

'Oh—sorry—one minute.'

The foreign boy wore a white coat; he set the breakfast tray down on top of the maps she had spread out over the writing-table. A small irritation: the plans were complex and important, and allowed of no interference.

But by the time she had eaten her breakfast and taken the small blue pill, she found she could embark on today's business. She made her notes with the aid of her map. The note-book was small, leather-covered, containing train-times, shopping lists, accounts both in dollars and sterling. She wrote quickly: figures, distances, all theoretical, but it seemed likely that she could keep to this rough time-table even if today's business lengthened into night. And if—she laughed suddenly—this journey should prove to be the end of Jane Rolf? Well, she could contemplate that without fussing. She dressed in the whipcord slacks of yesterday, adding a leather belt and an alpaca sweater. She transferred the necessary minimum from the suitcase to the rucksack; but one must be very careful here; one must forget nothing; one must be prepared for every possible variation of the game.

When it was full, she tested it for weight. Years since she had worn a rucksack and the straps were inclined to cut her shoulders. She tried it over her fur jacket. The look of herself in the glass amused her, so elegant a hitch-hiker; far too elegant. Far too conspicuous. After another look, she put the fur jacket into her suitcase and substituted an olive-green windbreaker. Better.

'Your newspapers, Madame.'

She sat on the side of the bed, turning a page of the paper. But her eyes were on her nails; they were begin-

ning to irritate her. Needed a coat of varnish. With a
towel on her lap, the polish-remover at the ready, and
the tiny brush skilfully directed, she made a pretty job
of her right hand. (Most women, as she recalled, painted
the left before the right. Ambidextrous since childhood,
Jane preferred using the left.) While she waved her
fingers in the air to dry, she glanced over the paper
again. The news seemed irrelevant, not concerned with
the all-absorbing hours that lay ahead of her. She turned
a page.

And then paused. She read:

SUDDEN DEATH OF NORTH ROYAL CANDIDATE
CEREBRAL HAEMORRHAGE ON EVE OF BY-ELECTION
MR RUPERT LEDYARD

'Well, well—the poor old bullfrog finally blew up,'
Jane thought unkindly, looking back to her glimpse of
him at the party. She saw him in the drawing-room,
loud, purple and disastrous. She saw the circular fringe
of women, the organisers and the helpers. She could
imagine the hen-roost squawking there must be now;
the emergency meetings, the fluttering chaos, the word
election—

Jane sat where she was and said, '*Oh.*'

She read the paragraph again. No mention of
Blessington. Not yet.

She put the paper aside and sat still. Then she pressed
the bell hard. 'Fetch me an A.B.C., please,' she said to
the boy. 'Quickly.' When he had brought the chunky
catalogue of train times, she rapidly turned the pages.
One newly-painted nail followed the tables carefully.
Then she turned once more to the note-book, murmuring, 'Faster, faster, as the Red Queen said.' She wrote
quickly, smiling a little.

When she had finished she stretched herself; then with

absorbed concentration began painting the nails of her other hand.

Lesley Fenton was bored. Nobody could blame him. Gravely Bridge on a wet Saturday afternoon in March would have bored men with quieter natures than his. In summertime he liked it. In summer this small town, this dump, this huddle of slate and dark northern brick at the river's edge became a lively focus for his imagination. Girls in shorts, girls in swim-suits, hiking girls, holiday girls, bound for the moors and the river, each and all lit up his internal torches most pleasantly. When he went off duty, returning to his bed on an August Saturday night, he would frequently dream of being locked in the desirable position with a really splendid girl; say Miss Anita Gilroy. Miss Gilroy was sometimes to be seen at her father's house, only a short walk from Gravely Bridge. Lesley looked forward to these times.

No holiday girls today. A few local girls in mackintoshes. He went on, his feet hurting, patrolling the little network of streets where nothing happened. A grey forty-six-year-old, stubby and wearing police uniform, toting the burden of the baffled Casanova inside. (And another two hours till opening-time.) He stood awhile before the stationer's window; the postcards were unsatisfactory, local views, mainly of the Garfe River and the grouse moors, he knew them by heart; but there was one agreeable calendar; expensive, unsold; he couldn't remember how long it had been there; an Italian picture of Venus scantily veiled. Old Mrs Grance, the stationer concerned, shut her shop at one p.m. on Saturdays, so Lesley could justifiably test the lock on the door while his eyes were busy stripping the veil off Venus.

His next port of call was the public car-park behind the corn-merchant's; in summer quite a pleasant place; at this time of year a deserted shell, spied on by a shed of green corrugated iron and a blind grubby window in the wall of a disused outhouse. Its only inhabitant would be Georgie Withers' scooter. Wise however to check on Georgie Withers' licence and if necessary give Georgie another warning. He took a last swig of Venus.

'Excuse me, officer.'

Officer . . . foreign talk, summer visitor's talk. And it *was* a girl. No, it wasn't: he looked into a mature made-up face, but he sniffed an exciting smell of scent. Her body brought to his mind other bodies; she was slim and strong. She might have escaped from summer to stand here in the light, raw rain; with a rucksack on her shoulders and those well-cut pants ending in ankle boots of bright brown suede. Sophisticated, Lesley's reading signalled. She could make him feel shy if he didn't look out.

'Can I get a bus from here to Borrowgate?'

American, too.

'Well, now . . .' He knew the bus timetable by heart, just as he knew the postcards. But he wanted to prolong this small moment with its unexpected suggestion of adventure. 'You'll have come down the valley,' he said, with a jerk of his thumb that vaguely indicated Garth-waite. She shook her head and laughed. 'No. I came on the bus from Ripon. I've been wandering all over,' she said. 'Not that way, though. Some sort of a lake, isn't there? Well, I won't have time now.' Friends, she explained, were meeting her in Borrowgate.

'You'll have to wait till four-forty; four-forty-five, more likely. They drive slow when the road's wet.'

She looked at her watch. 'Half an hour. Think I'll start walking.'

'Not much of a day for it,' said Lesley and added, 'Long way from home, aren't you, Miss?'

'About six thousand miles,' said the woman with the rucksack. She added, 'Thank you. Which way?' 'I'll take you to the corner.' Walking beside her down the tilted High Street, past the small shops with the crowded, inelegant windows, he found it hard to keep up with the long, loping stride. 'Anyone can see you're a walker, Miss.' She didn't answer. 'Now,' he said, as they passed the Green Dragon, 'here's the valley road; just follow the river; signposted for Borrowgate all the way. Keep your eye out for the bus, it'll catch you up.' He saw her glancing towards the head of the valley where the great clouds hung low. 'Yes,' he said; 'that's Garthwaite up there; a very wonderful achievement, Garthwaite.' He began giving her dates and figures of the reservoir, talking guide-book as he would do to a girl in summer. Usually the girls seemed bored. This woman listened politely. She said, 'I'd have liked to see it; I suppose there's a bus that goes that way too.'

He nodded. 'You could walk it, Miss. But you need a better day.'

Unexpectedly she blew him a kiss.

He felt quite sad when she walked down the road. Turning, he stumped back past the Green Dragon; something on his mind now, besides the usual images. What? Something that nagged. Something out of line, a picture hanging crookedly . . .

Her feet, he thought. Those elegant brown ankle boots were as clean as though she had only just put them on. She hadn't been 'wandering all over' in those boots.

Well, possibly she'd changed them somewhere, stopped off and put the wet shoes in her rucksack.

The afternoon began to hang heavy again as he turned into the car-park. On the soaked asphalt, set against the south wall stood Georgie Withers' scooter, draped in grey tarpaulin, looking muffled and dead. The park was L-shaped; he paced over the wet ground, looked round the corner. Unexpected, the car there; a black car, an impressive car, a Millaux. 'Whose is that, then?' Lesley wondered. He walked round it, trying the handles, as duty demanded. All the doors were locked, the windows wound up. On the front seat he could see a piece of luggage, white leather, woman's luggage. He was interested. He strolled away, looking back once or twice and presently stuck his head round the door of the Goode Goblinne tea-rooms in search of a possible owner. But the scatter of customers were all women he knew by sight. No strangers here. He went on being interested.

8

ALL DAY the liquid scurry of the water, the always-
sound but louder, fuller, the downward stream faster and
blacker, fed from the rain on the heights. Out on to the
bridge to watch it slide and swell, hear it make its little
thunder through the cleft. You would pace out, pace
back, wait and wonder and be sure she would come.
'We have—or had—a friend in common. Name of
Blessington.' A challenge thrown down.

So, to the wakefulness and the dreams.

But it was coming close now; no more need to go
squirrelling in your head asking again and again what
this was all about. You would discover.

There had been the ordinary outside day; beginning
with the telephone call to make sure. 'Yes, sir, there was
a Mrs Rolf here last night but she left the hotel about
half an hour ago.' Proceeding with the ordinary outside
day, walking down to the village and the shop, posting
off the usual packet of designs that seemed as though
someone else had drawn them. The headache throbbing
a little, threatening to grow stronger.

Hullo to the ordinary outside people you met; talk of
the weather and the reservoir rising, danger of floods, the
inspector worried, more rain to come. Hullo to Mary
Cattle; Mary Cattle turned into an ordinary outside
person, flat face of a stranger. Back with the week-end

supplies, to the house and the inside day, the true dark day of waiting. Because she would come, you knew that. You weren't fooled—not altogether. You hadn't cooked lunch for her; you had put lunch off a little while, destroying the jig-saw, the Tower of London, 1700 pieces, all turned right way up now; not begun but not strictly abandoned as soon as the last coloured piece lay face up; to eat your lunch alone.

I don't decide to do things, I just do them.

Where was she?

Who was she?

You'll know.

At half past two Matthew had begun to work on the edge; by four o'clock the thin jagged frame lacked only a few pieces at the top. He rose, stretched himself, and moved away to light the fire. He made himself a cup of tea in the kitchen. He returned to the jig-saw. Now, below the front windows, somebody came walking, whistling.

When he opened the front door she said, 'Hullo, there; sorry I couldn't make lunch.' Different today, with the rucksack, the bulky windbreaker and the scarf tied over her head; almost a stranger. Briskly she began to unload in the hall. With the removal of the scarf and the windbreaker she returned, bright head and bright eyes, careless hand smoothing her hair, not looking in the glass. But the night thoughts had made her younger; now he noticed the heavy make-up, the metallic shine on the curls of the close-fitting hair. The body young, though; with the lean-fitting slacks, the bulky shirt and loose sweater, it might have been the body of a boy.

All this was highly important, to be studied and absorbed while she said Yes, she would like tea, and he directed her to the visitor's chair. She spread out her hands to the fire, in the conventional gesture. He noticed a scatter of faint brown marks on the back of each beautiful hand; the vividly painted nails.

(Not long now. Soon you'll know.)

He felt the air in the room tighten; he felt the forceful, insistent beat of his heart. 'Now tell me,' he said.

The gleaming eyes, with the firelight in them. 'Tell you?'

'About Harvey Blessington.'

'Oh . . .' Faint amusement; her eyes went to the fire again. 'Did I mention him? I'd forgotten.'

(Not true.)

'Just a friend of mine,' she said. 'An old friend from way back.'

'But you've seen him lately?'

'A couple of days ago.'

'In London?'

She nodded.

'And he gave you my name?'

She didn't answer, smoothing the back of one hand with the fingers of the other.

'He must have told you. Otherwise—'

'We spoke of you; yes.'

'So you've come with some kind of message?'

'You could say that.'

'He's told you about Anita?'

'He's mentioned her.' She was watching him now as she drank from her cup. The light in her eyes beneath the thick lashes—*were* they false?—was teasing; not pleasantly teasing. 'This puzzles you?'

He paced to the window. The sound of the waterfall was like another voice in the room; it gave him the sense that they were not quite alone. He said, 'There's something I don't get; something missing. Because I feel as if I knew you; as if you'd been in this house for a long time.'

147

'Maybe I have.'

'You mean we've met before? I would have remembered.'

'Yes; maybe you would. Maybe you're the kind who remembers.'

'I think I am.'

'When you've lived the way I have,' said Jane Rolf, 'you don't look over your shoulder too often.'

'Conscience? Bad dreams?'

She said, 'Perhaps.'

'I have dreams sometimes.'

'About the past?'

'Mostly.'

'About your trip to America, perhaps?'

The eyes were very brightly on him now; he met them, and met also a challenge that he could not fathom. 'Sometimes,' he said.

'Not happy dreams?'

'Are any dreams happy?'

The answer seemed to have pleased her; she sat back in the chair, relaxed, with a small satisfied smile. She looked like a gambler who's seen her number come up. He said, 'But it's you I want to know about—your life-story, not mine.'

Her eyes, gleaming with a grim amusement, were set upon something that he could not see. 'I haven't got a life-story,' said Jane Rolf. 'I've got one thing I remember, one person I loved. After that, the dark.'

'Who was he?'

'My guy? The one they took away?' A flame spurted from the fire and showed suddenly the lines on her face; now she didn't look young any more; the lines were deep, speaking of old, hated things. She said, 'So long ago now.'

'Tell me.'

A flash of laughter then: she said, 'Why not? Why not? Tell you a story first, bedtime story, and then—' She looked young again, quite restored, wickedly gay. Matthew heard a crescendo of rain outside and the new urgent sound of the river, as if it went with desperate speed to some appointed place. (And that other river; the dark remembered river with the dead there, strongly haunting him; the past and the present, both in this room.)

He said, 'Go on, Mrs Rolf.'

The room had darkened. Jane watched him as he lit the lamp. Her eyes narrowed as if she made calculations in her head: she observed his body and the width of his shoulders and the shape of his hand as it fell away from the lamp. The river and the rain's sound enclosed them; she was aware of the blinded moors stretching beyond the house, swept by the curtains of rain.

'A drink, perhaps, to help you along?' he asked.

'Maybe a small one. I don't drink as a rule. And I don't need any helping.' (And one must be careful with the drink; a second could tip the scale, and the scale must not be tipped. One must go towards the beckoning danger with the balance and certainty of a man on the high wire.)

She took the glass, leaned back in the chair. Power and strength went slipping through her blood; now she was enjoying herself; this was the old accustomed feeling of excitement and command.

'She was another person, of course. That's how it is, isn't it? One looks back and sees—not a stranger, but someone divided from oneself—I guess you know about that.'

She saw him nod his head. His eyes were on her,

black eyes with the sparks of the firelight in them. (And if ever I had a listener, I've got one now.) 'There was this girl,' she said, 'a long time ago, a girl who lived in California. And the boy she loved was the other half of herself. Truly the other half—d'you understand what I mean? Born of the same parents, within a few hours of each other. She was as strong as he was, and as beautiful—they were beautiful kids, everyone said that. And not only strong: they could be ruthless, both of them; they liked power, and using power. Other people were afraid of them. The boy . . . the boy could go off into a silence sometimes, an enclosed, brooding silence, where even the girl couldn't reach him. But he'd always come back, and then it'd be just as good as it had been before. They had a whole language of their own: a whole set of characters, quite secret, not known to anyone—you quoted your Mrs Gaskell yesterday: something like the Brontës' Gondal stories—know what I mean? And part of that was a phrase, a warning phrase, belonging to them alone: "Take it easy, Araminta." '

She held his glance for a moment: the silence was suddenly deep.

'Go on,' he said.

'Anything he could do, she could do. They were a couple of star athletes in the making. They were too close, you might say. After a while it wasn't only swimming and ski-ing and riding and fencing and mountain-climbing. She was his first in bed and he was hers. At what you might call a tender age. Nobody knew—or maybe somebody guessed. Anyway, the family moved in and broke it up. When they were seventeen. They packed him off to England. She never thought he'd take that edict, but he took it. They cried their eyes out and said goodbye. He never went back. He grew up without his other half. She didn't. She lived by him and in him and through him all her life.'

She saw him move in his chair, but he was inexact, not quite apprehended; now she was held within the private walls of someone walking back alone through time, remembering.

'She dedicated every adventure she ever had to him. And there were plenty of adventures. She slipped in and out of jobs: she was a model, a movie extra, a grease-monkey—what you call a garage-hand. She travelled alone; she had no loves and no loyalties; people were there for her pleasure, and when they ceased to please her, she walked out on them. No loves; only him. She kept a diary over the years, meant him to read it some day. She wrote to him sometimes—he didn't answer—not ever. But that made him no less alive—more alive, she thought. He was living in her; that was the way she saw it. Crazy woman; as one looks back one sees she was crazy. But she'd get anything she really wanted. In the end she did find him again, because he came back. He came back to San Francisco, after their parents died. He saw the lawyer, about the inheritance. She trailed him all the time. Finally, she caught up with him. She went with him to their ranch. She thought life was beginning again; she thought she'd triumphed; that all those years of living in him and for him were justified. She made only one mistake. Only one.'

She paused. The wind sang by the house. Beyond the firelight the craggy, attentive face was still; the voice said sharply, 'What mistake?'

'Why, the poor silly lady,' said Jane, 'she never realised that he hated her. She'd turned into a night-mare. He had to tell her that. The memory of her was his curse, his cross, his shadow. He was her angel; she was his devil. Tough. Took her a long time to understand. She'd brought the diary. She gave it to him. He said it made him sick; that it was part of the nightmare; he never wanted to see it again. You can imagine, can't you? The devil you thought you'd escaped forever, come back not only to haunt you but to rub your nose in the filth you'd tried to escape from . . . He couldn't stand it. So—what did he do?'

For a space she saw the dark eyes fixed on her; heard the weather sounds outside the house, and within the room the little pulse of the clock.

The dry voice said, 'He—got rid of her.'

'You could put it like that,' said Jane Rolf.

She saw him rise suddenly from his chair. She rose too, swift, ready, welcoming the danger. She drew the piece of paper from her pocket, the message signed with his name. How many miles . . . She said, 'And what was that about, Matthew Gilroy?'

He said, 'It was about a murder, Colonel Blessington.'

A brave man, Matthew thought; in spite of all, a brave man. (As the stranger beside him so long ago had been brave.) One amused lift of the eyebrows before the matter-of-fact voice asked, 'When did you guess?' The change of accent was palpable.

'Not sure now. But I rather think I've known from the first minute you walked in.'

'Good for you,' said the gay cultivated British voice.

Matthew said nothing. These charging, furious thumps of the heart left him breathless. The thing that was happening before his eyes had the quality of a contrived nightmare. One moment there was the menace, the man showing through the woman's disguise; then the woman began to disappear. With a casual flick of thumb and finger Blessington pulled off the wig; he dropped it on to the chair beside him; rubbed his flattened white hair. He peeled away the false eyelashes, throwing them into the fire. Then he took a wad of tissue from the pocket of the whipcord trousers and began to scrub his face, taking the lipstick first. He did not use a looking-glass; when he had finished the colour was dimmed and smudged, but not gone: the lips still reddened, the skin patchily brown.

'Messy stuff,' he observed, rolling the tissues and pitching them after the eyelashes. 'Never really cared for it.' He stretched himself, then shook his shoulders as though he tried to shake away the last of Jane Rolf. But he could not, Matthew thought, quite escape her; Blessington still carried, obscenely, traces of the woman about him. Here indeed was a man who could slip easily into a woman's disguise. It was a handsome head; the face appeared thinner with the blurred make-up; the green eyes larger without the little frieze of lashes; his own lashes were short and fair. One saw these things while the heart inside one's ribs still plunged and one's breath was still harsh and uneven.

'Excuse me, Gilroy. Can't treat you to the complete transformation scene, much as I'd like to.' He spread out his hands, studying the painted nails. 'Those,' he added, 'will have to stay as they are.' As he turned from the fire his movements were heavier than before, movements not of a cat but of a padding tiger.

Matthew felt his hands clench at his sides. In this room belonging to now, the old river and the war-time hazard were back again; he could see in the handsome head the blackened face of the man who had leaned over him. The murderer. A man who had murdered not only the poor French fool, but had loved and hated and murdered his twin sister. And was ready now to—

With sudden recognition, Matthew pushed the long windows open. He was unprepared for the neat dancing movement that took Blessington past him through the billowing curtain; out on to the path; on to the bridge. He heard the light, taunting voice: 'Take it easy, chum. Take it easy, Araminta.'

He was out on the bridge himself. Now the graceful figure was ahead of him, speaking words that were lost in the wind's roaring and the plunging cataract of the river. Now he was moving in a confusion of time; this darkness full of its violent sound might have been the old darkness, so long remembered: the time of battle and death. His own voice was shouting, but there was nothing in his ears but the wind and the sound of the waterfall; and in his head a sudden oil-gush of anger as he thought of Anita, and the pain that must come to her. Danger cut as close as the tracer bullets and the heavier guns: he went towards the figure which seemed to be laughing now, and holding one hand behind its back.

As Matthew Gilroy came towards you, you had the old warning in your head, childhood's warning: 'Take it easy, Araminta.' You were reduced to this; to the last resort. The easy ways were shut. No long walk over the moors and the stab from behind and the body of Matthew Gilroy rolled down from the reservoir's height; no chance to slip the pills into the whisky and send him sliding through drugged layers of darkness to the last layer. You had to think fast, as you had thought fast before, in the silence of that Californian night. But then there had been no need to use the last resort; the lethal dose, slipped into the glass, had been taken: only after, as the poison began to work, had the face been turned towards you, blanched and silly with astounded fear.

Now, in this moment, you could see the face; remembering came easily; it always did in time of danger.

Now you were ready for him. Now the calculations you had made, the width of his shoulders, the degree of his strength, were on the top of your mind. With the knife in your hand you were simply giving yourself orders. 'Into the throat. One quick, upward jab before those searching hands get a chance. You'll have all the time in the world to figure it out from there.' Here was danger, forever delightful. Here was the thrill of power, turned to its highest point, an orgasmic shudder of release.

You felt no fear.

You felt nothing.

The chopping stroke of his own arm came with such ease that he might, Matthew thought, have practised it only yesterday. He struck, as the knife came up; the knife fell, rattling at his feet. 'So he had a knife.' The words flicked through his head, but he was not concerned with them; there was nothing now but the crumpled body, sliding in the sodden dark. With one violent movement he took it on to his shoulder, tipping it over the bridge; he leaned on the rail to see it go, down, down, down, a sort of messy doll, a rag-figure, a Guy Fawkes figure, broken and twirling through the dark water for merely a moment; drawn, lost and tumbling, through the cleft and on down to the great rocky swirl where the waterfall met the Garfe.

He stood still, wiping the rain from his eyes, feeling nothing but a large exhaustion, and a little awakening wonder: '*Why, it's done.*' Only himself, here on the bridge, standing as he had so often stood, watching the downward plunge of the water . . . But with a difference.

Something done now that couldn't be gainsaid; the world changed. He wouldn't think about that now.

He stooped to retrieve the knife. The little patter of drops falling on his hand was warmer than the rain. He became aware of the sharp sting at his collarbone; odd, not to have felt it before.

He went back into the house and pulled his shirt from his shoulder. A small clean cut. He washed it at the sink and plastered it over. He washed the knife, wondering idly what to do with it. He left it on the drawing-board. He did these things mechanically, shutting away the recognition that must come. He stepped back into the room. Here were the echoes: tea-cup, empty glass; most strongly the scent that 'Jane Rolf' had used, lying on the air. He pitched two more logs on the fire, and found that his hands were shaking. He poured himself a whisky and downed it. The scent was still in his nostrils.

What now?

He stood, hearing the wild assault of the rain. His hands were still shaking. But there was much to be done. He brought 'Jane Rolf's' windbreaker and the rucksack in from the hall, dumping them on the hearthrug. He crouched, looking at them for a moment, forcing back an impulse to put them straight on the fire. Better to know more, perhaps; to find out all there was to know of Blessington. For Anita's sake, he had to know.

He thrust one shaking, reluctant hand into the pockets of the windbreaker. Nothing but a bottle of pills and the scarf she (one goes on thinking 'she') had tied over her head. The scent again. He rammed the scarf back into the pocket. He left the bottle of acid-yellow pills on the rug.

Now he unfastened the straps of the rucksack . . . His head jerked up; was that the sound of footsteps? No;

only the rain; nobody would come walking here any more.

A neat packer, Colonel Blessington. Matthew found a grey suit, accurately folded in a square plastic bag; socks, underclothes, shoes, a shirt and tie. A map-case, a wallet and a wet-pack toilet case, all in new, gleaming pigskin. A man of expensive tastes: one who had abandoned the old commando preference for rough clothes and few belongings. (The commando ... So he had escaped; slipped through the hands of the enemy on that desperate night; been one of the lucky ones ... till now.) Matthew opened the toilet case. Toothbrush, toothpaste; razor. The razor brand-new; no blades that he could see ... What was he? A man, perhaps, who'd never had to shave in his life. He opened the wallet. Money; fifty pounds in tens and fives, a few pound notes. A driving licence in the name of Harvey Blessington, some cards with the name and the North Royal address. A blue leaflet: The *True* Tory Party of North Royal ... No keys. Where were his keys? The keys of his car? For a moment he wondered about the car. Where had he left it? Some way from here, most likely; to be later discovered. This did not trouble him ... What else? Only a snapshot, blurred and yellowing with frayed edges; a young boy mounted on a pony.

And a small notebook. He examined this with a sudden pounding curiosity. Several pages filled, covered with neat, intelligent writing. Shopping lists, train times, accounts, both in dollars and sterling. He turned a page. He read:

Leave Thursday, March 9th

Two days ago. Feverishly attentive, he read on:

Return Sunday 12th or Monday 13th
Friday, 10th—Ripon? (Dark by 18.25)
M.G.'s house—case the joint.
If proved necessary—

157

> *Pentobarb. 1,000 mg.—15 gr.?*
> *Height of reservoir—appx. 1,000 ft. Better?*
> *Or—the last resort?*

Scrawled in the margin beside 'If proved necessary', one word: *Yes.*

He turned another page. Growing in his mind was a deeper image of Blessington: a man of ruthless courage, of elaborate contrivance, yet so self-absorbed that he ignored the danger of putting his plan into words. He read on:

> *Car. On foot to G.B. Then*
> *A 614—A 638—A 38*
> *Turn left on A 38 2 m. N. of Lichfield.*
> *Countryside? Car park better?*
> *Bus to B'ham? Then B'ham—Bristol.*

There followed a list of train times. After this, the writing grew more hurried.

> *Damn Ledyard. Where was I? Faster, faster.*
> *Return Sunday 12th latest*
> *Birmingham—Padd. better?*

A further list of train times. Below these:

> *Anyway, no choice now. Goodbye, J.R.!*
> *Been nice knowing you.*

On the last page before the blanks, written with a flourish:

> *I love me.*

He crouched there by the fire, holding the little book in his hand. He picked up his own message: *How many miles to midnight* . . . It was like the jig-saw; the pieces fitted, if only he knew how . . . Why come here as a woman? Showing off? Maybe, but I'm not *quite* sure . . . The formula? The reservoir? The last resort? . . . His eye fell on the drawing-board. He thought suddenly: The last resort was the knife.

Wait a minute. *Leave Thursday March 9th. Return*

Sunday 12th or Monday 13th. I'm getting it; I'm after you now, you're only a little way ahead of me, as you were on the bridge. This is a trail, a false trail. You had to get away somehow without being seen. So you went as Jane Rolf. Maybe drawing attention to yourself as Jane Rolf. And here in the rucksack are the things you need for turning yourself back into Blessington . . .

Bristol. What was the echo in his mind? . . . Anita's voice: 'He's got a family business in Bristol.'

Yes; I believe I've caught up with you. You change your clothes. You drive south. You abandon the car. You plan to get a train from Birmingham to Bristol. And from Bristol Colonel Blessington arrives at Paddington Station as usual. *Damn Ledyard?* Something happened to speed you up; you thought of going straight from Birmingham home. Harvey has made his accustomed business trip to the West Country. He's never set foot in Garfedale. There was a woman called Jane Rolf wandering around these parts, staying at Ripon overnight. She vanishes. Her car's found some time, far away. Who was she? What happened? Nobody knows. End of trail.

Yes. Fairly brilliant, sir. Bad luck it didn't work out. It's all clear enough, as far as it goes. But there's one mystery, one thing I can't see: you got my message; you came up here prepared to kill me.

Why?

You *were* the man who killed beside me in the war, all those years ago. But—to kill me for that? You were so sure you were going to kill me, you boasted of another murder; of the girl who had haunted you . . . *Why?*

The blank mystery faced him; a final mystery; not to be answered now—

Not? Are you sure?

Yes, because you can't speak any more. The dead

give no answers . . . I wish they could. I wish you were here, so that I could ask the questions . . . And this is no night to be out. You'd be better here by this fire, talking to me . . . But of course you aren't out in the rain, are you? You aren't anywhere . . .

He felt the shiver go through him again; recognition was coming nearer. He could hear the storm, still riding down the valley; the crescendo of the waterfall. (And where is the body now? When will they find it? The flood water's rising; it could be carried a long way.) Do you remember the river, Blessington? No; you don't remember anything any more.

He stood up suddenly, drawing his hands over his face. *Well, what are we going to do now?*

The voice in his head sounded like Blessington's voice; he gave a shake of his shoulders to be rid of it, and began a sudden feverish tidying of the room, as if he could tidy away the memory that was beginning to turn his stomach. He made a pile of Blessington's clothes; took them with the rucksack and the windbreaker out into the hall. Back in the room he shook up the flattened cushions of his own chair. When he came to the visitor's chair, Blessington's chair, and shook the cushion, something fell on to the hearthrug, a soft something, unexpected as a dead bird, falling with a little flop. He felt his heart kick, and the sudden cold sweat on his forehead.

It was Blessington's wig.

Matthew stared down at it; he felt his stomach contract and the beginning of saliva in his mouth. The wig had fallen wrong way up. It showed its fine network lining, darker than the curls at the edges. A faint smell arose from the wig; Jane Rolf's scent.

Matthew found himself gagging violently; he gagged until his eyes watered. He couldn't lift it, not even with the tongs. He reeled away, looking back along the floor, as if the nasty little cap could come crawling after him.

'Bloody fool,' he told himself, wiping his eyes. His hand shook as he poured the drink. 'Get rid of it, can't you? Pick it up. Shove it in the fire. No, it'll smell to heaven.' The drink gagged him too. He put down the glass with a shivering hand.

This was idiotic. One couldn't stand here, shaking like a fool, sick at the stomach because of a wig . . .

'Reaction. Delayed shock.' Blessington's voice again. 'A killer's occupational hazard.'

'Is it? You should know.'

'I like that. We belong to the same club now, don't forget.'

Teeth chattering against the glass he swallowed the whisky, struggling to keep it down. When he looked at the wig again the nausea was less. But he still couldn't touch it, and it couldn't stay there. He found the thing to do. A moment after he was sliding half today's news-paper under it. This tipped it right way up, so that it squatted on the paper, looking round and lively. He fetched the shears from the tool-basket. He knelt by the newspaper and chopped the wig methodically to pieces. Here and there it was tough, making the shears stick. He went on snipping at it until it was only a heap of hair and netting. He bundled the paper around it, folding the edges as if he were making a parcel. Carrying the bundle at arm's length he went out through the garden door. The rain was like the sudden assault of an army, claiming and half-blinding him. Under-foot the path was greasy; Matthew slithered his way to the bridge. The wind was snatching at the bundle already; the wind caught it before it left his hands. As he hurled it over, the paper flew apart; one or two soft little pieces of hair came blowing back into his face.

Sick now, no help for it.

He leaned out over the rail.

Presently he went lurching back into the house.

Wash, wash, wash—your face, your head, your hands; gargle the mouthwash again, clean your teeth; strip right down and wash.

Better now. Clean underclothes, clean shirt; clean shoes; your other suit. Better. A pale face in the looking-glass, the face of a man convalescent after a long fever, beginning to come back to life. Some sort of sanity returning; and with sanity, knowledge.

I've got to get out of here.

To escape? To give myself up? I don't know yet. Going's the point; it doesn't matter where. Lock up and go.

'And leave the house to darkness and to me?'

'Go away. Go away. You're dead.'

'Am I? Wasn't there always someone in this house?'
Out of here.

Take only the things you need in a small hold-all. Take Blessington's clothes; take the note-book and his wallet . . . What for? Maybe to dump them on the road; maybe to hand them in, as proof of what you've done . . . Tidy up after him; wash his cup and glass . . . Off with the lights. Now there was only the fire's glow, the lonely dark cavern of the room, beseiged by the rain.

Last light out; key turned; along the path with the skies falling on him. Clumsy going, with his own case and the unwieldy package of Blessington's clothes. He pitched them all into the back of the car. He started up the engine. The headlamps caught the rain's hurrying lances: they caught the gate-posts as he turned, they gave him the wet black road, the downward-plunging hill; and the storm.

9

THE WINDOW of Mrs Vernon's living-room was set
below the level of the garden. This gave the impression
—only too appropriate, Anthony thought—that they
were all of them very slightly sinking below ground.

The room itself contained an air of restlessness and
disorder, somehow emphasised by a large sheaf of
flowers which someone with more sentiment than sense
had delivered (too late for the funeral) in memory of
Ledyard.

'It's all so *strange*,' said Miss Appleby. 'I really don't
under*stand* . . .'

A tremor of the voice; a suggestion of threatening
hysteria?

For himself, Anthony thought, he couldn't entirely
blame her. Had he been of hysterical mould he would
by this time have been climbing the curtains and
screaming. From the point of this Tuesday afternoon,
he glanced back on the sorry confusion of the last four
days. In his own mind it resembled the middle act of an
opera (Anthony was allergic to opera) when characters
dash to the centre of the stage, scream passionately and
indecipherably of some fresh anguish and then swirl off
again. Or you might call it, he thought, the Lament of
the True Tories. Ledyard's death had been one thing.
But the strange and continuing absence of Colonel

Blessington was another. What had begun as a small frustration was growing hour by hour into a source of speculation and alarm. Blessington had failed to turn up for his luncheon engagement with Anthony on Monday. He had failed (causing havoc in Stonehenge's arrangements for scampi) to keep his dinner engagement with Miss Gilroy. He had sent no message; no explanation of any kind. He was not in Bristol, nor could anyone in Bristol suggest where he might be. He was not in North Royal. He was not, it seemed, anywhere.

'Oh, Mr Price, where *can* he be?' He couldn't remember which one had said that; perhaps they'd all said it: he had a picture of a composite True Tory woman, clasping her hands before her chest and looking up at him with yearning enquiry. 'We *must* have a candidate: surely something can be done. What about the Police?'

He had, Anthony said, been to the Police. A clear memory of North Royal Police Station: the man-to-man expression on the face of the policeman on duty as he'd said, 'Now, sir, if we were to get fussed about every gentleman who takes a week-end off without giving chapter and verse to his loved ones ... Well, sir, you can see.'

Anthony could. So much for the Police.

But Blessington? Anthony went on thinking about Blessington. After long protest, Stonehenge had agreed to look through the drawers of his desk. But this, Anthony thought, had been a Pyrrhic victory; seldom, surely, had a man left so faint an imprint of himself on the place in which he lived. No personal telephone book; no address book; no personal letters. Blotting paper, writing paper, a neat clutch of receipts (tailor's, wine merchants, the elegant local grocery store); a road map of London; a desk diary, with only the most prosaic appointments noted there. Grudgingly, Stonehenge had

165

parted with this ('I'd like it back *right away*, if you don't mind, sir') and it lay on the table before him. One puzzler: on Thursday, March 9th, there was scribbled in pencil 'J.R.' followed by a question mark.

And one drawer of his desk—the upper left-hand drawer—locked.

'I'm not opening *that*,' Stonehenge had said. 'The Colonel would never forgive me. Never forced a lock in my life without permission, and I'm not going to start now. Privacy's privacy, that's what I always say.' The baffling little drawer held its secret, unyielding as a closed mouth. Anthony found it kept recurring in his mind, like an unsolved crossword clue. Privacy's privacy. All very well; but there might come a time, if the Colonel didn't return . . .

The doorbell, followed by a shrill, familiar voice giving off the meaningless little exclamations of arrival, brought him back to the sunken living-room on this grey afternoon.

'A meeting,' Mrs Vernon had said; 'we must have a meeting; *pool* all our knowledge; it's the only way.' Well, they'd got a meeting, thought Anthony, they'd got so far Mrs Vernon, talking him down as usual; Miss Appleby contributing no more than a few unfinished bleats; Miss Crutt giving toothy agreement to everything that was said, however contradictory; and—the only enlivening thing in the whole unwelcome sequence —Anita Gilroy, sitting with her chin in her hands and her palpable anxiety almost—but not quite—in control.

As the voice from the hall advanced, Anthony gave Anita a conspiratorial wink. She made a brave show of returning it, though a sadness came quickly back into her eyes, and they fell again to the Colonel's desk diary, open at the page with the pencilled entry—'J.R.?'

Now he came to think of it, she'd barely taken her eyes from it for the last half-hour.

The voice from the hall was now close at hand: Beryl Crawshaw, the Pink Aunt, was sitting at the table, scattering jets of talk this way and that . . . 'Hoped she wasn't late . . . always difficult to get away . . . so many things to do . . . just leaving when the telephone . . .' Anthony gave a few moments to imagining an enormous dustbin filled with all the unnecessary things Beryl Crawshaw said. He saw them in a huge writhing pile of ticker tape.

She beamed on him; he tried to shut the thought away. She said, 'I've come because I feel I really *can* contribute to this meeting. I have an idea—not a very nice one, I'm afraid, but we do have to look facts in the face, don't we? And after all, I *did* know the Colonel long before anyone else.'

Here, Anthony noticed, Anita Gilroy sat upright in her chair, as if she prepared to gallop towards Mrs Crawshaw with a lance.

Unobserving, Mrs Crawshaw went on: 'You see, what I think we must be prepared to face is that something untoward has happened to the Colonel—'

Anita was sitting rigidly still; Mrs Vernon began, 'We've absolutely no reason to think—' but went under to Mrs Crawshaw, slightly to Anthony's pleasure.

'We have to remember two things,' she said, and added, 'one lump please,' to Miss Crutt who set a cup before her with a not quite steady hand. ('Or two lumps and one thing,' whispered Anthony to Anita; but she did not respond.)

'Two things,' Mrs Crawshaw went on. 'First, that the Colonel is a most courteous man. One to think of others, not to give anxiety. Dear Mr Ledyard's death was in all the newspapers. Is it really possible that the Colonel should make no effort to contact us—no effort at all?'

'Is that one thing or two?' muttered Anthony, but, paying no attention, Beryl Crawshaw flowed on.

'Secondly, that when I met him, all those years ago, he was a man in the grip of *fear*. He was afraid of something—something that he never explained. It's my belief that this person, thing, whatever it was—has finally caught up with him—'

'Oh no!' exclaimed Miss Appleby.

This was followed by a silence, broken by the doorbell again; and the chattering, explanatory arrival of Miss North Royal Echo.

Anita, paying small attention to Miss North Royal Echo's bright journalistic enquiries, sat with her arms on the table. Moodily she crumbled a macaroon on her plate, making no attempt to eat it. She was, she found, meeting two pieces of knowledge head-on; and she didn't like either of them. First, she was the only person in this Mad-Hatter's tea-party who'd got hold of the right end of the stick. And secondly, the right end of the stick was unbearable.

Beryl Crawshaw could go purling on in that silly voice about Harvey being hunted down over the years by some nameless Thing (if one weren't so miserable it would make one giggle); she, Anita, could snuff the whole thing out with one blow. She knew what Harvey was doing. He hadn't come to any harm; he wasn't being chased by a kind of Hound of the Baskervilles over the moors; he wasn't doing anything so uncomfortable. He was warm, safe, happy. He was far beyond thoughts of Ledyard.

He was with Jane Rolf.

Anita was sure of it now. Ever since she had seen that

sinister little entry: 'J.R.' in the desk diary, she had been miserably sure. The printing-press *hadn't* been a printing-press, after all. Bristol was a cover-up for a romantic adventure; a sideshow, he'd say, if she challenged him (which of course she wouldn't dream of doing); a diversion, having no effect on his love for her. All the same he was there now, intimately happy, so happy that he had forgotten their dinner engagement for Monday night: left her to wait and wonder and pace round the telephone, and finally to lie wakeful through the nastiest night she could remember—

Anita had to prevent herself once again from saying 'Ow!'; she did indeed give a small repressed groan, as for toothache; and was aware of Anthony Price sending her a glance of sudden sympathy.

The women were still chattering on. Mrs Vernon was tossing aside the idea of foul play; the Colonel might, she said have been taken *ill*; got off the train, perhaps; but any idea of—

All a waste of time, Anita thought. She brooded: should she put an end to this needless waffling by speaking the name of Jane Rolf? They said there was a locked drawer in his desk; Anita knew what *that* held; love-letters. From Jane Rolf. Maybe others as well. She had no wish at all to see them.

Miss North Royal was saying that she could get in touch with the Press Association; sometimes a brief paragraph about a disappearance worked wonders; someone saw it and then . . .

Under cover of this Anita murmured on an impulse to Mr Price: 'I know what "J.R." stands for.'

'Beg your pardon?'

The clear blue eyes were set attentively on her. She made a small gesture to the desk diary on the table before them. ' "J.R." That's Mrs Jane Rolf. A friend of his. He was expecting her to come to the party.'

The loud voices had fallen into a momentary lull, letting her words ring clear. Anita found all their faces turned to her; she felt the blush swarm over her face. Mr Price kept his eyes on her, as if he were beguiled by the blush. 'A friend of his,' he said, and added, 'I remember. I remember your asking about her; asking me if she'd come—'

The silence round the table was broken by Mrs Vernon who said, 'I do think that if there is any new information, it ought to be given to the meeting as a *whole*—'

Anita glared at her; Mr Price, with diplomatic charm, explained about J.R. He was interrupted by a cry from Miss Appleby. This being the loudest utterance of Miss Appleby's so far brought another alert silence to the table.

'*I* remember her,' Miss Appleby said. 'She came downstairs, and I was a little upset about that, because of what the Colonel had said, trespassing, you know— but she seemed—well—how shall I put it?—'

How indeed, thought Anita, held in an agony of attentiveness.

'—so well-dressed and sure of herself and *expensive*, if you know what I mean—'

(Oh, we do. We do indeed. Death, hell and damnation.)

'—She had the most *beautiful* scent, I remember; spoke in that kind of husky American—Why!' Miss Appleby gave another little scream. '*I* know. Where's the visitors' book? She signed it—she was the last person to sign it—*that's* how I know her name—'

It was Mrs Vernon who produced the visitors' book. Anita watched the pages being turned, her heart beating in her throat. Absurd. What did one expect to see? Only a name. And yet . . . Odd how sinister it all seemed; it was as if up till now, in spite of everything, she had not *truly* believed in Jane Rolf. Now—

'There!' cried Miss Appleby, triumphant. Anita looked at the page, with its column of varying signatures. The last seemed indecipherable; it could, surely, have been anything—

'Yes, I know it looks very difficult to read,' said Miss Appleby, 'but as a personal secretary I have to read some *very* difficult signatures; people are so careless, sometimes nothing more than a long squiggly line with a larger bit at the beginning, yet I *do* manage to decipher them, I don't know how it is; I suppose it's a gift.'

The general silence that followed might, or might not, have been affirmation. Anita went on looking at the page. 'The hotel in W.1.,' Miss Appleby was saying; 'now *that* I couldn't read; nor the number in Pacific Avenue—'

Nor were you meant to, came into Anita's head. She met Mr Price's eye; he was, she thought, thinking the same.

'Well,' he said; 'puzzle: find Jane Rolf.'

Anita looked at him squarely; he met the misery in her face with a look of deep understanding. Anita turned away; being pitied made it worse.

Of a sudden, she found she couldn't bear the chattering women, the half-sunken living-room, the cups of tea; even the palpable sympathy of Mr Price. She had to get away; to find out something more. She had to get as close to Harvey as she could; if not his presence, at least his dwelling-place.

The somewhat Biblical phrase stayed with her as she excused herself from the meeting, and hurried, taken by her long stride, through the blowy streets of North Royal. The occasional head that turned, the voice caught on the air: 'Anita Gilroy . . . *Salvation Road* . . .'

slid away from her, scarcely apprehended. Two people warred inside her head: one who accepted with pain that Harvey, beguiled by Jane Rolf, had given no thought to Anita waiting by the telephone: and another who said, remembering so much. But he *couldn't* have forgotten: he *couldn't* have; think of all the things he said . . .

The dialogue of these two opposing voices was, Anita found, an exhausting thing: this morning at the Television Studios she had played her part, imposing the discipline of her training on the fog of weariness.

Stonehenge's face, as she opened the door, said plainly, '*You* again.'

'I was just passing,' Anita said. (*A likely story* seemed the unspoken comment.) 'I thought perhaps you might have—'

'Nothing at all,' said Stonehenge. She was, Anita perceived, torn between a reluctance to ask her in and a need to vent her grievance. 'I must say, it's very disturbing. Not knowing where I am or what I should do. People asking questions. That Mr Price wanting me to *open* things—' A gust of wind with rain on it whipped down Heath Hill, and Anita shivered. Stonehenge stood a little to one side and said without enthusiasm, 'Come in.'

Anita stepped into the elegant voiceless hall. No place so empty, she thought, as the house of the man you loved, without him. Stonehenge was opening the door of the drawing-room with an expression she could not quite fathom: like one who pulls a curtain aside to show something nasty behind it. But, of course, in Harvey's drawing-room, there couldn't possibly be—

Anita stood still. Sitting at the end of the sofa, with an ashtray in front of him, and an expression of doomed anxiety, was the young man from Bristol. Quentin

Something. He wore a pink shirt and black velvet trousers, and his golden hair was awry. He stood up guiltily. He looked pale, and there were shadows under his eyes. Anita said—the Dowager mysteriously taking command—'Good afternoon. We spoke over the telephone.'

'I know. I had to come. It's all been so *frightful.*'

Taken aback, Anita said, 'Yes, hasn't it—'

Stonehenge was looking at the young man as if she dared him to sit down again. She said, 'I'm afraid it's no good waiting any longer, sir. I've no information from the Colonel, and until I have—'

'Very well,' he said; 'I'm going. I just thought he might come back. He sometimes rings me Tuesdays.' He gave Anita a look of appeal. 'Are you coming too?'

Surprised, perplexed, not without a pang of pity, Anita gave this a moment's thought. Anything to be gained by lingering here under the hostile eye of Stonehenge? Clearly not. 'Yes, I'm coming,' she said, and turned to Stonehenge. 'You *have* got my telephone number in case—'

Stonehenge said she had everybody's telephone number; when the Colonel returned she would, in time, make use of them. She shut the front door with the satisfaction of one who has swept something unwanted out on to the mat.

Together they walked up the hill. On the windy corner by North Royal tube station, Quentin paused. His face, still anguished, looked now a little pinched from the cold. He said, 'Come and have a cup of coffee. *Please.* I must have someone to talk to. And that beastly woman at Minster House looks at me as if I'd come with a flick knife and a knuckle duster. Which heaven *knows,*' he said, giving a slight twitch of his shoulders, 'I haven't.'

Dubiously, Anita followed him into the café with the flamingo on the wall. He sat with his elbows on the table, smoking, running one hand through his hair, talking at speed. 'Surely somebody must know something? I mean, a man like Harvey, all that money and all those friends—it can't just be a blank?' He took a sip of his coffee and a nervous pull of his cigarette. His hand was shaking. 'I mean, there *couldn't* have been an accident, could there, we'd've heard. We *must* have heard.'

Anita, watching him, found herself gradually engulfed by a kind of fascinated horror: Quentin was not only in love with Harvey, he was as much in love as she was herself. *And where does that get us?*

'You see what worries me so dreadfully is that I broke my promise.' He was, Anita observed, one of those whose self-absorption in trouble is so complete that they have no power of hearing more than a word of question or agreement.

'Promise?'

'Yes, you see I came to the house. And then I rang up, that Friday afternoon. And he'd told me never to.'

'Never to come there? To Minster House?'

'Nor to ring up.'

'Why not?'

'I don't know. It was a rule. Inviolable. Not to be broken. I belonged in Bristol'—(the faint echo of a song went incongruously through Anita's head)—'and I was supposed to stay there. It was for *him* to get in touch with me.'

Anita received this in silence. A pattern was taking shape: not, for the sake of his feelings, to be offered to Quentin: a tiresome young man, a nuisance, noisily and obsessively in love, having to be kept at bay by strong-arm methods, by rules: no visits, no telephoning. Yet all the same . . . Anita dodged the alternative. The alternative wasn't possible. 'Well, if he made a rule,' she said, reasonably, 'why did you break it?'

'Those frightful leaflets,' he said. 'Getting mixed up with a great blue bunch of Tories. *Tories*, for heaven's sake. *Why* should he get involved with them? I couldn't help thinking there was someone, some reason . . . perhaps that rather stiff city-gent, blue-eyed type I saw at the—'

'Mr Price?'

'Yes; I went to the Committee Rooms this morning, and I thought—'

Anita found the Dowager was briefly taking over again. 'There,' she said, 'you are quite, quite mistaken.'

Quentin blinked the long lashes one or twice. He said, breaking for a moment through the cloud of self-absorption, 'I've seen you on television.'

'I make no doubt,' said Anita; 'it's my job. As to which, if you're working at the Bristol printing-press, what are *you* doing in London on a Tuesday?'

He rubbed both hands over his face, then looked up, the pretty pouting face a mask of tragedy. 'I've run away,' he said. 'I only worked there because of Harvey. I can't stay there, not knowing what's happened to him. I'm going to stay here in London. Until he comes back.'

Anita faced him. Again, there were tears on the long lashes. A small shudder of distaste went through her, because it was Harvey—however unwillingly (and of course it *must* have been unwillingly)—who had aroused this spectacular anguish. She took a mouthful of tepid coffee and told herself, 'Take it easy.' And then the words came into her head, spoken in Harvey's voice: 'Take it easy, Araminta.'

The café with the flamingo on the wall dissolved, and she was seeing the house in Hawkeswell; the rising moors

175

behind it; and Matthew sitting in his chair, his familiar face suddenly strange to her, because of the four silly words.

She sat, lost to the young man before her, while the question began in her mind.

10

THE DARK showed a tracing of light that was, Matthew found, disturbing. He closed his eyes and opened them again. The illusory clamour of a dream slid away, leaving a stillness in his mind, the blank moment of waking. The edge of light took on shape and meaning: the outline of a window. But what window? The puzzle stayed with him until he thrust himself up in bed and heard the harsh city-sound of traffic on the road.

In one blink, it was all there. Outside, a strident jungle, lay the streets of the city: here, a small dingy nucleus of quiet, was the room he had come to last night, in Roper's Town, North London.

The question first. The same question each morning, the same movement of his hand: a click from the small transistor radio set on a chair beside the bed. Listening, eyes on it, as if it were an oracle, seeing nothing, merely waiting to know . . .

'The Chancellor has given grave warning . . . Voting on the Bill for . . . Vietnam . . . The Middle East . . . The death is announced of . . . Sunny intervals and showers.'

He switched it off. The familiar words in his head: the words that in these last four days had come to be expected: Not yet.

Quickly he got out of bed (odd that he moved fast,

felt compelled to move fast). He went clumsily about the strange room, like an animal in an unaccustomed cage. Dingy furniture; drawers that stuck; a small mottled looking-glass; a hand-basin, cracked and stained, whose tap gave tepid water. These things lay outside his thought, were not quite real.

Only one thing was real: the moment on the bridge, dividing his world in two, cutting him off for ever from the easy days, now past. That, and the sequence of time which followed it, wholly absorbed him; he was, he thought, haunted, accompanied, possessed.

As he stripped and washed in the hard, unwelcome water, he traced the pattern of the time. There seemed some compulsion to keep it in his head, as if no detail must be forgotten, as if he were under oath to remember it all, a story later to be told.

When it was done, I drove away. I drove fast. Still with him were the long monotonous miles, the motorways showing their lighted signs with feverish clarity, the anonymous company of cars that travelled with him: all of it seen from far off, through a cloudy horror which sapped his strength. It was done. It wasn't a dark fantasy, part of the old dreams; no temporary oblivion could blot it out; he would wake to it always now.

Done. He had driven on, with the wet roads gleaming, only dimly aware that he was driving south. Somewhere, in the beginnings of this journey, there had been a reason for driving south: he was too exhausted now to remember it. Weariness, like a great animal, suddenly sat heavy on his shoulders: he had pulled into a roadside parking place, climbed into the back of the car and there slept.

The next morning he had woken to the headache, savage, new in its force. He had got out of the car, taking gulps of white misty air. Stiff, aching, sourly haunted, he had yet been able to keep the horror a little way from him: enough sanity had returned to send him on to an anonymous roadside hotel, whose prim fake-Tudor trappings received him with startling incongruity.

Here he stayed, like a man who sits outside time. Held in a grey miasma of thought, he had paced the prim patterned carpet, he had watched the travellers come and go, with their dogs and their suitcases and their innocent irrelevant words. Up and down. To the window and back. To the bar and back. Waiting for news; waiting for some agent from outside to enter and change the course of things.

By evening, feverish for knowledge, he had telephoned to Mary Cattle. 'Away for a few days,' he had said; 'went on the spur of the moment. Forgot to leave a note for old Oakley. Would you mind telling her?' These few sentences had left him breathless; he could hear the puzzlement in her voice as she asked, 'Where are you speaking from?' 'Oh—some Inn or other, roadhouse sort. On my way south.' 'South? To see Anita?' No words would come to answer this; he said at last, 'Perhaps. Any news in the valley?' 'Only the floods; the water's still rising.' Casualties? No, none, except three of Oakley's sheep. Saying goodbye, he had been briefly aware of her there in the Hawkeswell house, concerned for him.

All through the next day he had been waiting. In the paper had been news of the Yorkshire floods. Photographs on the picture page: 'Eighteen inches of water after torrential thunderstorms ...' For a moment he had seen the floods; and that burden on the floods. *How far down to the river* ... When would they find him? Where?

'Bit of a fool to run, weren't you?' The jolly clubman's voice was still in his head.

179

Maybe I was. But I had to get away; to find Anita. That was the reason for driving south; I had to get to her. See her; tell her, before the news came some other way; comfort her.

Then why are you here?

He took the question with him, round and about, up and down.

Because I can't face her yet; because it was I who killed him.

There were two forces within him: this increasing anguish for her; and the fear. Between them he was held immobile; the hours passed, and another night; and still he was there, chained by the conflict, unable to move.

And then, in the evening of the next day, wandering through the meaningless spaces of this transient place, he had come into the television room. A little group of people sat in the ghost-blue half light. He stood in silence behind them. On the screen, Anita stood, hair dishevelled, sleeves rolled up, cooking something on a stove. A voice pursued her from off-screen: she made flat replies which brought laughter to an unseen audience, and to the little group of people in the room. He heard nothing of the voice. The large familiar figure with the lovely face, the unicorn who had walked alone, was desperately vulnerable; it was all at once beyond bearing, to watch her there.

He had packed and paid the bill; he had got into the car; he had driven south to London; he had, last night, come to this place.

He dried himself and dressed quickly. Alone here in this dingy lodging house with the traffic outside, he was, he thought, in enemy country. Nothing new in that: it was what he had been trained for: to move quietly, without help through the dangerous places. He pulled on his soft, rubber-soled shoes: like the commando boots they wore, going silently so that the enemy could not hear him.

Enemy? He looked from the window: saw the lorries and the early workers going by; the innocent, harmless people, beginning to turn the wheels of the city round ... Yes, enemies; because he had made them so. He was alone, outside them.

A knock on the door. A metallic blonde with no shape and a mauve overall came in with a tray. She said, 'Your breakfast,' without enthusiasm, then stood to give him a long stare of passive enquiry, as if she wondered what he was doing there. Well, what? he asked himself as she turned to go. Some instinct to hide, some wish to escape the polite ordered society of his own kind, perhaps. He ate the breakfast hurriedly. Sausage a little cold, tea over-strong; none of this mattered. More and more he found himself taking on the old pattern of the commando he had once been: unconcerned with the comforts of living, concerned only with harsh and desperate things. The man who had lived in Hawkeswell, who had composed comic rhymes and crossword clues, was becoming gradually obscured, belonging to another time and another reality.

The noise from the road increased, weighted now with the flood of incoming cars, the jagged rip of motor-cycles: somewhere the high-low horn of a police-car.

The Police. They were part of the enemy. What did they know? How soon would the questions start? He needn't wait for the questions. He could go to the enemy: men had done that before. 'I've come to make a confession.' As if he were acting this out, he got up from the table and collected the wallet, the notebook, the True Tory Leaflet, his own letter, the verse crypto-gram. The police would show no surprise, of course; they were used to confessions: some were true, some were the fantasies of the psychopath. The story was clear enough. 'He came to my house, dressed as a woman. He came at me with a knife. I killed him. With the old unarmed combat punch across the throat. I had no choice.'

Self-defence.

Truly?

Sitting there, he pulled and plucked at the words 'Self-defence'. He was uncomfortable with them: they took no account of his rage for Anita; the poisoned memory; the long cherished hatred and revenge . . . So then? There was an answer here, but his head, with the pain beginning to clamp down, had not the energy to pursue it.

'Colonel Blessington.' He said the name aloud, still staring at the small belongings before him on the table. He saw again the masquerading figure; heard the husky American accent of 'Jane Rolf'. What had they talked about? About a visit to Garfedale, years ago; curiosity about his house . . . none of it true, of course . . . There had been something about America—about his own journey with Wallader . . . What was this remind-ing him of? . . . Solving. Faced with a cypher, in the small war-time room, searching for a hidden clue.

Something still hidden. Something he didn't know.

He rose abruptly from the table. He wasn't here to ponder the riddle of Blessington. He'd come here to North London to be near her; to get to her; to find her.

You must find her. Or else—

He stood still in the room, as if listening. Through the throbbing of his head, he met the old fear again; and beyond the fear, a danger and darkness that he could not yet fathom.

Move on, then. Take each minute as it comes. There'll be an answer of some kind; there'll be an end.

He pulled on his duffle coat, went quickly from the room and down the stairs. The soft-soled shoes made no sound. Out into the street, with the clamour of traffic sounding rawly in his ears. Strange country. Enemy country.

A newspaper. When he had bought it he stood scanning the pages on the pavement. He swore as the wind ruffled the edges, and a passer-by jolted his arm.

Nothing. Nothing—Wait.

A paragraph in Beresford's Diary, headed *Where is Colonel B?* Lost to the street, he read: 'The True Tories of North Royal are in trouble. With a by-election on their doorstep, and the sudden death of their candidate, they are anxious for news of Colonel Harvey Blessington. "He is the perfect candidate," said Mr Price, their organizer. "We are doing everything we can to contact him." Anita Gilroy, star of Television's *Salvation Road*, also a supporter of the True Tories, said she appealed urgently to anyone who could give news of him.'

He stood there, the paper in his hands. The wind was strengthening, and the blown edges of the paper made a sound like the faint but rapid beating of a drum.

Mary Cattle parked her car in the small public car-park at Gravely Bridge. From the park a little flight of stone steps made a short cut to the High Street; she went this way. Thursday: a busy day in Gravely Bridge. The narrow tilted street, washed now with pale threatened sunshine, carried a lively burden of shoppers and traffic. Every now and again the shoppers came together in a little thrombosis, discussing, likely as not Mary thought, the floods. Floods were nothing new in Garfedale, but each time they happened they swamped the valley not only with water but with talk. Who'd had it waist high in the front room; whose electricity had stopped working; whose stores had been ruined; how many sheep had been lost. And as they talked, always in their minds was the reservoir with its sluice gates, and the steep fall of the ramparts, with the water suddenly pouncing through like great white tigers, over and down to the river far below. *Worse than anything for twenty years* Mary heard as she passed; each flood, apparently, was always the worst for twenty years: difficult to explain. Though the sun faintly shone, there was dampness in the air and drying patches on the road, the feeling of an aftermath of disaster. It recalled, Mary thought, London in 1940, the time after the All Clear; the time of splintered wood and broken glass; of calculating damage and clearing up.

Mary edged her way round a knot of three women, who, with shopping baskets and a dog apiece, made an extensive barrier across the pavement. 'Excuse *me*,' she said, and heard the unaccustomed edge in her voice; unlike her to show irritation, or, indeed, greatly to feel it. Not hard to find the source of this: she knew well enough what niggled uncomfortably at the back of her mind. Nothing to do with the floods: that telephone call from Matthew, late on Sunday night.

Going down the sloping street, Mary went over the call in her mind. Somewhere about half past ten; Dorothy already in bed and crying Who's that? in a maddening way before she'd had time to answer. Her first thought had been that she was glad to hear him; he'd passed her in the village on Saturday morning, his face remote and unsmiling. But there had been something strange in his voice; an unexplained sadness. Disturbing; a question left unanswered. It had fretted her now for four days.

This morning she had met Mrs Oakley at the bus stop by the green. Ten minutes before the bus was due; Gertrude Oakley was all set for a natter. No news from Mr Matthew? Strange, going off so suddenly; he'd said nothing to her on Friday when he drove her home. Though he *had* been more absent-minded than usual on that Friday afternoon; perhaps he was tired; good thing, she dared say, if he had taken a bit of a holiday, though usually he sent a post-card—

No, Mary said; no one had heard from him since Sunday night.

Well, of course, there wasn't anything really to worry about; maybe they'd hear tomorrow. He'd left the house much as he always left it; bit of a muddle of things on his desk—no dirty plates, he was good about that. Only one thing. Mrs Oakley leant a little closer. She hadn't mentioned this to anyone else; didn't want to start any gossip, perhaps it didn't mean anything: but on the floor under the chair by the fire place, must have rolled there, she'd found a little, well, couldn't really call it a bottle, more of a phial, really, of pills. Odd looking pills, nasty, bright yellow. Never seen them before; Mr Matthew never took more than aspirin; of course it might not mean anything, but you heard so much about drugs just now, didn't you, that when you saw—

Mary had soothed this down, saying that the mildest cure for stomach-ache in these days resembled nothing so much as a cross between a party-balloon and an atom bomb; and Mrs Oakley had given a dubious nod, mounted her bus and been driven off up the valley to the farm.

But—pills? So much out of character for Matthew, who shrugged off doctors and medicines and sleeping drafts as the pastimes of old women and hypochondriacs. She still had this in her mind as she came out of the small local library, a new book under her arm. Here she paused. There, just ahead of her, was Lesley Fenton.

Off duty, thought Mary, in more senses than one: he was out of uniform, and he was lost in contemplation of a young woman's behind as she crossed the road in tight-fitting jeans. Mary waited till this was over, then tapped him on the arm.

Lesley jumped, then smiled as he saw her. Not greatly different from the smile of the boy who'd sat in her classroom all those years ago, making markedly slow progress in *Twelfth Night*. In spite of this she'd always been fond of Lesley, and this fondness, she thought, was returned. Certainly this afternoon he seemed anxious to accompany her; walking with her to the car-park, asking questions but not really paying attention to the answers. As they turned into the park, he put a hand on her arm, and glanced right and left to see who was near. 'Got something interesting to show you,' he said. 'Come and see.' He had the satisfied knowingness of one in command of a secret. Mary went with him, as, she thought, one would follow a child to see its hidden treasure. Lesley pointed to a large black car parked round the corner, out of sight from the road.

'That,' he said, 'has been there since Saturday.'

She looked at the car. A Millaux; its gleaming body marked with rain. It had the slightly sinister quality of all inanimate abandoned things.

'When it was still here on Sunday night,' Lesley said, 'we started making enquiries. Checked the number against the list of stolen cars, but it wasn't there. Then we got in touch with the Registration Authorities and established ownership.' (No amount of school-teaching would stop Lesley talking like that.)

'A fairly expensive owner, I would think,' said Mary.

'You'd be right there. She talked to me, here in Gravely Bridge, that Saturday afternoon. Though I didn't know it at the time.'

'Didn't know she was talking to you?'

'No; didn't know she was the owner of the car. But she *must've* been. Couldn't have been anyone else. She was an American; quite an eyeful in her way; very nice and friendly, as Americans often are. She was asking about buses to Borrowgate. But *I* don't believe,' said Lesley, as one who has perceived some deeply hidden truth, 'that she really wanted to go to Borrowgate. What did she want with buses if she'd got this car? I think she was trying to throw dust in my eyes. Not only that, I think she was trying to make sure I remembered her.'

'Whatever for?'

Lesley looked a little downcast. 'Well, I don't know. But why go out of her way to ask me about a bus she wasn't going to take?'

'Perhaps she got a lift.'

'Well, maybe; but the fact remains, her car's still here, after six days. *And* there was something else.' He told her about the boots; the clean boots in which she had been 'walking all over'. On a very wet afternoon. 'She hadn't been walking all over; she'd been in that car.'

'You've found out who she is?'

'Her name,' said Lesley, rather as if he were giving evidence, 'is Mrs Rolf. Mrs Jane Rolf. The address registered with the licence number is 54 Shepherd Street, Chelsea. But when the local Police got on to it, they found she only used it as a garage. An old girl lived in the house, and said Mrs Rolf had taken the car out on Thursday night to go and stay with friends in Chiswick Mall. But she didn't know the address. Not surprising,' said Lesley, 'since she didn't go to Chiswick Mall, but to Yorkshire. At least, we know she spent Friday night in Ripon. *I* remembered her saying that. We telephoned all the best hotels and found her name in one of them. After that, we lose sight of her. She asked about the buses, as I said, but the bus driver never picked her up—'

'You mean she's disappeared?' said Mary.

'Well, it looks like it, doesn't it?' said Lesley. 'At least, it's rum. You can't say it isn't rum.'

Driving back to Hawkeswell, Mary brooded only briefly on Lesley and his vanished American. There was, most likely, some perfectly reasonable explanation for her disappearance: she would turn up again, drive off in that rather splendid car, and Leslie's burgeoning hope of excitement would droop and fade.

Meanwhile, Mary was still concerned with Matthew. As she drove past Squaretrees she glanced hastily sideways. The orderly stone front with the gleam of daffodils in the garden showed no sign of life; Dorothy was indoors. Mary drove on with increased speed, through the village and up the rough road to the familiar house. She parked the car outside the gate-post. As she switched off the engine, the sound of the waterfall came clearly, ceaseless and industrious in the silence about her. She went towards the house. Mildness in the air; sun on the yellowish stone; cheerfulness abounding, Mary thought, were it not for the locked doors and the silence. She walked round the house, tried the back door, peered in through the drawing-room window. The familiar sitting-room, the cluttered and loaded desk; the logs on the unlit fire; and on the mantelpiece, the little phial of pills Mrs Oakley had spoken of—she turned away; something about the room she didn't like.

She went towards the bridge and the waterfall. Sun made a brilliance of the water, something marvellously constructed of snow and light. On to the bridge, and the sound enclosed her now; it was like the sound of many voices shouting at once in her ears. As she turned to walk back towards the house, the glint of something at her foot made her pause. She bent down. Caught between a stone and the path, a small twist of hair. Gleaming, metallic hair. She stood there with it held between her fingers. The wind divided it, blew a strand away. Not animal hair; it looked like the touched-up hair of a woman.

She let the strands blow, drifting off on the wind. Curious, still fretted, she drove back down the road. *On my way south*, he had said. They were, for some reason, not comfortable words. She drew up before her own house, to be greeted by a sudden irruption of Dorothy in a royal blue shift, bursting through the front door and crying, 'Quick!'

'You ought to know by now,' said Mary, getting placidly out of the car, 'that I don't believe in—'

'The telephone! From London!' Dorothy always reacted to long distance calls as if they carried an immediate threat of fire. 'They're holding on—'

'Who is?'

'Anita. She wants to know—'

Mary moved to the telephone. The young voice sounded strained, its beguiling cello note altered in a way Mary hadn't heard before. 'Aunt Mary, do you know where my father is? Because I've tried and tried to telephone—'

Her own misgivings instantly revived, Mary explained what she knew, adding, 'He said he was on his way south.'

'*South.*' The word was sharp. 'Then perhaps—Aunt Mary, I thought I saw him—'

'Saw him?'

'My father. Here. In London.'

'But—' Mary began.

'I was in a bus. Going to work. Not far from my flat. There was a man with his head down—I'm almost *sure* it was him.'

'But surely,' Mary said, trying to keep her own fears from sounding in her voice—'surely, if he was in London he'd get in touch with you—'

'I don't know. I don't know. Something odd seems to be going on, Aunt Mary; I just don't understand.'

'Something odd?' Mary repeated, liking this less and less, and aware of Dorothy circling like a huge attendant question mark.

'I can't explain,' Anita said. 'Not over the telephone ... but *why* did he suddenly go away? Has anything happened in the village?'

'I don't think so. Only the floods.'

'No visitors?'

'I don't think so,' Mary said again. 'Except that an American woman drove into Gravely Bridge and then—according to Lesley—disappeared.'

'American?'

'Lesley was full of it, but you know what he is. Her name was Rolf: Mrs Jane Rolf.'

An astonished silence. Then: '*Golly Moses,*' said Anita.

Now the tunnel of time was narrowing, the air darkening, the sense of outlawry more complete. The ordinary commerce of the world was at a greater distance, like the diminishing shore to a man on an outward voyage.

The small drab room in Roper's Town was blurred, as if he had already left it and forgotten how it was disposed. As he moved silently, putting the few things of his own into a case, Matthew glanced at his watch. Half past five. Morning darkness at the window; only a little traffic on the roads.

Moving quickly, because his plan now was clear, the time of indecision past. The small agony of failure, the sudden dying of his courage on his way to Anita, had left the future plain. The message had been written; it was the best he could do.

The full story, the detailed story, wasn't completed yet. He took the writing-pad from a drawer, with the several close-written pages: that would be finished somewhere along the way. The whole story. Or as much as he could tell.

Pack the things away. Put the note-pad in your pocket, ready to be completed. Move quickly and quietly. Take the wallet, Blessington's wallet, glance once more at the note-book, at the blue True Tory leaflet, at the name of the house there; thrust them safely away. The parts of the puzzle; nearly all of the puzzle; not quite all.

Everything packed. The room now anonymous, nothing of him there; only the tumbled bedclothes and the damp towel to mark his passage. His bill paid last night; a pound left on the dressing-table for the girl.

As he went from the room he saw clearly again the image that had recurred through these last hours: a small, brightly coloured image, like an advertisement in a glossy magazine. The little phial of pills which he had found in the pocket of Blessington's windbreaker.

Left in the house. Somewhere in the house. Brightly, vividly clear.

Down the staircase. Out into the cold darkish morning air; drying pavements and a smudge of dawn-light staining the puddles. Out; on his way; the plan made, and the journey begun.

11

Ivy Stone woke and was instantly alert, sitting up, looking about her, as if her name had been called. She waited, making adjustments to her hair-net. Nothing, of course. Merely her room, darkish in the early hours of a March morning; silence of road and the Heath beyond; silence of the house.

She looked at the clock. Ten past six. She wouldn't sleep any more; once awake now she stayed awake. 'Things can't go on like this,' she said, and sought for her slippers. Better if she moved around, giving to the house the illusion that it was an ordinary place where ordinary things happened; where people pursued a commonplace day. She'd go downstairs and make herself a cup of tea; she would—

Tying her dressing-gown about her, she sharply lifted her head. What was that? Surely a footstep on the carpeted stairs, someone abroad in the house ... The Colonel. Come back. Moving with that light, catlike tread, moving noiselessly so as not to wake her. Must be the Colonel. Ivy stood still, ears straining. She felt cold and her hands shivered. Daft. Nothing to be afraid of. If the Colonel was back, all problems were solved. He'd quiet her down, have some perfectly reasonable explanation for his disappearance; cover the whole thing over with a light, laughing apology. Still she did not move.

The house was silent again; the sound was not repeated. Ivy moved firmly to her bedroom door, opened it and went out into the hall.

Nothing there. Merely the accustomed silence of the house, shaken by the grinding of gears as an early lorry trundled up the road. A fading darkness; things beginning to take shape. Heart beating heavily, she began to climb the stairs. Well, what are you afraid of? she asked herself. Grown woman, getting on for fifty; jumpy as a child without a nightlight. Well, it's the house, she argued; living here alone, not knowing where the Colonel is; a week since he's gone now and not a word. You can't help feeling tensed up, waiting. You begin to imagine things.

She went on climbing the stairs. Silence. Silence. Silence—wait. Another sound? No; only her own breath and the fall of her slippered feet on the carpet. No one in the house but her. Yet sometimes she could *hear* that voice; the light, pleasant, laughing voice: 'Come along, Ivy; what's all this about? Thought you'd lost me? Gracious no; I'm not the kind that gets lost easily; I was just—' Well, what? Where was he? Not here in the house; of course he wasn't; how could he be? And yet, more and more, as she moved about she felt a prickling at the back of her neck, as though someone followed her; a reluctance to open the door of a room, as though the room would not prove empty but reveal something unimaginable—

Now stop it, Ivy said to herself. Never been fluttery like this; you've always been very sane and sensible. That time Florrie had hysterics when you were both in that farmhouse late at night, and there'd been a murder not far off, and someone came knocking at the door, it was you what kept calm . . .

Yes, but this is different. She went on climbing the

stairs. It's different because of the Colonel. Having admitted this, she paused for a moment. Now that the Colonel was gone, he had left a legacy, not of the pleasant and friendly things he had done, but of his strangeness; the way he walked so silently; the way he had gone by the back door; the funny feeling he sometimes gave her when the bright gaze looked beyond her shoulder, or when she saw his figure disappearing into his own room, shutting the door very quietly, as he always did. And then locking it.

On the landing she paused again. Locking it. The little sound of that key turning now came back into her mind, isolated and strange. Always that locking of the door. Why? It began now to seem very odd. He really couldn't have imagined that she would plunge in suddenly without knocking; he couldn't have thought she was likely to lose her mind (as that poor Florrie did with *her* employer) and dash uninvited into his bed . . .

She still stood on the landing. His door was open now. The light had come up further, and she could see its gleam on bedspread and dressing-table. Heart still beating strongly, she went in. A different silence here. The silence of an absent person; familiar things untouched, bed unslept in; a silence that reminded her, Ivy thought, of her mother's room after her mother's death.

She shivered again. A reel of pictures went over in her mind; the Colonel in his dressing-gown, accepting his breakfast tray; his pyjamas, folded on the bed; the confusion in the bathroom of damp towel and shaving-brush . . . His voice calling, 'Morning, Ivy! Bless you; put it on the table; I'm just coming.' Silence now. No sound, no movement; no one here.

'Not far off, ducky.'

She gave a spiralling jump; her hands shook.

195

Nothing; the voice had been in her head.

But wasn't there a sound downstairs? Someone moving?

You couldn't go on like this. Ivy passed one trembling hand over her face. More of this sort of thing and she'd end up with a nervous breakdown. You had to take yourself in hand; you had to decide on some sort of action; arrest this ghostly sequence of silence and more silence, with the Colonel haunting your dreams.

She crossed the room. An increase of traffic on the road; an ordinary friendly sound belonging to the unghostly world; it gave her courage. She went into the bathroom. Unused soap, unused towel. Dry bath mat, hung over the rail. Bottles of mouthwash, hair-cream and after-shave lotion stacked neatly on the glass shelves as the cleaning woman had left them. And—

Ivy paused. On the shelf, razor and shaving-brush. It had been there all the time; she had noticed it before; noticed it and not noticed it, as it were. She picked up the shaving-brush and put it down. Quite dry now. Did it mean anything? He'd forgotten to pack it, perhaps; or had another one, a travelling one, that she didn't know about. All the same . . . She fingered the brush again. Odd, the way it never looked worn . . .

Mingled with Ivy's fear was now a strong curiosity. That bossy Mr Price had said, last time she saw him, 'If this goes on the Police may *have* to take an interest.' Ivy had no wish at all for the Police to come snooping; if anyone was going to snoop, Ivy was going to get in first . . . Suddenly unwinding in her head was a splendid history: Mr Price and all those silly ladies of the True Tories were congratulating her, shaking her by the hand: 'You've been absolutely wonderful, Mrs Stone; without you we should have been . . . How could we have all been so foolish; you were the only one who . . .'

Who what? Well, to begin with, thought Ivy, there's that cupboard. She stood looking at the long floor-to-ceiling cupboard, shining with its glossy white paint; shining and shut. Locked. Ivy tried the little handle; it rattled and did not give. *Privacy's privacy; that's what I always say.* Well, so she did, but this was something new.

Ivy went downstairs, treading firmly now, to her room. From a drawer she took a large ring of keys. Keys of all sizes, some a little rusty. Came in useful, quite often; someone lost a key to a suitcase or a drawer: Ivy would appear, smoothly helpful, 'Perhaps one of these might do it, sir.' Frequently, it did. She went upstairs again, a bubble of excitement in her throat. *The Colonel'd never forgive me.* But the Colonel had become, in these last days, not so much an employer to be feared as a taunting stranger, an enemy. Someone against whom she had to protect herself.

Back in the bathroom again, her hand trembling only a little, Ivy tried one key after another in the hole of the cupboard door. No. No. Still unmoving. More light in the room; more traffic on the road. Silly, but she had a feeling of hurry, as if this had to be done urgently, before ... Well, before what? ... She thrust the seventh key into the lock, hearing the loudness of her own breathing.

It turned. With difficulty, it turned. Ivy opened the cupboard doors wide.

The first of her senses to be astounded was not sight but smell. From the closed cupboard came a strong, sweet scent; woman's scent, expensive, powerful, by now a little stale. Ivy drew a hand across her mouth; at this hour of the morning, it made her feel slightly sick. She mastered herself, and looked more closely at the things hanging there. Woman's clothes. A fur coat, a tweed suit, two gleaming elegant dresses, a pair of woman's slacks. On the floor of the cupboard, several pairs of woman's shoes. On the shelf above, gloves, handbags, a bottle of scent.

Ivy stood looking. After a few moments she realised that her mouth was open. She closed it. She took one of the dresses from the rack, holding it by the hanger. Black with a shining gold thread; cost thirty pounds if it cost a penny, thought Ivy with one half of her mind, while the other scurried about, trying to make sense of it. Kept here for one of his lady friends? Must be. Yet she had the feeling that these clothes had been recently worn; and there wasn't one here, thought Ivy ungenerously, that would go half-way round that huge Miss Gilroy.

I don't like it, Ivy said, putting the dress back. The limp, uninhabited clothes had a menacing look as if someone might be hiding between them. Scorning this, Ivy shook them with her hand. Nothing but a more powerful drift of scent. The clothes hung still again, spelling their message that she could not read.

Baffled, shaken, still intensely curious, Ivy shut the cupboard door and locked it again. As she did so there was suddenly a different image in her mind: the little left-hand drawer of the desk, which was also locked.

Breathing hard now, Ivy turned and began to go down one flight of stairs, towards the study.

But on the landing she paused. From the window she had caught sight of a sudden movement, down there at the back of the house. Ivy stood still with her heart beating. So there *was* someone there. Not in the house but outside, prowling around. Nerves screwed tight, Ivy went on down the stairs. At the back door she hesitated. These were violent times; no part of Ivy's plan to be laid out cold before the mystery of the Colonel was solved.

Go on, said Ivy suddenly to herself: *have a go*. A new image presented itself: Ivy as heroine: Housekeeper resists bandit; the Judge (would it be) in his summing up commended Mrs Stone . . .

Ivy opened the door and stepped out. 'There's someone there,' she said to the silence. Rounding the corner of the house, she came face to face with a man.

In spite of herself Ivy gave a small shriek. A ruffianly man, with a beard and dark eyes and a duffle coat.

But he said, surprisingly, 'Don't be afraid. I only wanted to see the house.'

'I don't know who you are,' said Ivy; 'but the Colonel doesn't like trespassers, and I'd be glad if—'

'I wanted to see the house,' he repeated; 'to know where he lived. If you'd just let me in—'

'Certainly not,' said Ivy. 'The Colonel—'

'I shouldn't stay long. There's just one more thing I wanted to know; I thought perhaps the house might give it me—'

(Mad? Ivy thought. Something very peculiar about the eyes. She began to grope her way backwards to the door.)

'Letting strangers into the house; I've never heard of such a thing. The Colonel'd be—'

The man gave an odd smile. He said, 'The Colonel wouldn't be anything.'

Chilled, Ivy said, 'What d'you mean? Do *you* know where he is?'

The smile again. 'No. I suppose no one knows that.'

Fear made Ivy speak angrily and fast: 'Coming round here at cockcrow and frightening people to death—'

He said, 'There was no need to be afraid.'

He turned away.

Transfixed, Ivy watched him go. Then she went back into the house.

She found she was trembling so much she had to make herself a cup of tea before she climbed again, with increased determination, to the study.

Anthony Price strode quickly through the streets of North Royal. He walked with his head down, one hand guarding his bowler hat from the wind. The often-commended air of North Royal was today, Anthony thought, overdoing it; at every corner a strenuous assault of dust and flying newspaper, and a sense that you were being pushed backwards from wherever you wanted to go.

This seemed all of a piece with the day. He had woken this morning, haunted by a disastrous dream. Shaving, dressing, eating his breakfast, he had tried to push it out of mind, but it had pursued him, popping up evilly between him and his morning paper. He had dreamt that Ivy Stone was the new True Tory candidate. Enthroned on an orange-box, a duster tied round her head, she had shrilly addressed the citizens of North Royal. He himself had been explaining at length and with small success to a policeman, that something had gone awry. *A laughing-stock*, said a voice loudly in his ear, and he awoke.

The dream had been given a nasty emphasis when, after breakfast, Ivy Stone herself telephoned. Having no relish for coincidence, he met the shrill voice of Mrs Stone with distrust. She was, he decided gloomily, in a state. The words 'urgent information' forced themselves upon his attention; he would, he said, be round right away.

He hurried on, still guarding his hat. Down the steps of Mansell Passage (with a passing salute of mixed reverence and exasperation to Ledyard's ghost) to the windy road running by the Heath. For a moment before he entered, he looked up at the graceful front of the house. Not an imaginative man, he nevertheless seemed to see a shadow on it.

Stonehenge received him into the house and shut the door again with the swiftness of one under siege.

'Trouble?' asked Anthony.

A man, said Stonehenge, still slightly trembling. Lurking at the back of the house; a strange man with a beard.

Anthony nodded, as if he understood about beards; he was disappointed. 'A sightseer, perhaps—'

'At half past six in the morning?'

Anthony agreed this was early for sightseeing.

'What's more, I believe he knew something about the Colonel—'

'About the *Colonel*? And you let him go?'

Abashed, Stonehenge said he had looked *very* peculiar; she was, after all, quite alone. Perhaps aware of failure, she added, 'But that was by no means all. Come upstairs.'

As he followed her, she said, reviving his curiosity, 'There was a time when I wouldn't have told *any*one of what I've seen today. Wild horses wouldn't have dragged a *word*—'

Though I never really see, Anthony thought, why they should try.

'And even now, I'm only telling *you*. Not any of those silly women. They'd talk; I don't want talk. But this morning has been . . . well, I'm still shaking *now*.'

Anthony said he could see, and followed her into the bathroom. When she flung wide the cupboard doors, he took a smart step backwards.

'I don't know what you make of them,' said Ivy Stone.

Anthony thought he didn't either. Various nasty little hares were starting in his mind; none of them seemed suitable for discussion with Ivy Stone.

'It was a terrible shock. It made me feel . . . I find it hard to explain. And then the man . . . But after that I went upstairs to the study.'

She paused. Anthony repeated, 'The study;' and then looked at her and said, 'The *study*?'

'The desk there,' she said. 'The drawer that was locked.'

Anthony found his heart beating fast. The strong heavy scent from the cupboard, the elegant feminine clothes, Stonehenge and himself, somewhat oddly, together in Blessington's bathroom, all fused to make a moment of expectation and importance. He said, 'You opened the drawer?'

'I tried very hard,' said Ivy Stone. She was, Anthony saw, much put out at not being able to answer Yes. 'But it's a very valuable desk; all the Colonel's things are very valuable—' (a faint echo here, Anthony thought, of her old veneration, diminished now by the clothes in the cupboard and his absence)—'and I didn't like to take the responsibility of damaging it. I said to myself, I should be happier if Mr Price were here.'

It was an admission; Anthony saw that. Not one she would have made, except under stress. He gave a very small bow, at which she gave in turn a surprising blush, and became voluble. '. . . always known he was a gentleman . . . confident in his discretion . . . the sort of person one could rely upon . . . times when a *man* is needed . . .' Diverted by this image of himself, Anthony followed her down one flight of stairs to the study. The quiet elegant room was shadowed; here and there a wan light from the window showed the top of the desk, the swords, the globe. Entering, they became silent as if it were a sacred place. Perhaps we should take off our shoes, Anthony thought; he moved his shoulders, aware of a sensation in the room that did not quite please him. Perhaps it was the carpeted silence, combined with the memory of those extraordinary clothes. He could recall clearly the night of the True Tory party (it seemed a lifetime ago), with himself, the Colonel and Miss Gilroy in this room: the Colonel opening the wall cabinet to reveal the drink cupboard; the handsome, white-haired figure with the glass in his hand. Very vivid; one could almost see him still standing there, the courteous and prodigal host. Anthony controlled a small shiver, and approached the desk. On its top were a number of screw drivers and a bunch of keys. The small left-hand drawer looked inviolable, smugly shut.

'I've tried the keys,' Stonehenge said. 'None of them would make it turn. Dark, isn't it.' She switched on the lamp; the desk became suddenly isolated, lit in the shadowed room, a focus of drama. Aware of Stonehenge at his shoulder emitting some sort of challenge, Anthony took the bunch of keys and tried each one in the lock.

'As you say, they don't fit.'

'No,' said Stonehenge. Anthony wondered if his image as the all-efficient male was slipping. He crouched down, eyes on a level with the drawer. The small blind hole confronted him, baffling, unco-operative. Tentatively he felt it with one finger. He was aware of Stonehenge still waiting. He rubbed his chin, as if making calculations. At the back of his mind was a small memory, beginning to emerge. Himself, a schoolboy of sixteen, packed and ready for a journey to France. An hour before the train; his passport in a locked drawer, for which the key had been lost. Sunday: no locksmith available. His mother becoming hysterical; his father by contrast Olympian in his calm, calling for vaseline and stout wire.

203

With the controlled authority of the expert, he demanded these from Stonehenge. The idea seemed to please her. After a few minutes she returned with a round tin of vaseline, a coil of wire, a pair of rubber gloves and a plain green bibbed apron.

'Rather messy stuff, vaseline. Thought these might be useful, sir.'

He perceived in this a transference of loyalty to him from the Colonel. He said, 'Thank you,' putting on the apron and the rubber gloves; and feeling a bit of an ass. His heart beat steadily with expectation. He forced vaseline into the lock. He took the wire and bent it; then, holding out a hand to Stonehenge said, 'Pincers, please,' hearing overtones of surgeons on the cinema screen. With the pincers he shaped and twisted the wire. He did this, he found, with a certain expertise. (Perhaps he had mistaken his calling.) The wire began to resemble a piece of modern sculpture. With Stonehenge giving out an air of huge expectancy behind him, he gently urged the wire into the lock. The wire turned slightly; there was a small sound in the lock; he heard a sharp breath from Stonehenge. He pulled at the drawer. It slid a fraction, then stopped. He pulled further.

No result.

'Damn,' he said.

'You see,' said Stonehenge, with a trace of satisfaction.

'Pincers please.'

He shaped the wire again. There was sweat on his forehead; he wiped it with the green apron. The secret, difficult operation, done in the circle of lamplight, now had urgency in it; though the house was silent, there were moments when he thought he heard a footstep, when he could feel the approach of someone behind him, the quiet tread, the pleasant clubman's voice, 'Well, now!

Bit of housebreaking?' He knew now he was afraid of the voice.

Once more he inserted the wire. There was a satisfying sensation of grip; he turned his hand slowly. Stonehenge seemed to be bent double, and breathing hard. There was a small, completed click. He pulled. The drawer slid open. Stonehenge gave a small cry.

He looked into the drawer.

He didn't know what he had expected. Some revelation, some instant answer to the mystery. There was, faintly mocking him, a small tin box. Nothing more. He could feel Stonehenge deflating beside him. She said, 'Just a box, sir.'

'Yes,' said Anthony, anger gaining on him; 'a box.' He shook it. A rattle inside as of something small and hard. A little padlock, securing the lid.

'I'm not standing any nonsense from *this*,' he said, and grabbed a screwdriver. 'This isn't valuable; I don't care if I break it in two.'

He thrust the screw driver below the lid, prising upwards. The lid fluted, buckled. The next levering movement forced the lock. He was faced with a broken tin box containing a small leather-bound note-book.

'A book,' said Stonehenge.

'Doubly locked,' said Anthony. 'In the box, in the drawer. So . . .' He pulled off the rubber gloves. He sat at the desk and with his hands still shaking a little, opened the book. Pig-skin cover, grey-blue paper (the colour of the True Tory leaflet, Anthony reflected.) On the first page was written 'California—Summer— 1953'. Undoubtedly the Colonel's handwriting; the neat intelligent writing, with the ink a little stale. On the following page 'Rogue River Ranch' underlined, and then the words: 'It is important to record this time. Important for whom? For myself, I guess. There have been other things; nothing like this. It was all of fear, all of misery, and yet—all of satisfaction; the final achievement. When it was done I burned the other diary; this overtopped it all. Only this remains—a last will and testament? No, because there is no one with whom I am at all concerned; it is a world now of strangers, and I despise them. More than despise them; they fill me with disgust. No, I write this for myself, the only person now I love.'

'Mercy on us,' said Stonehenge, who had been reading over his shoulder.

Anthony turned the page. Here was written 'Night of 17th July. About 01.00 hours. Great warmth and quiet. It was quite easy. Not much fear. The high lonely place deserted; the mountain heads, and the river making its secret way to the coast of the Pacific. Suitable ground.'

He turned another page.

And then swore.

A blank. And then, after that, a column of figures. Pounds, shillings and pence. Impatient, he turned the other pages. Nothing. He turned back to the column of figures. Sums of money, added up. Accounts. At the top of the page 'O.K.' with a question mark. And nothing more.

So why lock it up?

As if she sensed that the moment of drama was past, Stonehenge switched off the lamp. After one more baffled look at the note-book, Anthony said, 'If I may take it . . .'

'Yes, sir. But I'd be glad if you'd keep *what we saw in the bathroom* to yourself.'

Pleased by this phrase, Anthony said he would try. 'But you have to remember that the time may come when the whole thing's taken out of our hands. If the Colonel doesn't come back—'

Stonehenge faced him across the desk. 'I don't understand,' she said, 'how the Colonel could do this to *me*.'

Anthony sat that evening at a table in the Oak Apple, North Royal's historic pub. The place was thinly occupied; he sat alone, watching the door, nibbling a sausage and occasionally glancing down at Blessingtons' note-book.

He was aware of a rising irritation. First with the note-book for being unintelligible. Secondly with Anita for being late. Why was she late? She had seemed to him the kind who would be most blessedly punctual.

He bit angrily into his sausage; then started to rise from the table with a smile, which was wiped off his face a moment later.

It was absolutely no part of his plan that his date with Anita should be turned into a triangle by Quentin Payne. But there, a little way behind Anita, looking a size too small, was the slight feminine figure with the troubled blue eyes. No one, Anthony thought, that he wanted to see less. During the last days, his fluting presence had been an increasing irritation. Plaintive and distressed he hovered, hands clasped, at the edge of events. Like those maidens, Anthony thought sourly, who give useless little bleats of anguish and encouragement at some mediaeval confrontation of knights.

They came towards him. Anita had on her face an expression that resembled, Anthony thought, a fire-alarm. While Quentin lingered to hang up his coat, she whispered, 'I'm sorry. I *had* to bring him. He simply won't go. It's like a dog; and he's so miserable. I think he looks on me as a mother.' Anthony received this improbable hypothesis with a gloomy nod. She went on,

'Mr Price, things have happened. The strangest things. I don't know where I am.'

'Sit down,' said Anthony, giving a brief nod to Quentin who was full of apologies and nervous chatter. Leaving these to wind off on their own, Anthony brought drinks from the bar: a glass of red wine for Anita and with less enthusiasm a pink gin for Quentin Payne. He sat down, giving Anita all his attention. 'Now,' he said.

The large beautiful eyes were fixed on him. He found the confusion and distress in them disturbing. She said, with urgent emphasis, 'Mr Price, I don't know whether or not to go to Yorkshire.'

It wasn't what he had expected. Quentin pushed one hand over his hair and said, 'She's in the most *awful* fix, poor girl—'

Anthony gave him a brief paralysing stare: this rapport between Quentin and Anita he found inexplicable and deeply irritating. 'Yorkshire?' he repeated.

'Two things have happened,' she said. 'A woman called Jane Rolf has disappeared. Near Hawkeswell, where I live.'

'Jane Rolf. Our mystery girl. And the other thing?'

She took up her large handbag. He saw that her hands were trembling. Quentin was watching the bag with sad expectancy, as if she were about to reveal the body of a pet hamster.

She was showing him a piece of writing-paper. Ordinary writing-paper, torn off a block. 'Look,' she said. 'From my father.'

He stared down at the page before him. The words were written in heavy black chalk, large letters conveying something of fear and desperation.

> *Do not search further for Colonel Blessington*
> *Do not search further for me*

The story is to come
You must forgive me

He looked up sharply. 'What does that mean?'

She said miserably, 'I don't know. I don't know. It wasn't posted. It was put through my door. He's been in London. Been to my flat. But I don't know where he is now.'

'You can see,' said Quentin, moodily taking a sausage, 'that it's the most ghastly fix.'

Anthony ignored him. Eyes on Anita, his thoughts turning, he was aware of the strange facts piling up: this message, Jane Rolf, the clothes cupboard, the man who had come this morning to Minster House. She couldn't—perhaps would not want—to be finally protected from them.

She said, 'Something's happened in Yorkshire. I'm sure of it. Something to do with Harvey. I want to go there—desperately—but I can't until I know where my father is. If he's still in London . . .'

'Have you any idea where he might stay?'

She shook her head vigorously. 'He hardly ever came to London. He hated it. He was always crazy to get back to his moors and the waterfall. He hasn't been here for years. When he came, he wouldn't stay more than a night or two. That's why I believe—'

'You think he's gone back?'

'I don't know. I can't be sure. But somehow I feel— *yes*—I do feel that he wouldn't stay here longer than he need.' Her eyes from looking at nothing gradually focussed on the note-book under his hand. She said, 'What's that?'

Anthony made rapid calculations. How much to tell? Not yet the clothes cupboard. But the note-book . . . yes, she must see the note-book. A first step; a warning of things to come.

He explained about the desk drawer. He said, 'We found—this.'

Her eyes came up to his face. 'Not letters?'

'Nothing but this.'

'Pretty cover,' said Quentin with brooding nostalgia; 'Harvey had lots of things like that.'

Anthony passed her the note-book. 'I'm afraid—' he began, but she shook her head. She was, he thought, prepared: stricken, apprehensive, but prepared. He watched her as she read the opening words; saw her eyes darken with pain as she came to: 'No, I write this for myself, the only person now I love.' She stared at this for a moment, then turned the page.

He saw the sudden frown on her face as she came to the figures. Quentin who was reading beside her looked up, bewildered. 'D'you mean, this is *all* there was?'

Anthony nodded. His eyes were still on Anita. Very pale, she was turning the small blue pages back and forth. He said, '*Why* lock it up? A few windy words, and a page of accounts? A page of figures?'

'Quite large figures too, aren't they,' said Quentin. 'Six hundred and thirty nine pounds; four hundred and sixty nine pounds; one hundred and eighty five ... That'll cover a day's shopping at the Supermarket all right.'

Anthony shrugged. 'He was a wealthy man; no problems there.'

'And "O.K." ' said Quentin, still frowning over the book. 'What's that in aid of?'

'Means has he added them up right, I suppose.'

'Can't help feeling,' said Quentin, 'that there's something a bit odd about the figures ... such *peculiar* amounts, somehow ...' He turned to Anita. 'Don't you agree, dear?'

Anita sat biting her thumbnail, eyes on the book.

Then she said, as if she were thinking aloud, 'Unless of course they aren't figures after all.'

Anthony stared at her. 'What did you say?'

She looked at him, a little dazed at the sharpness of his voice. 'Unless they're—something else.'

'My God,' he said, 'it could be. It could be. A cypher? Let me look . . . Let me see . . . You know, I believe you're right . . . Figures *do* seem a bit odd . . . Oh, you brilliant girl. You absolutely *brilliant* girl.'

Anita was looking at him as if this description came as a surprise.

'I'm sure you're right,' he went on; 'sure you're right. Why didn't I think of that? Slow. Dumb. Getting old. Needs a young mind like yours. An interesting man, the Colonel: perhaps a bit of a cypher himself.' He stared at the figures before him. 'A cypher,' he repeated; 'but *what* cypher? Never been good at those. Not got that sort of brain; never been one for crossword puzzles—'

He stopped at the sudden bark from Anita. She said, 'Crossword puzzles.'

'Well?'

'My father. He does them. Not only does them, *he makes them up*. He used to break codes in the war. He could—'

'You mean,' said Anthony, a sudden excitement rising in his head, 'that if it's what you think, he could solve it?'

'Yes. Yes. Oh, I'm sure he could. *But I don't know where to look for him.*' Her eyes were on him, in a torment of indecision. 'Here or in the North? I don't know. And we haven't got much time.'

'You mean—'

She pulled the written message towards her and looked long at it. 'I believe he's in trouble. I don't know what's happened. But I'm afraid.'

'So we have to make a decision.'

'Always my least favourite thing,' said Quentin.

Anita sat, as if submerged, brow puckered, eyes on nothing. Then she suddenly said, '*Got it.* I think.'

Anthony looked at her. Quentin pushed his curls back with troubled expectation.

She said, 'I shall go home to my flat tonight. If I've heard nothing more by tomorrow morning, I shall go up to Yorkshire by the earliest possible train. And *you,*' she said, turning to Quentin who gave a small jump as if something had stung him, 'you are going to stay in my flat all tomorrow and *not move*—'

'Me?'

'Yes, you,' said Anthony, releasing some dammed-up force of irritation: 'you're going to do something useful for once.'

'*Not move,*' Anita repeated. 'And if my father should come, you're to hold on to him—'

'Hold on to him, dear?'

'I don't care how you do it: you're to keep him. I shall telephone you the moment I arrive—'

'You can telephone before that,' said Anthony.

'Before—?'

'You're not going by train. You're coming in the car, with me.'

12

DOROTHY CATTLE strode out between the puddles on
the slippery path. The first truly fine morning since the
heavy rains let up; March as March ought to be, with
a high wind racing the shadows over the moorland,
white clouds, blue sky; all about her in these low lying
fields the long blue lakes left by the flood water.
Uplifted, she went quickly on, seeing herself as an
Atlanta on her way, a slim athletic shape going through
the Spring (though half of her mind was aware that the
person who breasted the slippery slopes was a very big
lady panting in a bulky tweed coat and a wool pixie
hood, carrying a stick; and that Spring was not yet here.)

She skidded on a film of mud. Mary would say she
was foolish. Defiant, Dorothy went teetering along
beside the river, hoping for a sight of primroses, awed
as she heard the noise of the fall going down into Orson's
Pool. Strange that the river, which flowed for many
yards underground, should emerge, welling up with
such force, then fall to the still, secret pool. No sun here;
the opaque brownish water, risen high, frothed in the
green gloom of tree shade. It had fallen a little since the
floods; there was a line of dark dripping weed along the
bank, where the water had been.

There were primroses. One pale yellow star shone
through the willows. It would, normally, have been

well above the waterline. Not today. She could see the water seeping through the moss; the spur where it grew had almost vanished. Her usual approach to this spur was by way of the rocks at the pool's edge, but they were three-quarters covered, only their tops visible, smooth brown humps like the backs of tortoises. Dorothy went perilously down the bank, and paused on the last dry stretch. If she squatted here, driving her stick into the ground and holding on, she might reach the tantalizing flower ... No, she couldn't. Dared she risk setting one foot on the nearest rock? No. Crazy. She would have to leave the primrose till tomorrow.

Baffled, she stood leaning upon her stick; consoled by the sharp gust that whipped over the pool making little peacock-feather shapes on the surface and then leaving it still again. Still as a mirror. There was a face looking up, thought Dorothy, looking up at her from the mirror. Only a trick of the light, making a face come in the shallows, close to the rocks, the ragged likeness of a face. The face went. Still she stood staring.

That wasn't a rock at all, the pale brown hump in the middle ... not a rock at all but an old sodden sweater. Swollen up and floating. It moved; the gentle flux of the pool was swaying it to and fro and now two more little objects bobbed up like corks, just a few feet from the sweater. Not corks; they were the tips of somebody's shoes.

Slowly, Dorothy inched herself nearer to the edge. A sudden, stronger drift of light. She could see the dummy, the big bruised doll, whatever it was, head, arms, tattered hands and twisted legs, a-sprawl, just under the surface, resting against the rocks, caught there, moving up and down, up and down.

*　　　*　　　*

214

Mary shook flour into the bowl and began mixing. Martial music from the radio at her side (somebody's brass band), the strong sunlight at the window and the prospect of steak-and-kidney pudding all combined to lift her spirits; this was a morning of good omen. On such a day as this she was content, looking back with amusement and no regret on the busy class-room years, the noisy, difficult, absorbing time of teaching the young. Alone in the kitchen she could hear the shrill echo of their voices; see the young faces, given to her, for a little while her own. Done now. Now there were the quiet even days, the shallows of life, enlivened by martial music and steak-and-kidney pudding.

Only one shadow, she thought: Matthew. Still no news of him. Yet on such a day as this, her worry seemed to thin and fade. Matthew was a puzzler, the unknown quantity in their lives, but he was safe. Today, she was sure of that. He would return suddenly, and she would have the comfortable knowledge of his being back in that house, working away at some absurdity, arriving unannounced to see them with the piratical beard and that extraordinary red shirt. She would like it to be soon.

As she rolled the pastry out on the board, she heard Dorothy come in through the front door. Mary called, 'Hullo! Make you some coffee in a moment. Had a nice walk?'

Most strangely, no reply. She could hear Dorothy's step in the living-room. Perhaps Dorothy was going deaf—there were times when she'd had to speak twice ... She called again, '*Had a nice walk?*'

Another pause. A further step. And then Mary looked up from the pastry-board to see Dorothy standing silent in the doorway of the kitchen. She stood quite still. The large-eyed tragedy queen's face was pale. Reminiscent, Mary thought, were it not for the tweeds and the pixie hood, of a performance as Hecuba, long ago.

'Whatever's up?' said Mary.

Dorothy slowly removed her hood. She spoke at last, saying, 'I want you to keep perfectly calm.'

'I *am* perfectly calm—'

'Something terrible has happened. I have to make a telephone call immediately.'

'But what on earth—'

'I went for a walk, along by the river.'

'Well?'

Dorothy looked, if anything, paler. She paused, and then said, 'There's a body in Orson's Pool—'

'A *body*?'

'A dead body. I'm afraid it's been ... there some time.'

Mary's first thought was that Dorothy had gone out of her mind. She began, 'Dorothy dear; sit down. I'm making the coffee—'

Dorothy said with dignity, 'I shall be grateful for coffee in due course. First of all I have to telephone the Police.'

'But—'

'You needn't think I've imagined it. I made very, very sure.' She slowly unbuttoned her large tweed coat, and removed it with the sweeping gesture of a queen renouncing her robes. 'I'd just like you to notice that I'm not at *all* hysterical.'

'No, you're not,' said Mary, finding that a small chill was beginning in her chest, because this was beginning to be true. 'You're being very brave—'

A faint, queenly smile. 'It's been a particularly horrid experience. Something that's never happened before—'

'No, well; finding people drowned isn't—'

'I couldn't help thinking, it's a pity I can't play Gertrude again—'

'Gertrude?'

'Ophelia. All that about the willow . . . It would have *meaning* now.'

She moved slowly into the living-room, Mary following her, wiping floury hands on her apron. She said, 'Dorothy dear, you do look very pale. Perhaps a little brandy—'

'A very small one, Mary dear. It is, I must say, rather nice to have you. I shouldn't have liked to come home to an *empty* house—'

As she poured the brandy, Mary heard Dorothy's voice: 'I want Gravely Bridge Police Station, please . . . This is Miss Dorothy Cattle of Squaretrees, Hawkeswell . . . Yes . . . Yes. Good. I have to report a body in Orson's Pool . . . No, I am *not* raving: a body of a—a man, in trousers and a sweater. Yes. No, there's no doubt at all, I'm afraid. There is a dead person in Orson's Pool.' She put down the telephone.

'Here,' said Mary, offering the brandy. 'Sit down and drink this.'

Dorothy said, 'Thank you,' and sipped the brandy. The large moony eyes were raised to Mary. She said, 'It isn't very nice, dear, is it?'

Mary shook her head. The bright morning had died; the shadows had come back. 'No,' she said; 'not nice at all.'

Strangeness in the valley. Leaving Dorothy comfortably by the fire, Mary went out of the house. Already the village was alight, groups of people talking together; the ambulance had gone through, and a police car; rumours were abroad. In her mind's eye Mary could see the grim drama at the water's edge; the poor wrecked thing, lifted from the water: not merely a body any more, but the start of a long process of inquiry, even of trial.

'Someone drowned;' she heard Sally Moore from the shop say as she passed; 'can't be one of us; no one missing hereabouts; must be a stranger. Orson's Pool; got lodged underground, most likely; then drifted out ... A man, they say. Not just an accident; they've got an Inspector there and a chap taking photographs ...'

Not just an accident. Mary went quickly on. All her fears for Matthew had returned. Perhaps it was absurd, but she kept seeing the small twist of hair which she'd found on the bridge ... Quickly on, away from the village, towards his house.

Half way up the road, she stood suddenly still. There, half hidden by the trees, stood Matthew's car. He was back. Relief out of all proportion poured through her: he was safe; all was well. She went more quickly, panting, stumbling. Near to the house she found she was calling, 'Matthew! Matthew!' I suppose I must love him, she thought; in a perfectly nice, sisterly way, but yes, *love*—wanting him to be safe and happy and fearing for him ... '*Matthew!*'

Of course he could not yet hear. She went through the stone gate, along the cobbled path. The front door shut. She rang and waited. No reply. No sound of steps. She went to the back door, tried the handle ... Yes, open. She walked in. 'Matthew?' she called again. Silence. She moved hesitantly into the house. The place, though quiet, seemed in some way alive; she called, 'Matthew?' again, but with less conviction now. She went into the living-room. Here she paused, looking about her. The untidy desk, the unlit fire ... this was the room she had spied on from the window. And yet ... no, not quite the same. A difference; an envelope. Addressed to Anita. Frowning, she picked it up, turned it over, then put it back. She moved to the desk. Here, on the drawing-board, lay a knife; a sheath knife, leather-handled. New? She could not remember it. Something in the room was troubling her; some small niggle that she couldn't yet capture . . . Her eyes went over the room, coming back to the mantelpiece again—

The pills. The phial of bright yellow pills, retrieved by Mrs Oakley. They had stood there, on the mantelpiece when she'd looked in from the window. Now they were gone. Why was it frightening?

Of a sudden she was out of the room, out of the house, scrambling uneasily over the moorland, a large woman, more than sixty, wishing she were smaller, wishing she were younger; panting and gasping and afraid.

Anita rubbed her eyes with her hands. The long drive seemed to be singing in her head like a drug; the motor-ways, pouring past; speed and more speed; the conges-ted, tangled roads with the trail of inching traffic; the small cabin of the car; and always the sign, *To the North*. They had left while it was still dark; now, though it was only ten o'clock, the day seemed old.

She sat forward, watching the spinning road. Mr Price said, 'Don't do that: you might go through the windscreen.'

'I'm wearing my safety belt.'

'Even so,'

With a small sigh, she sat back in her seat. It would not be polite to Mr Price, who had been so consistently kind, to say that the thought of going through the windscreen was not without solace. The thing that he had just told her seemed too painful to be borne.

Last night she had slept little. Tormentingly in her

mind had been those words in the notebook: '. . . the only person now I love.' Still haunted by them, she had set out on the journey with Mr Price. And become aware, as they drove through the darkish morning roads, that he had something he wished, and did not wish, to tell her. At last, his pleasant young-old face pleated in a frown, he had said—'I think I should tell you something. I've wondered . . . but I think you should know.'

Frightening words. She had made a small meaningless sound and waited.

And then Mr Price had said there was a cupboard full of woman's clothes in Harvey's room.

She had turned her head sharply from him. She wondered for a moment if she was going to be sick. When he said, 'Should I not have told you?' she shook her head, and murmured, 'Better to know.'

'Are you all right?'

She said, 'Yes;' but then sank into a silence; a dark place, where she was alone.

These facts were true. The note-book was true. She could try to persuade herself that someone had forged it: the writing was all too plain. What Mr Price said must be true: he had no reason to lie. Somehow she must accept them; and the small childish person within herself who cried out that they *couldn't* be true, that she *wouldn't* believe them, must be brought under control.

She sat now, watching the needle swing, climbing to seventy on the motorway. The speed induced vivid memories, like dreams: she could see Harvey sitting opposite her at the dinner table, hear his voice, feel again the gentle, controlled caress—

She put one hand against her mouth to stop the sudden '*Ow*' of pain that nearly escaped her.

All these once joyous things carried now a dread, a vast uncertainty. The voice that had been the only voice in the world had now a hideous echo, as if it had spoken from behind a mask.

She glanced for a moment at the firm concentrated profile of Mr Price. This now signalled a friend; a companion in adversity. She began to be aware of how long she had been silent, and how he had accepted her silence.

He said, 'Will you telephone home again?'

She shook her head. 'Not till we arrive.'

Three times she had telephoned to Quentin in the flat: he had answered at once, his light sad voice breaking oddly into this fevered journey: 'No, dear, absolutely nothing: only the milkman, and a postcard from Amsterdam... Call again whenever you like: I'll be here.'

Lonelier country now; here was the rising ground and the dry-stone walls; near to the journey's end. She said to Mr Price, 'I believe he's gone North. I believe so. I *think* this is right.' The strange message lingered in her mind: *You must forgive me.* 'Oh,' she said, 'I do pray it's right.'

From her bag she took the note-book, Harvey's note-book, and stared at the baffling figures. Pounds, shillings and pence. Above them, 'O.K.?' Figures. Figures standing for letters? They had tried that; it made nonsense. So *what* then?

'Let it be,' said Anthony, giving a quick glance her way. 'We shall discover.'

She shifted a cramped leg. 'What shall we find?'

'The answer.'

'To Jane Rolf? To Harvey?'

'To everything. Have no fear. You've had a perfectly bloody time. And you've been very brave ... we're getting nearer. Soon we shall know.'

Now the tunnel was narrower still. This day of wind and sun, with shadows racing like rabbits over the moors and the pools of water blue as the sky, belonged to a different time. His time was all of darkness, the old darkness: not Now but Then.

He moved quietly, steadily, walking upwards and alone. Deliberation marked it all; this was what he had been trained for: to keep the mind alert in danger as one keeps a flame burning in a strong wind; to be on easy terms with death.

All this was close about him. Close too were the remembered names, Philip Carlson, David Ballam, Jack Forge. Vivid, the many dead with their savage, ugly wounds. Most vivid of all the blackened face that had leaned over him: the man who had killed, who had haunted him over the years; whom he himself had killed.

Perhaps we were all meant to die.

He walked on, still climbing. Fading from his mind was the drab room in London; his spying on Minster House; the long journey north. Why had it seemed necessary to come? Was place any longer important? No; yet he had travelled like a man under orders, obedient, unquestioning.

The house had not welcomed him. It was no longer the friendly place where he had played a game. On the drawing-board where he had left it lay the knife; and Blessington was there; the savage encounter in the room was there; the final moments on the bridge . . .

He had lit the lamp; he had lit the fire; he had sat at his desk with the writing-pad; he had finished the story.

Not quite got it all? Something missing, wouldn't you say?

Never mind. I've told all I know. If there's still a question it'll never be answered now.

Never? Why don't you wait to find out?

Because you're the only one who can tell, and you

222

can't speak any more. Only silence now, except in my head.

The story done, he had left it in the house. He had left Blessington's clothes, his wallet, rucksack and windbreaker: all the proof they would need.

And then the battle had begun.

This is too easy. Anita deserves better than this. You should see her once more; give the letter into her hand. One last thing. It ought to be done.

He had waited then, fighting the battle. Up and pace the room. No sleep; the long hours of the night falling gradually away. Out on to the moors, tasting the sharp air of very early morning, seeing the greyness slip over the grass, a sudden dim whiteness of stone. Back to the house. Time slipping by, unregarded now. Thought so deep that the brightness of the day came only gradually upon his consciousness. Dazed, head throbbing, he had walked out again, the battle still unresolved.

And then, as he walked, gaining ground, with the river sword-bright below him, he had suddenly paused. Standing there he had seen the day change; the battle die out and cease.

Beside Orson's Pool, where there should be nothing but the bare ground and the blowing trees, was a knot of people. At their feet was a stretcher, and a burden on the stretcher. The blue uniforms shone clear. Beside them an ambulance had been driven over the rough path. It was all very small, very distant; and it was the only real thing in this day.

Move on. The time is going now. The time when the dark enemy coast comes nearer; when the light goes off the past; when the malignant air is full of death and there is nothing beyond this: the astounded brain has clear before it the prospect of an end—

His hand went to his pocket, and felt the small glass

223

object there. Clearly he could see the note-book: Pentobarb. 1,000 mg.—15 gr.

He held the phial in his hand. How many? One needed to be sure ... There were, of course, the other words: *Height of reservoir—appx. 1,000 ft. Better?*

He stood there. Maybe it is, chum. Maybe those pills don't work any more: I don't know much about pills; never dealt in them, except the benzedrine they gave us before the raid. 'Better?' He saw the ramparts, the bridge, the culverts, the steep fall.

He would go that way.

Now he moved fast. Time had stopped; he was over the edge of the dark. Up the steep slope; up the steps; meeting the harsh wind; meeting the great depth; not long now; so little time—

He sharply turned his head.

A voice? Calling his name? He swore. No one must come now; it was too late; he'd done with them all—

But the voice came again; his own name sounding clear, '*Matthew!*'

Such desperation, such appeal in the voice, it held him still. And then, appearing on the upward path, grey hair blowing, one arm waving excitedly, the large body of an elderly woman, trudging with difficulty over the stony ground.

Mary. Coming breathless towards him with such joy on her face that he could not move. He stood there on the bridge, watching her. Hair blowing, coat flapping wide, sturdy legs trudging. An absurd figure, perhaps; he saw no absurdity. She was coming with gladness towards him, and he must send her away.

She climbed the steps; she stood before him, panting, triumphant, speechless.

Then she put a hand on his arm. 'Tell me. The whole

story. You must tell me.' She added, 'I've been so afraid.'

Mary felt calm, no longer breathless. They sat together on a large boulder beside the moorland path. He had spoken for a long time. The words had come with difficulty; sometimes she had had to lean close to hear him. When he had done she sat for a few moments looking at the bowed dishevelled figure beside her. So men looked, she believed, after battle, dazed and bewildered to find themselves still alive. It was necessary to work quickly, to cut through into the lonely place where Matthew was: no time for ease and sympathy.

'And you believe,' she said, 'that at this moment, when Anita has to face the extraordinarily unpleasant facts about the man she loved, the best thing *you* can do is to remove yourself entirely as a source of comfort—'

He muttered, 'What comfort can I be to her?'

'A great deal.'

'I killed him.'

'In self-defence. Oh yes; I know all about your dark memories, the "river running underground" as you call it. Leave it alone. We all have our dark rivers—you're not the only one. Even fat old ladies like Dorothy and me have our buried serpents, you know—have you ever thought of that?'

The muttering voice again: 'She'll be better without me.'

'Guts and brains,' said Mary crisply; 'it surprises me that you should have lost both at the same time—'

'You don't know—you don't know—'

'Of course I don't know. I can't get inside your head and you can't get inside mine. But I've known you for many years; you've been of great importance to me—I really don't know quite why, but you have—and I'm perfectly clear what you've got to do now—'

'No one can know that but me—'

'Yes they can.' Mary folded her hands together in her lap. Very odd, but in this difficult and dangerous battle, she was aware of reserves of power. 'Because Anita is the one who is important now.'

'She won't want to speak to me—ever again—'

'Oh yes, she will. Anita has plenty of guts. I always thought she got them from you. And if you come back and face her, you'll give her a great heave over the hurdle she's got to take, poor darling.'

'I killed him, Mary.'

'All right. All right. If it's punishment you're after, you'll get it, I daresay. Not heavy punishment, because he came at you with a knife—but punishment, all the same. And when it's over, you'll come back—even to that house, I believe, because you're not one to be afraid of places, and you've lived all your life there.'

Mary sat watching the craggy, tormented face. Eyes bloodshot with weariness, hair ragged in the wind, the beard unkempt—yet the sharp blowing light showed—what? A small change perhaps; the look of a man making some new discovery . . .

She felt the excitement of ground gained; she went on, 'It needs courage, of course. More courage than *that*.' She gave a jerk of her head towards the reservoir. 'Weren't you trained in courage? The kind that goes beyond the edge of possibility?'

He was looking away now, over the long lariat line of the moors. 'I was trained for death,' he said. 'To give it and meet it—'

'*Nonsense.*' (And it was, she thought, her classroom voice. Useful, even here.) 'All that's finished now. It was finished when Blessington was killed. Now, you begin again.'

Once more she saw a little change on his face; the look of one suddenly attentive; who has caught through the undemanding sounds of some conversation a word relating to himself. Silent, he picked a little heap of stones from the ground, letting them run through his hand.

'And,' she said, 'there is one more thing.'

He did not look up, but his hands became still, letting the stones fall.

She said, 'You told me you had a question—'

His head was still down. 'Maybe. What difference can it make now?'

She said, 'It isn't time to go yet.'

Again he bent and picked a handful of stones. In the silence she could hear the wind in the grass, and the treble cry of a sheep.

She waited.

13

ANTHONY STOOD, looking over the room; at the tall desk in the corner, the wide grate, the windows showing the sunlight and the moors. A townsman, he felt a stranger here, at odds with the space and the silence. He did not speak. Anita stood by the window; she had not moved for some time. She had one arm up against the sash, her forehead against the glass. The large figure looked concentrated, lost, as children do when they dream, deprived of the garden, on a wet day.

His eye went to the table. There was the torn envelope with her name on it; the pages filled with her father's writing. There was the message, 'How many miles to midnight'; there was the whole story: 'Jane Rolf', Blessington's death; the night of the Labrière raid: all of it told. She had read it in silence; without a word, she had given it to him.

He began to speak, but she gave the smallest shake of her head. He looked beyond her to the sunlit moors. So gentle a day, giving the lie to the darkness now in her mind. Yet the darkness was true. How did one balance this? Some such harsh arithmetic, he thought, occupied her now. He could not foresee the final sum.

His eyes went again to the table. There, amongst the pages of writing, lay the small leather-bound note-book with its abiding question. The stillness after the long journey sang in his ears: this was a strange patch of time, removed from its normal sequence: a time of waiting.

Anita had moved from the window. She was looking at him as if, on a moment of waking, she was trying to remember who he was. She said, in a voice without expression, 'My father's been here, of course. His car's outside; the fire's been lit; there's a used cup and plate in the kitchen.' She spoke as of facts which did not greatly concern her. Yet she was waiting now, listening. The silence of the room deepened. Far off in his mind was an image of Quentin Payne, sitting obediently in Anita's flat, waiting for the telephone. She had, Anthony thought, quite forgotten him.

She stood before the table. She picked up a page or two of the closely-written story; put them together, as if this were a letter in which she had some slight curiosity.

But then she froze, her head lifted; alert; very pale.

He heard footsteps on the path.

'Baffled you, has it? Do I keep my secret?'

Matthew shut his ears to the voice. About him was the silence of the room; the strangeness of sitting here, with Blessington's note-book in his hands; a companion to the note-book he had found in the rucksack on the night of Blessington's death—but this one found in a locked drawer of Blessington's, two hundred miles away ... He stared at the page of figures. Concentrate on them. Forget the desperate moments just passed; forget —if it's possible—the misery on Anita's face; concentrate, dredge up the old skill; forget the past and the future: let there be simply Now. Work hard, work quickly. Time must be running out. They had found the body. They might come to ask questions. Someone must have seen 'Jane Rolf' when she came to the house; somewhere there must be a clue that leads this way ...

Before they come, solve this. The last question; the last words of Blessington's story.

Come along. This is your country; the crossword clue, the cypher.

They all had their eyes on the note-book. Mary lit a cigarette, but otherwise was still. The young man called Price sat with his chin in his hand, wearing the expression of one who cannot now be surprised by anything. From time to time he turned to look at Anita, but she did not return his glance.

Matthew drew his breath. 'All right,' he said. 'Take it step by step. The figures stand for letters or words. They can stand for the pages or the lines of a book—but *what* book?' He stared down at the neatly written figures on the blue-grey paper. And the scrawled 'O.K.?' above them.

He went on looking at it.

I think I'm after you. I think I'm on your tail. Odd to feel the muscles of the mind reviving; the skill coming slowly back. He said, 'It's there. The title of the book. Somewhere in those two letters—*O.K.*' They were all leaning forward. He could feel his heart racing. Let there be time. Please let there be time.

'O and K,' he said. 'Omar Khayyam—is that it? . . . No; no—not enough lines in old Omar: there's a figure here, six hundred and thirty nine pounds. 639? Can't be that . . . Try again.'

'*Got you, has it? Can't quite solve it? Too bad. Never could do your crossword, so it's tit for tat.*'

Shut up. You're dead. You can't speak any more—only through this.

He said, 'Try the letters *before*—try N.J.—'

Am I getting it now? 'What the hell does N.J. stand for?'

'New Jerusalem,' said Mr Price.

'Somebody's journal,' said Mary.

'Nuclear jurisprudence,' offered Mr Price. 'There must be a—'

Suddenly Matthew said, '*Wait*.'

They were all still. Anita's eyes were on him now: he couldn't read her glance; he mustn't try; he must keep to this. He said, '*Not the letters before. The letters after.*' He looked up. They were all staring at him. 'I've got it. Don't you see? The letters after O and K—'

'P and L,' said Mary.

'Exactly. Something with enough lines to account for everything, enough words—*Paradise Lost*.'

'Paradise Lost,' repeated Mr Price. 'My goodness me.'

'Quickly.' Matthew was up from his chair, running one impatient hand along the bookshelves. 'Always had it here; where is it; how is it, *always* the book you want . . . *Here*.'

The close-printed, old-fashioned book. His father's book. Decorated with steel engravings, long out of date. Is *this* the answer? Am I wrong after all? £468–11–2 . . . He muttered as he worked, 'Thank God the lines are numbered . . . Line 468—but there aren't eleven words in a line . . . No, surely I can't be wrong . . .' He turned the pages, reading here and there: *The reign of chaos and old night . . . Evil, be thou my good . . .* '*Book* 11; try that; Book 11, line 468, word 2: *Death* . . .' He paused. 'I think we're on to it. I think we've got him. What next? 4–4–1 . . . He liked to jump about, didn't he . . . *Came*. It must be right . . . next: £187–4–5, 6: *with ease* . . .' He looked up. Silence in the room; their eyes all on him. 'A little more,' he said; 'a few words more . . .' Still silence. As he found the words he wrote them on a sheet of paper from his desk. He wrote them in black chalk in capital letters: as he searched for each hidden word, fingers trembling, going back and forth in the great river of a poem, the message grew.

DEATH—CAME—WITH—EASE—NO—HORROR—MERELY—SLEEP.

This was the murder. The murder of the sister. Yet the small neat figures beckoned him on; seemed to have something more to tell him.

Go on. The next word. And the next. I—TOOK—THE—BODY—DOWN—RIVER—

He looked up at them. '*The river*,' he said. 'I begin to see.' Nothing now but the small inked figures, the close-printed pages of the poem, the tremendous trumpet blast of the words—and the message, Blessington's message, unfolding on the paper beside him. He thrust one shaking hand through his hair; bent again over the note-book.

LAID—IT—IN— Where?

'£469–11–4 . . .' Book 11, line 469 . . . He muttered the words aloud: '. . . "*but many shapes of death, and many are the ways that lead to his grim—cave.*" Cave. And then . . .'

I—TOOK—THE—BODY—DOWN—RIVER—LAID—IT—IN—CAVE—IN—

'639–12–7 . . .' Now he could feel himself near to the edge of discovery; quickly turning the pages; here it was: '. . . *the hastening angel caught Our lingering parents, and to the eastern gate, led them direct, and down the cliff—*'

'Cliff,' he said. '*The river and the cliff.*' There on the table was his own message—he said, 'It begins to make sense. What more? A little more.' As he sought for the words he saw the body of the girl left undiscovered there; undiscovered until—as Blessington believed—Matthew's message had discovered it. Go on.

LAID IT IN CAVE IN CLIFF—

What more?

AND—THERE—

He turned the pages. 185—2—1, 2, 3:

UNRESPITED, UNPITIED, UNREPRIEVED—I ABANDONED—

One further word. 44–1–4. He turned the pages again . . . Book 1. Line 44 . . .

'*Him.*'

He blinked at the word. '*Him?*' For a moment there was nothing in his head but silence, the silence of unbelief.

He went back. He counted the lines again. There was no mistake. '*Him the Almighty Power hurled headlong flaming from the ethereal sky . . .*'

'Him.' Fingers shaking, he wrote it down, so that the message was complete.

DEATH CAME WITH EASE NO HORROR MERELY SLEEP I TOOK THE BODY DOWN RIVER LAID IT IN CAVE IN CLIFF AND THERE UNRESPITED UNPITIED UNRE-PRIEVED I ABANDONED HIM

And now the revelation was swarming up in his mind, beginning to take shape—

'My God,' he said, 'do you see? . . .'

They were all looking at him. Anita, Mary and the young Mr Price. Mr Price said, 'What do you mean?'

'I mean it was the *girl* who killed. The sister who killed her brother. And then—'

'The *girl?*' Mary's voice, bewildered, incredulous.

'It was the sister who killed,' he repeated. 'Killed her brother, and then . . . *she took his place.*'

'My God,' said Mr Price.

Anita was sitting very still. Mr Price put one hand on her arm, but she did not seem to be aware of it.

'No . . . I can't believe . . .' Mary's voice again, quiet,

233

protesting. But after a taut silence, Mr Price murmured, 'I think I begin to understand . . .'

'A woman,' said Matthew. He was seeing the figure, here in this room: Blessington, trying to scrub make-up from his face: a man, Matthew had thought, who could most easily slip into a woman's disguise . . . He said, 'It makes sense. She took on his clothes and his accent and his life. She played his part—'

Clearer and clearer he could see her—Jane Rolf Blessington, sitting here, telling the story of her love, asking, 'So what did he do?' 'He—got rid of her,' he had said. And she had answered, 'You could put it like that.'

'Sometimes she was Colonel Blessington. Sometimes she was Jane Rolf. A dangerous life, but she loved danger. And the murder of Harvey Blessington was deep in the past, his body hidden in the cliff's cave. But then the message came from me. She believed that someone knew. And no one must know.'

He paused. Very lightly Mr Price was beating a tattoo on the table with one hand. Anita sat still. Mary carefully shed the ash of her cigarette; there was a little sharp line between her brows.

Matthew gave one sudden glance round them. He was still held in this odd excitement, the tightening spiral of revelation and discovery. The vivid figure of Jane Rolf Blessington seemed to stand somewhere in shadow behind him, with the gleaming hair, the bright make-up, hands in her pockets, the lazy unloving attractive voice mocking him, saying, 'Well, well! Got it at last . . . Bully for you.'

He said, 'She had to find out. She had to get to Hawkeswell and see what she could discover. So she shed Colonel Blessington; she left the London house—'

'Lord above,' said Mr Price. 'Jane Rolf. Talking to Miss Appleby. Signing the visitors' book—'

Matthew saw Anita's hands tighten on the table. He said, 'She came North—'

'Leaving her car,' said Mary, still frowning at the ash-tray before her, 'at Gravely Bridge, and making her mark on Lesley.'

'And making it clear,' Matthew said, 'that a woman had come this way. So that when my body was found, people would remember a stranger in these parts, a *woman*, not a man—'

'*No, it can't be true!*' Anita had thrust her chair back from the table, risen suddenly to her feet. The long silence was broken: her voice was passionate in anguished protest. 'I don't believe it. Harvey was a man. Whatever he was like, whatever he'd done, he was in love with me—'

'My darling girl,' Matthew said, 'Harvey was Jane. And Jane loved no one but herself. Her fun was to take people's lives and spoil them—the love of power. A common love, brought to extremes—'

But she was shaking her head, not listening to him, turning from him, going from them all, out from the house.

The young man got to his feet, as if to follow her, but Matthew said, 'No. Let her go. Let her be alone.'

There was quiet in the room. Then Mary said, 'The news. It's nearly one o'clock.'

He switched on the radio.

'Fine in the South East; rain spreading later from the West . . . winds strong to gale force . . . rather cold.' Strange to hear that ordered, civilized voice; listened to with such attention in these last days . . . different now.

He waited. The pips sounded clear in the silent room. 'It is announced from number 10 Downing Street that

. . .' 'New regulations concerning the sale of . . .'
'Accident, involving a goods train and a locomotive
outside Rugby . . .' And then:

'The body of a woman has been recovered this
morning from the Garfe River in Yorkshire. Police are
now investigating the cause of death, and want to see
anyone who can give any information about her . . .'

He looked at Mary and Mr Price. He said, 'A
woman . . .'

'And now racing—'

Matthew switched off the voice.

Mary stood outside the house. The air had darkened
a little; the bright morning (as it so often did) had given
place to cloud; perhaps a promise of rain. She watched
Matthew as he loaded the car. His own bag; and the
other things: the rucksack, the jacket, the suit in its
plastic cover.

She said nothing. She was aware of Mr Price looming
behind her, a strange, out-of-place young man in his
city clothes. She felt a certain friendly pity for him: he
was so sombre and well-mannered; a little like an
undertaker.

Everything nearly ready now. Matthew was giving
her instructions about Mrs Oakley; about the keys;
about any letters that might come for him.

She nodded, taking this in with the top of her mind,
while at some deeper level she saw the young man of the
Labrière raid; the haunted, piratical figure; the lone
tiger, pacing over the moors . . . The end of something
now. A dark dream brought to its conclusion; purged
in violence and death.

Now he stood by the car, waiting. Mary, looking out
over the moors, said, 'She's coming now.'

Anita's large figure came towards them. She strode with her hands in her pockets, her face impassive. 'Went for a walk,' she said, smoothing her hair against the wind; 'bit of a walk.' She faced Matthew. Mary saw their eyes meet: his with a question, hers without answer, but steadily. Anita said, with a glance at the car, 'You're going—'

'To Gravely Bridge,' he said. 'To talk to Lesley.'

Anita gave a brief nod. 'Coming with you,' she said. 'No—don't argue. Let me get in.'

Mary caught the flicker of light on Matthew's face, the small vanishing pleasure. For a moment, she took his hand. Then she watched as he got into the car and, with Anita beside him, began to drive off down the steep rough road.

The car diminished; it turned the corner into the valley road; it was gone.

Quiet came back to them, standing there. Mary stayed for a moment, looking at the cloud-shadows on the empty moorland road. The wind strengthened, bringing the first touch of rain.

Mary turned to Mr Price, who was looking sadly after the car, as if he would like it to come back. She put a hand on his arm.

'We'd better go in,' she said.